RATS

RATS

JW HICKS

TRISKELE BOOKS

Cover design and typesetting: JD Smith Design

Published by Burleigh Publishing.
Printed in the United Kingdom by Lightning Source

All enquiries to essorer3@virginmedia.com

First printing, 1st October 2014

ISBN Paperback: 978-0-9929823-0-0
ISBN ePub: 978-0-9929823-1-7
ISBN Mobi: 978-0-9929823-2-4

Dedication :- For Alan and my four monsters.

1

My father's dead, buried under a pile of rubble, yet he's still carping; still grumbling at me. I'm burning hot and sweating rivers one minute, shivering cold the next. My hand's worse, like it's been knife-stuck not nail-poked. Should it hurt so much? I pulled the nail out, didn't I? I let it bleed—that cleans the wound, right? Knew I was in for it soon as the swelling started. Now the hole's oozing green gunk, and there's red worm-veins crawling up my arm. Zip it, old man. Stop nagging—you're breaking my brain.

Wind's rising, shaking the plastic, letting in rain, but I can still smell his oldness, his stinkbreath … his dead flesh.

Cass girl, he's gone—it's just his smell that haunts. Okay, so why is he sitting at his desk giving me gyp? It … he … can't be real. That desk went up in flames along with the rest of the narding house. Can't get away, can't run. Legs too heavy, arm too sore.

So what's it gonna be this time, *Father*? Did you spy me pouring ink on your prize orchid? I been playing my *common* music too loud? Not another frinking lecture on the way I speak. Did I use a bad word?

'Slang, my dear Cassandra, is the refuge of the uneducated. You should be aware of the correct mode of expression and use it at all times. It may be street slang *de rigueur* for 2034 but I expect a higher standard from my daughter.

'You are thirteen in a month's time, old enough to conform to the dictates of grammar and clear speech.'

But now I ain't a kid any more. It's 2036, I'm fifteen and he's dead. Yeah, and it's the old him talking at me, same as he useta.

Okay then, anything you say, *Father*. You're always right, yeah? Like the time you said your old pal Frink was a true blue patriot and was gonna put the country to rights. And just what did that solid gold patriot do? Juded the country to the troopers. Didn't see that coming, did you?

I close my eyes to shut out his voice, but I can't get him out of my head. Why was it always Ca-*sand*-ra, with him? Never Cass or Cassie. And he always talked to me like I was an idiot. Powerful with words, he took pride in never losing an argument. Mother? She was all, 'Don't upset your father, Cassandra, he's doing it for your own good.' How they ever got together I never could figure out. Hell, a gnomish pedant and a vid-star beauty— you couldn't make it up. Small wonder I ran with *unsuitable* companions. What's he gonna do now he's dead? Can't touch me now, old man.

Pity I take after him in the looks department. Always wanted to be tall and blonde like Mother, 'stead got stuck with dark and scrawny. Got her green eyes, though. Cat Eyes, the other kids called me, till I showed them the error of their ways. I might get tongue-tied but I won't be stepped on.

My mother loved me, I could tell. Thing I couldn't fathom was how come she loved a stiff-faced old fossil like him. But she did, I could see it.

'He loves you, Cass,' she'd say to me, after a scolding. 'He's just not good at showing it.'

'Way he goes on at me you'd think I was the worst kid in the world.'

'He only wants the best for you.'

'Best for me or best for him?'

See, when I was a *little* kid, me and him were tight, but soon as I hit the teens he changed. Started looking at me like I was some alien from another dimension. So I played the part he handed me, played it to the narding hilt.

Mother tried to smooth the road, get us walking in the same direction, but guess what? All the coaxing in the world wasn't gonna level *that* broken highway.

One time when the tension grew toxic tight, she took me to the attic, pulled out a battered tin trunk and showed me a pack of photos. 'Your father's,' she said, laying them on the dusty floor.

I rooted through pics of fabulous landscapes, dinner parties and Cinderella-type balls, and didn't find one picture of *him*.

'So, where's father?'

'Your grandparents were in the diplomatic corps. They worked in consulates all over the world and your father was brought up by nannies, until he was six, old enough to be sent back home to boarding school.'

'But he was only a little kid. What happened holiday times, did he go back to his parents?'

'No, he stayed with his grandparents who were used to living a certain way and refused to change. They made sure he learned to fit in.

'Your father lived a lonely life, Cassandra. His only friends were books.'

Okay, so now I knew how come he turned out like he did, but knowing didn't make me like him any better. S'pose I should've been grateful he didn't have the gelt to banish *me* to some hi-toned school. But though we lived in the same house it was like we lived miles apart. Anyway, it wasn't my job to heal rifts, it was his.

For a moment, I picture my mother's smile, then she's gone, and I'm shivering worse'n ever and Dad's talking again, but his voice is different, *he's* different. No longer the stern-faced Father, but the dying Dad; hair dirt-full and straggly, eyes rheumy, skin sagged and wrinkled. He's huddled in the sleeping bag he was buried in, and he's on a preaching streak. 'They *will* catch you, child. You cannot outrun them.' And I'm crying, not because he's right, but because I miss the Dad I came to know in our two years on the run, the Dad I forgave, the Dad who called me *good child* and *my dearest Cass*.

'Templeton's troopers mean to round up every fugitive and place them in work camps. They have their orders and will obey them to the letter. Face reality, surrender. It will be easier for you in the long term.'

'Dad, give it a rest, will you?' I say through tears, then start coughing and can't stop. Time I do my chest hurts and my ribs ache like they been punched.

I don't believe it, I'm talking to a man buried under a pile of rocks to keep the feral curs from cracking his bones. I'd laugh if I could get my breath. If I could quit crying.

Now he's quiet. He's gone and I'm at the burying pit watching my mother's body slung on top of the rest of the bagged corpses. But this time she's not in a bag, her hair's bright in the sunlight and her eyes are open. She's calling to me to come and get her. I'm too weak ... couldn't save her then, can't save her now.

I want her back, to be a child again sitting on her lap before a roaring winter fire, listening to my father reading a scary tale about ogres. But that was back before I turned awkward ... and he didn't know how to handle it.

The scene judders, and I'm somewhere else wrestling an old woman for a tin of baked beans. I cry out, spun to a smoky place where people swoop down a giant slide straight through the gates of Hell, to the demons who rip off their heads and lap their blood with great forked tongues. I scream and a demon looks at me, drops a body and runs towards me. I try and escape but can't, because my legs are tangled in a sticky net. The demon's closing fast, I smell hot breath, feel claws ... and suddenly Hell-gate's gone.

I'm back, safe in the shelter. But not alone, I brought the demon with me. Freeze, don't move. Breathe and it'll pounce, tear my head, lap my blood. It's man shaped, got snakes instead of hair and its Cyclops eye is staring at me. It's hypnotic, that lone eye, pale and grey and luminous, set in flame dark skin. Gotta get away. Can't move. The demon's coming for me, mouth open, spike-fangs bared. The hair-snakes writhe closer. I'm demon food. NO! Fight. Don't be snapped up like some timid mouse. Get that arm up, go for the eye. Yell like he's the old man, 'bout to tear a strip.

'NOOO,' the demon yells.

I got it, got the eye. It's bleeding, the demon's bleeding ichor down its leathered skin.

'Frinking hell, girl!' a voice cries. The demon! No, not a demon, but a solid 3D human who speaks same style as me.

'Fighter are you?' grates the voice and a pair of strong hands grip my shoulders. 'Still yourself, fighter, you bin honourably captured.'

The strength leaves me, my heart pounds. I stare at the demon's face and see the man behind it. He's no cyclops, just a guy with a missing eye. One socket's sunken, seamed by an old knife wound and painted ebon black. The snakes? Wiry dreadlocks. But the teeth *are* pointed like the demon's. I could still be prey. I relax, his hold loosens and I tear free, kicking and gouging till he knocks me out.

I wake, fever down, hand bandaged, and pain free. 'Who be you?' says the voice as I stir. Not threatening, curious. I try for a word and croak dry-throated.

The one eyed man feeds me water. 'Cass,' I whisper. 'Name's Cass.' His smile makes me shudder; the teeth are all too real.

'I'm One Eye,' he says calm and quiet, the skin about the living eye wrinkling with the smile. 'One Eye of the Whip Tails. Best fighting clan in all the city ruins. Wanna join us? Always room for another fighter in the clan. And I'll attest you ain't no faint-heart.'

So, having no place else to go I journey with One Eye. 'Take all you can carry,' he says, 'You'll need a shelter when we reach camp.'

As we walk I study the guy. He's wearing a mish-mash of hide and cloth under a trooper greatcoat customised with myriad sewn-on cap badges, braided lanyards and the regimental tags from at least three trooper units. None of the doodads obscure the triangle of bullet holes placed neatly on the upper chest area of the coat. He's toting at least two knives, a handgun shoved into his belt and a full pack over his shoulder.

We walk in silence, at a speed I struggle to maintain. When we stop for a rest he shares his water flask with me.

'Not far now,' he says. 'So you'll need to know what to expect. Listen close.

'First I present you to the tribe leader, Man Ear. You just keep yer mouth shut. As sponsor I puts in the request. Don't you worry, Man Ear trusts me, knows I see more with my single glim than most Rats with two.'

He reads the question in my eyes and shakes his head.

'You ain't never heard of Rats? Hell, girl, where you bin living? Rats are the scavengers of civilization and the sole resistance to that murdering creech Templeton.' He spits on the ground. 'There's wrangling about how Rats came to be. Me? I was a wanderer well before the bad years hit, so they kinda passed me by. Never had no job to lose, no house to give back to some money man. Came the sickness I stayed healthy. Came the Crash of '34, I wasn't battered like most folk. Didn't have no 'sponsibilities, no family to lose. Yeah, when the world went to hell and Templeton took his chance, I carried on as usual. I joined with some like minded souls and laid down rules to give us the best chance of surviving. Clans that don't lay rules fell apart, and Templeton picked them off one by one. You acquainted with Templeton?'

I nod. 'The General? Course I am.'

'Wants a kingdom, does Templeton. Join him or die, he says. Aims to remake the world, and heaven help you if you don't like the shape he wants it.' He stops to chuck a stone at a withered oak tree. 'How long you bin cut off?'

'Cut off?'

'Surviving chaos on yer own.'

'Dunno, I lost count long back. My mother died in the first wave of Sickness. I was thirteen, and we stayed in the house all through the Crash. We managed okay till dad caught the second wave. He recovered, but never got his strength back. When Templeton turned the screws and it got so bad, we left the city. Kept moving till he couldn't walk any more.'

'Yer dad?'

'Dead. Cairned days past.' I hold up my bandaged arm, 'When I got spiked.'

'Crash was around two years ago. You're 'bout fifteen, then. Done all right for a young'un. Your dad much help?'

I look at him, hard. 'Not since he got sick.'

'What was he before?'

'Professor of Literature at the University of Wales.'

One Eye laughs. 'So, not much help even before he got sick, eh?'

'Did his best,' I say, realising it was the truth.

'Right then, last lap. Let's be walking.'

We get to Main Camp at sunset. An escort of plait-haired weirds loaded with guns, knives and spears walk us through what looks to be a squatter camp.

'Why is it like this?'

'Like what?'

'Ramshackle.'

'Rats don't build permanent. Keeping on the move's the safest option.'

'That's why you told me to bring my plastic.'

He doesn't answer. The path winds in and out of tents and teepees, brush huts and corrugated lean-tos till we get to a small bright fire and the man waiting there. He looks up at One Eye's whistle and stands to greet him. From a distance he's nothing much to look at, thin, mid height and bald. Close up he's completely different, his eyes hot as fire coals and his smell overpowering. Animal-like. He's greased his skull and it catches the fire flickers The red circles tattooed around his eye-sockets dance in

13

the firelight and the lines in his cheeks look chasm deep.

'You bring a stranger to the camp, One Eye?' He says in a voice of grinding gravel.

'I do, Man Ear. A candidate.'

'You claim her? You vow to train her to the testing point?'

One Eye bows and Man Ear bows back, the string of shriveled ears dangling about his thick neck attesting to his name.

'Take her. Teach her to be Rat.'

And that's it, seems I'm in. But in for what?

First off One Eye razors my hair with his hunting knife. It hurts like hell, leaving me with rough stubble, uneven ridges and bloody notches where his knife caught my scalp. The watching weirds laugh at my winces, but cheer and whistle when I refuse to cry.

Shaving done, he dumps me in a barrel of ice-cold water and tells me to scrub everything, skin *and* clothes. As I scrub he lectures me in The Way.

'Girl,' he says, his scratchy voice loud in the evening air. 'Rats are given nothing. You keep your old clothes till you get yourself new.' He leans close and his breath smells worse than my clothes ever did. 'Rats steal or fight to get what they need … or die in the trying.'

Out of the barrel and standing in my wet clothes, Man Ear declares me 'prentice to One Eye. I'm his till I'm ready for my naming trial, or get croaked. Something tells me the learning won't come easy.

I go to pick up my stuff, my makings for a shelter, my water bottle, my carrisack, and all my stuff's gone.

'Yeah well, that's how things go,' says One Eye. 'Come sit by the fire.'

He talks as he builds up the fire while I sit and steam. 'Understand this. Rats do for themselves. From now on you fight for food, clothes, and most important you'll fight for a name. Till you're named you're bottom rank. You'll answer to a yell or whistle, sleep cold till you get yourself a shelter and fight for your food with the rest of the nameless.'

'When do I get a name?'

'When you complete Trial successfully.'

'How long before Trial?'

He shrugs. 'Depends. Any time from three months on. I'll spring it on you. A trialist gets no warning, so be ready at all times. Survive Trial, win a name and even Templeton's finest will be hard put to drag you down.'

It's my first night and One Eye lends me a blanket and I lie down close to his shelter, a teepee made from long sticks set pyramid-style, woven together with creeper and covered with fir branches. The blanket's the same colour as the one I carried from my shelter, smells of me as well. But for the first time in a long while I feel … sheltered.

The camp wakes early and I hand the blanket back. 'Right,' says One Eye. 'Go get some stuff. It'll rain tonight.'

2

Another rainy night, another *wakeful* rainy night, even though I'm lying soft and lying dry. Cost me a black eye getting my plastic back, a slashed arm and a wrenched shoulder to snaff a straw-filled bed-sack. With a knife instead of a tree branch I'd have fared better. I *have* to get a knife. It's thinking how that's keeping me wakeful.

Got to be realistic, how's a skinny fifteen-year-old newbie gonna wrest a knife from a long in the tooth Rat? Pick a weak one, that's how. Hell, what would Dad say? I'm turning Templeton? All right Dad, tell me what else can I do? Hand myself over to the troopers? Starve?

Sleep's out, I'm going walkabout, take a scout-around. I won't make it without a knife, that's for definite. P'raps I'd be better off on my own, away from this camp; outside and roaming free.

I wander through the put-ups, meeting sentries who give me the eye, and skulking behind wigwams and bashers when I spot a no-name wanderer like me. Hope I don't look as scared as them. Pray to God none them find my stash of plastic.

The rain stops 'ventually. The wind's freshening, the moon's in and out and I cut through a clump of canvas-covered shacks heading for the raised ground in the centre of camp. I'll get a good overview soon as the moon shines clear. Need to suss a way out, 'cos I got the feeling I could be making a run for it real soon. As a nameless, weaponless fem, I got a big target pinned to my back.

Climbing sparks the memory of the day Professor Rhys-Jones took me and his son Owen on an expedition to Skenfrith Castle, one of the castles the Normans built in Gwent. The prof was a pal of Dad's and worked in the history department. The guy lived and breathed history, loved it same as my father loved literature. But unlike my dad the prof also loved spending time with his one and only kid.

And wowee, what a day that was! Me and Owen did stuff my father would never have allowed. We climbed wonky steps to the top of a stone tower, and shot pretend arrows through real arrow slits to defend the castle from marauding Welshmen. Dinner time we ate shop-bought pasties and sucked fizzy pop through plastic straws while the prof told us about buried kings, pharaohs, and grave goods. Then he told us about Twmbarlwm Twmp, a mound built on a hill coupla miles from Newport. He said most folk believed it to be an Iron Age hill fort. Then he tapped his nose, looked over his shoulder and whispered that it might possibly be a barrow where a chieftain was buried.

Back then I never believed that tribal times would come again, just like I never thought I'd bury my father under a cairn of stones like some Stone Age king.

Back then I was a child, never dreaming how the world could change.

Hilltop reached, I take an all-round view of the camp, and it's big. Far bigger than I thought—shanties everywhere, set in a maze of passageways. A bank of cloud drifts across the moon and I lean against a boulder, my mind wandering back to the time before Dad died, and how close we got.

Footsteps? I been followed? Stay small, girl, and hope the moon stays hid. And here comes a burly guy, all curls and goat stink, dragging something heavy.

'Shut it,' he growls and there's a meaty slap. 'No noise or I'll slice your ears off one by one. Kick me again and I'll stuff that gag way down your gullet.'

As he dumps what he's dragging, the moon escapes a cloud and shows me that it's a girl, shaven-haired like me; bruised and blooded about the face.

The big guy grunts, 'I'm your finder, do as I say and give me exactly what I want.'

The girl struggles, he slams a fist down and she's still for a few seconds, then resumes the fight. The noise she makes hides my footsteps and the sound I make in grabbing up a rock. He's so busy he doesn't know he's easy meat till the rock hits, and then it's far too late.

Me and the girl split the booty, I get the knife and the greased hide shirt that'll keep the rain off. Girl gets the socks and boots, the carrisack and the food tins. The rest of the stinking junk joins the stiff in a shallow grave topped with slabs of shale.

Next morning One Eye starts me tracking. He spots the new gear straight off but he don't pass comment, apart from a fleeting grin.

Two months on I'm fit, strong, got a pair of good boots, hide trews to match the shirt and an easy-up easy-down shelter, far better than a plastic sheet. Best of all I got an ally in the no-name girl I 'helped out' with the rock. And I'm starting to feel part of something, a community ... a family. I've missed that feeling.

Today's move day. The Whip Tails have been rooted too long, the pack's grown too big, too fast and it's way past division time. Stay any longer, troopers'll sniff us out.

Last night's Meet was called to vote a new leader for the split-off pack and deciding who stayed and who went. The vote went to Throat Tearer and his new clan Questers. Throat Tearer's speech was finer than any Shakespeare Dad had me read. Nameless, I couldn't vote, but given the chance I'd have given him my aye. Even One Eye was swayed, but he stayed loyal to Man Ear and voted to stay Whip Tail.

Before the Meet he told me how Man Ear got to be leader of the Tails. How he snared his followers by exciting them with a plan to attack a small new-built trooper garrison on the edge of a city ruin. The attack had been a triumph, the troopers' toes so well trod they pulled out of the sector. Big man among the clan leaders, Man Ear.

Throat Tearer preached change. I sat at One Eye's side and sucked his words in deep. To look at he was striking, tall, strong faced with short black hair and a close-cut beard. Soon as he started speaking his blue eyes brightened like a torch had been switched on. Wasn't his eyes that hooked me, was his voice.

'I, Throat Tearer earned my name ripping out a trooper's throat with my teeth and endowing my pack with his clothes and weapons. I have fought against New Order troopers since their formation, and I tell you, brothers and sisters, we fight a losing battle.' He paused and looked from face to face, his eyes like polished sapphires. 'You have honoured me in voting me leader, and now I honour you with the truth. Let those who believe, follow me.' He took a draught of water before continuing.

'I say that we Rats must leave the ruins in which we live. The supplies we live off, the abandoned food, the scavenged equipment, grow ever scarcer. We exist on products of a past time; a time ended by the Sickness. We fight against the resurrection of the cities under Templeton's New Order. His troopers grow in number and his technology races ahead of our simple blades and guns. The city dwellers rise while we scavengers dwindle. They will grow stronger. They will spread from their compounds and colonise the ruins and us with them.'

A voice howled curses at Templeton. It didn't faze Throat Tearer, he just bulled on. 'We *must* leave the ruins and the shadows of the past, and search for fertile land to grow crops, sustain herds. We *cannot* beat Templeton. The Wilderness awaits. Who among you is brave enough to cease fighting for the past and begin the fight for the future?'

He got his volunteers and I ached to be one of them. Now,

today, the two packs were going their very different ways. Had Man Ear said the word I believe every Rat in his sept would have turned towards the Wilderness, but he was of the old ways and kept silent.

I watch the Questers leave, honing my knife and imagining the Wilderness, when One Eye marches up.

'Right girl, this is the day.'

'The day?' I say watching the last of the Questers heading out.

'Trial day,' he says, all quiet like. I start to shake.

He looks at me and I know what I have to do, I grab my water flask, sling on my food pouch and leave straight away, hoping he doesn't see my fear. You don't hesitate after Trial words are spoken. You hear them, you go. That's why my gear is always close to hand. Coupla weeks back some kid got the word and left without the food and water stashed in his tent. He never made it back.

Right, so I step out acting brave and feeling nothing like. Hell, it's one thing to know a Trial's in the offing, quite another to have it bite your throat.

Only the strong and well prepared return from Trial. Hope the tribe leaves clear track signs so I can find my way to New Camp —if I get the chance. So it's goodbye shelter, farewell bed sack. Who cares? If I die on Trial, nothing's lost. If I live I'll steal it back.

I'm scared. One Eye has to know I am, hell, every Rat must know, they've all been trialled. 'Girl,' he said early in my training. 'Never listen to the fear. Rats are fighters, it's what we do—what we are.'

I make for the ruins alert for hidden signs. 'No signposts in the ruins, kid,' was One Eye's favourite saying. All Rat tribes use stones, twig bundles, sand scrapes or earth pictures to convey messages and warnings. A known cycle of slash-tags give the date. These and our finger language are the same for every clan. As tribes split some signs might change, a new dialect might emerge, but always the core remains. It's how Rats communicate.

Sometimes tribes join for a raid or a vengeance attack. Mostly they keep separate, but are always Rat.

One Eye's a good teacher and I know to look for snoop bugs and how to keep my pacing irregular so as not to wake detectors. I been taught well, I know, but …

3

My food and water will stretch for two, maybe three or more days. Being alone in the ruins is the real killer. Got to watch for trooper patrols and set-traps, feral dogs after warm-bloods, and rabid two legged loners after meat, not to mention falling brickwork and chancy weather.

I've a rough plan, no details though, a too-rigid plan gets fouled up if the details don't run right. A basic framework leaves room for possibilities. True, the possibilities seemed greater when sitting in the middle of an armed Rat encampment; here on my own in the middle of nowhere they're a tad meagre.

To earn a name not only do I need to get back to the tribe, but bring in something of value. If I succeed I get me a name, an initiate scar and a tattoo. Fail and the dogs chew my bones. If … *when* … I come back no one's going to call me 'Girl' or 'Lefty' or 'Hey Green-eyes' without blood spilled.

My plan is to go back to where One Eye found me, on the outer edge of the ruins. Dad and I settled there because of the stream. If squatters haven't settled and if troopers haven't taken over, I'll stock up on wild meat before venturing deep into the ruins where the real treasures lie.

Closer I get to Dad's cairn, faster the memories run. On my twelfth birthday I got father's old microscope instead of the dog I craved, and a definite no-no to a trip to the fair with my friends. 'Money's tight,' was Mother's excuse. She was always the explainer while Father kept his stern mouth shut. But soon after that his department closed and he was home all day grumbling like a broke-down water geyser. He wasn't the only one, most of my friends' parents were on short time or laid off. Professor Rhys-Jones and his family had left for greener pastures long since; America, so I heard. Like everyone else Mother and I joined food queues while marchers protested and schools went half time, and Father retired to his study to write a history of the world.

One day when she was doling out yet another meal of potato soup we heard the New York stock exchange had imploded. Britain's followed suit and the news was so black for so long, the first flu deaths were lost in the gloom. That soon changed when the death toll rocketed.

A week after my thirteenth birthday Mother was dead and Templeton, aided by the Honourable Stuart Frink, had taken over a country that was sinking faster than a stove-in row boat.

The Sickness was unstoppable, taking old and young, strong and weak. Many survivors died the following bitter winter, while immunes like me lived unscathed. Countries already weakened by Aids copped it worse than us. Dad likened it to the Black Death and talked of the Spanish Flu, a bigger killer than the Great War.

Mother died early in the outbreak when hospitals were still accepting patients. As hospitals closed and food shops emptied, riots and looting were the norm. Dad mourned Mother by ranting at the government. 'Where's the vaccines? The food drops? Who's in charge? The Queen's flown off somewhere. This Government's worse than useless.'

He wasn't the only cit to cry those words.

Cometh the hour, cometh the man. This particular hour brought us General Julius Templeton, leader of the New Order Party which sprang from the ashes of a beat-down, death-wrung government. Templeton declared Martial Law. Unite and build, he called. Folk turned to him and marched towards his glorious future. He was the saviour; Arthur come again, Churchill re-born. And he grasped all in an iron fist.

My father refused to wear the NOP badge, wouldn't salute the troopers, or attend the rallies. 'It's no Second Coming,' he'd mutter to anyone to brave enough to listen. 'He's no Saviour just another Antichrist.' Friends and neighbours shunned us. There were no more oddments slipped into my hand when friends popped by. No more tins of beans, sprouting potatoes and wrinkled apples to eke out our rations, and no more bundles of firewood left at the back door. I missed the callers as much as the extra food. I lost contact with my friends when they joined Templeton's Young Bloods. They wore the badges, sang the songs, got the ration books, and looked away when we chanced to meet.

Like every other cit I queued for scraps, bartering my mother's clothes and jewellery for 'extras' like meat and eggs and soap. When Dad took sick I traded his beloved books. After he recovered, a frail old man, he cried over the gaps in his bookshelves.

Bargaining with food traders and avoiding Templeton's serf-recruiters, speeded my growing up. Not physical growing 'cos I reckon I'll always be a skinny black haired runt, but a hardening of mind and determination. I switched to parent mode as my father dwindled.

'You want to eat?' I said, peeling his fingers from a precious first edition. 'Then *this* has to go. Got to stock up on tins 'cos the word's out, Templeton's cracking down on barter.'

He shook his head, 'What about your mother's rings?'

'Gone for aspirin.'

'Her clothes?'

'Fuel. Look,' I said, trying for reasonable. 'He's bringing in the New Currency and you only get that by working. Workers have to be fit, not old and sick. They take me and I'll be shut in some work camp or trooper brothel, and then what'll you do?'

Still cradling the book like it was some holy infant, he sat on the stairs, shoulders bent, head down. Then, slowly he handed it to me. 'Who buys them?' he whispered.

'Guy in Radyr. He sells to NOP high ups, under the counter.'

'These books are treasures,' he said, 'and what is this New Currency?'

I sighed, 'Told you yesterday. It's scrip, paper money you earn by doing authorised work. Scrip comes alongside a party card. No card, no entitlements.'

'I could go along and request a card. I could take notes for officers. Keep accounts, that kind of thing.'

'Fat chance. Look, folk get scrip for informing on dissenters. Your name'll be on some list somewhere for slagging off Templeton. Mine too, because I'm no Young Blood. Soon as we're noticed they'll hoik you off to some old folks' refuge to be *disappeared*.'

I was shouting by then and after giving me the book, he got up and shuffled to his study, shutting the door carefully behind him.

I leant against that door, listening to silence, wiping tears from my cheeks and holding back the sobs best as I could. When calm, I set out for Radyr.

On the way I noticed an increase in the banners and posters that'd been cropping up lately. Pictures of the general dangled from windows, trees and no-light lamp posts. Today there was something new: ragged figures toting placards and sandwich boards urging citizens to join the General in his fight for peace and prosperity. One of the carriers called to me. 'Hey you. Hungry? Get down the Council Hall, tell 'em Parry Bowen sent you. They give scrip for walking these placards, and they give you a bonus for recruiting fresh meat.'

I shook my head, darted into an alley and took the quiet ways to Radyr. I got to the black marketeer late, and had to bang on the door to be let in. 'This is the last I can take,' he said. 'Troopers have been around, didn't find my stash but I ain't taking no more risks.'

He gave me a handful of scrip for the book. 'Got nothing else,' he said. 'And don't come back, I'm crossing the border to England. Been told things are better there.'

Next day I stood in the food queue staring at Norman-built castle walls, standing strong on Roman foundations in the wasteland that was Cardiff, and finally accepted that my world had ended: my future shrivelled to a meaner, shorter span.

But it seemed, as I listened to the queuers talk, that others saw a rosier future. Seemed the general was what the country needed. He was building a *new* Britain, giving us back our pride, giving the youngsters an aim in life. I kept shtum, thinking of conscription, work camps and *refuges* for the loony, sick and old.

I got home and for once, Dad was alert and eager to talk. So I told him what I saw and heard every day and watched his face turn grave.

'So,' he said. 'All is being safely gathered in.' He patted my arm, 'Soon it will be too late. Templeton will wrap us so tightly we will never move freely again. Come Cassandra, we must make plans to leave.'

4

On Trial and heading into the Ruins, I tread on the grass and weeds creeping over cracked pavements and see saplings rise through riven tarmac. I wade through streams flowing down gradients and filling bomb craters edged in moss and weed— green life reclaiming deadened land. Thoughts of Throat Tearer and his prophetic speech come to mind.

Further into the rubbled landscape there will be no green. I'll have to cut across much devastation before I reach my goal—the oasis where I can stock up on meat.

Here and now I must face a night alone in the ruins. Unlike that first trek from the city I'm no longer a no-nothing kid with an old man dragging at my heels, slowing me down: that same old man I learned to love, the one who changed from the father who wanted to mould me into something I could never be, into the dad who came to love me for what I was.

I build a small fire, for comfort, not for cooking. Tonight I'll dine on a jerk-meat twist, soon I hope to be reaping a fine harvest from the snares set near my dad's final resting place.

The night's clear, the stars bright and I'm no scared cit, so I should be cosying down to sleep. Been trained by the best and I know that rest fosters a clear mind. One Eye always says that worry is a waste of energy and won't stop troubles coming. But try as I might, sleep won't come. But memories do.

I remember the day we left the city, heading north, to Whitchurch. Father wanted us to move to Gran's house and I went along with it. It was as good a place as any. Out in the suburbs we could at least grow food in Gran's big garden.

We carried as much food and water as we could, plus spare underwear and toiletries. Father insisted on taking two heavy books, a Shakespeare and a Dryden. 'Can't you choose something lighter?' I begged. He shook his head and smoothed the tooled bindings. 'I'll carry them. I won't trouble you,' he murmured.

I was about to shut the front door when he slipped back inside. After another book, I thought, but he came out with nothing extra. Wasn't till we were half way down the street that I heard a splintering crash and turned to see smoke billowing from the study window. I looked, and he was crying.

A car ride to Gran's used to take half an hour tops, but now? I knew what we faced, did he?

I shook his arm. 'Listen,' I said. If I give the word, you do what I say, no quibbling, okay?'

'What do you mean, Cassandra?'

'I say run and hide you do just that. See these caterpillar tracks on the road? Trooper vehicles, right? They see us they'll want papers.'

'But we have no papers.'

'Right. So I say run, you run. I say duck, you duck. Hear me?'

'The gaps? Did the owners burn their houses?'

'Some did. Troopers did for others, or joy-boys seeking thrills. Early on a few streets went west after a gas main blew.'

Dad started walking slowly, and every street we passed through he got slower, till at last he sank to the pot-holed road. 'The city's dead and we're walking through its corpse. This is the end,' he whispered into the early morning silence.

'Quiet. Hear that? We gotta hide.'

I dragged, he crawled and we got behind a bus carcass as the armed patrol car rattled past, troopers' eyes glinting in the sight slits. We stayed crouched until the last cleat-rattle died.

'Where are the people that lived in these houses? Are they all dead, Cassandra?'

'Most. The rest? Guess they moved closer to the food kitchens or into trooper run compounds.'

The silence weighed heavy. I wanted him to walk faster but the books slowed him. 'Ditch them,' I said. He clutched them tighter. Round the next corner dogs fought over a heap of rags, only it wasn't rags but a body. Dad cried out, alerting the trio of prick-eared mastiffs. 'Look down,' I whispered, 'Don't give challenge.'

I dropped to my knees, grabbed a couple of bricks and lobbed them over. Full bellied, the dogs glared undecided, red chunks dangling from their jaws. A distant volley of shots spooked them, a closer volley set them running. I dragged Dad behind a garden wall. We moved off soon as I was convinced the shooters were gone.

About noon we came to the old bridge across the Taff, the quickest route to my grandmother's house. It was blocked by two felled lime trees. Dad sank to his knees and while he rocked and cried, I took a look-see.

The trunks were splintered with bullet holes and stained with blood. No bodies, though, and someone had hacked off a couple of branches making a squeezable hole. I'd get through it easy as pie, but Dad?

I took his arm. 'Leave me, child. Just leave me,' he cried. 'I'm done for.'

I tugged his arm, but it was the sudden outbreak of dog howls that got him moving. 'They're coming for us,' I lied, pushing him towards the splinted hole. Don't know how I got him and the books to the other side, but I did. Breathing heavily, he sagged to the ground.

'Let me rest. Five minutes and I'll go on.' Seeing he was too heavy for me to drag I let him be, and we crouched behind the tree trunks listening to the pack sounds fade.

'It's okay, Dad. They've gone, must be some other losers turn, but there'll be others on the hunt.'

Spurred to his feet, he staggered across the bridge. We passed huge gaps in the sides, through which I could see the carcasses of new-power travel wagons lying on the river bed.

'We got to keep going. The bridge ain't safe.'

'Don't say ain't, Cassandra,' he said. I smiled; he was perking up.

The air on the other side of the bridge was foul. We soldiered on, wrapping scarves about our faces in a futile attempt to keep it out.

'What is that smell?' he asked.

'Burning corpses.'

'At least I buried your mother. Don't burn me, Cassandra. See me buried, will you?'

'Do my best, Dad. Do my mizzing best.'

He didn't scold, he staggered on clutching his slipping books. 'Give them me,' I begged, but he wouldn't so I shut my mouth and kept walking.

Something, probably military dozers, had cleared Caedelyn Road, heaping abandoned vehicles to the sides in massive metal drifts. That night we sheltered in a doorless travel wagon, eating biscuits and tinned beans. I couldn't sleep for listening to his uneven snoring and when dawn came it was damned hard to get going.

Took us two days and two long nights to get to Gran's and all the time he mumbled about the nine circles of Hell. But he didn't give up, kept right on walking. It was the sobbing woman sitting next to an empty supermarket trolley that almost did for him … and me.

I was all for crossing the road and leaving her mizzing, but Dad had to go and help. Next thing, she had a knife to his throat and had me load our stuff into her trolley, even his creechy books. She'd have had the clothes off our backs if a gun hadn't fired close by. Soon as she heard it she scooted off with her treasure-filled trolley, after downing Dad by slicing his face from cheek to jaw.

We reached Gran's staggering like a pair of drunks to find

the body of a man rotting on the bed in the back bedroom. I parked Dad on the front step, nursing his bandaged face, while I tied a wet cloth over my nose and searched the semi and the one next door for anything useful. Didn't find much, a few food tins under the floorboards and a metal trunk in Gran's attic holding two sleeping bags and a couple of plastic drink flasks with shoulder straps and decorated with peeling cartoon decals. I knew we couldn't stay for long, so I washed and filled the flasks. The taps ran dry just after.

When I'd covered the body I put a match to the bed, and Dad and I stood across the road and watched the fire burn high and bright. Then we left. Back in the zone of flaming tombs, I said, and he managed a wheezing laugh.

'We need more water. Perhaps we should go back,' he gestured to the way we came.

'Back there?' I said. 'If the water's off here, bet it's the same everywhere. Think you're up to walking back through all that crap again? Dogs getting hungrier, crazies getting wilder? Want to be butchered for meat or taken by troopers? How long would you last in a labour gang? And where they going to put me, in a trooper cat-house? No. We can't go back.'

He sobbed like a child told Santa was a con. I put an arm around his shoulder and stood looking heavenwards, watching a tiny cross grow into the outline of an aircraft. Then I heard engine noise. Dad heard it too, and he rose from the wall waving and shouting.

'It's a rescue, Cass, he said—the first time he'd shortened my name. 'It's a food drop.'

It wasn't food they were dropping. A second plane appeared and then another and the crump of explosions soon followed.

'They're flaming disease sites.' I shouted. 'Let's go before they flame us.'

I grabbed the sleeping bags, stuffed the food tins inside, shouldered the water flasks and dragged him from the war zone, again heading north. We ran till he dropped. I hauled him up and we staggered on, through the noise and over the shuddering ground. I ignored his pleas to stop and hide, same as I ignored the dust and stink and rain of stones. Eventually the bombing ceased and real rain fell. Huddled under a corrugated metal sheet propped against a downed tree, we drank our water and listened to the rain. This time both of us cried.

I woke to silence and sunshine. Dad was up before me and he'd opened the flasks to the rain and they were full to the brim. I hugged him, a child again and safe in my father's charge. Then I turned adult and opened two tins of vegetable soup. After we'd eaten we trekked on, heading north towards the Valleys and the greener territory of the Brecon Beacons.

Days later we saw trees on the horizon which gave us hope. As we travelled closer, we moved slower, hellish slow, with Dad the limper, me the crutch. One night we rested at a broken water main and drank till we sloshed, filled our flasks, washed away the dust and then struggled onwards. The night after that we slept in a cottage built top of a crooked lane. From the bedroom window I could see the winding water course of a small river. Fresh water!

Early morning we trod down the pot-holed lane to the overgrown path beside the river which as we neared it seemed more like a rushy stream. It was hard going, that steep lane, but once we reached the flat path it got easier. But flat or steep Dad never grumbled, not even at the small portions of food we ate, or the stench from closed up farms, or me urging him forever onwards. He just forged on stoically.

Coupla days later we rounded a bend to find the stream blocked by a heap of mud and stone, and beyond that a great crater … and no more water. A deliberate bombing or a jettisoned shell? After that we walked past mud and stone and blackened weed. We slept nights in a ditch, fearful of sky craft.

'Next trail up, we follow,' I said. 'I spotted house-roofs on that ridge above us. Could be we'll find more hidden food and decent shelter. Anything to keep him moving.

Round the next curve we came to a humpbacked bridge and an overgrown lane leading upwards, hopefully to the houses I saw earlier. Half way up we stopped to rest and share the last tin of baked beans. After I massaged his legs, we carried on.

Top of the lane we found a group of pre-crash new builds, the once neat lawns littered with dug-up soil and scattered bones, and in the distance a dog pack bayed. We kept on past the houses and came to a kiddies' play-park with rusted swings and a broken see-saw. The sun came out as we sat on a bench almost swamped in grass and ivy.

'That's it, Dad. Tins are finished, and we need a fire to cook the veg.' I handed him a flask and he drank the last of the water. A loose skinned hand crept into mine, and we sat like that till the clouds crept over the sun. I didn't feel like getting up, felt like never moving again, but the sound of water stirred me into motion.

'Hear that, Dad?'

'Hear what?'

'Running water. Could be another stream. I'll go look. You rest here.'

'Be safe, child,' he whispered.

Fighting through the brambles, I pushed into an overgrown copse and followed the trickling sound till I came to a fast flowing stream. It looked and tasted wholesome so I went back for the flasks.

'Ambrosia, Cassandra, pure ambrosia.' My father said in his old pompous way, then smiled his new soft smile. 'But I've reached my limit. I'm done, my girl, really done this time.'

He was right. He was a walking corpse.

'You go on if you have to. Leave me here.'

'No, we stay together, near the clean water. I'll go check the houses. Back in a jiff.'

The houses showed signs of recent occupation, fresh ashes in the grates, a straggle of empty tins and buzz-flies everywhere. Could be they were drawn by the lingering smell of death. I didn't investigate further, scared of disease.

I found a roll of tough plastic under a hedge, a pile of timber that might once have been a garden shed, and a mattress stuffed into a crumpled van. Took me three trips but I got them to the park before dark. I made a lean-to among the trees well hidden from the play area, using the shed timber to support the sheeting and the rest of the plastic as a ground sheet.

'See, Dad, with the sleeping bags on the mattress we'll sleep soft and dry. We'll stay a few days, till you get stronger. Why don't you get an early night while I go back and cover my tracks.'

I helped him into the shelter and as he slid into the sleeping bag he spoke. 'Only be a day or two, Cass. Soon as I feel up to it we'll move on.'

'Sure, Dad,' I said. 'Few days and you'll be on top form.'

Last thing I did before turning in was shroud the shelter with branches, adding armfuls of grass and leaves till it merged into the undergrowth. Dad was fast asleep and snoring as I lugged flat stones from the stream bed for a hearth and screening for a cook fire.

Dad's few days stretched into a week, and if anything he grew weaker not stronger. We wouldn't be moving on.

He became attached to the hideaway and like him I felt we'd stepped out of the real world. Cut adrift we began a kind of hibernation. After that first week I roved, grubbing for supplies, finding the blade of a carving knife and a battered ladle. Small items to bring such joy.

Dad tutored me in edible greenery and beneficial fungi, resurrecting his role as father. I found myself unable to resent his teaching as I once had. We'd become companions.

'I studied fungi, when I was younger. Quite the expert, actually. This one here is the Horn of Plenty,' he said and pointed to the dark brown funnel-shaped fungus I found growing in a carpet of rotting leaves. '*It* is completely edible while this one,' he pointed to an ordinary looking mushroom, pale yellow with white gills on the underside. 'This one could kill an army.'

'Good job you're here,' I said. 'I'd have put money on the plain one being edible, shows how much I know.'

I stayed away from farms and we took to veggie living. But as autumn progressed I lost my squeamishness and after a few lessons from my father I snared a brace of fat rabbits and used the skins to make a soft headrest for him.

He faded, sleeping more and more, lying curled inside his sleep bag. When he did wake he spoke of days past, to people long dead and I gradually dimmed from his notice. On the morning of the first hard frost he didn't wake, lying stiff and still, gone to join my mother. A day later with the ground too hard to dig I lugged the sleeping bag to a ditch and piled bricks and stones over him to keep him safe from scavengers.

5

Takes me four days and a near-empty belly to get to the spot where One Eye found me. But *is* it the one? It doesn't feel the same——for starters the wood looks more like a forest with more saplings, more brambles, more of everything. And my guide, the tall pine tree has vanished. So I backtrack. And yeah, OK, the houses are where they should be, but they look decades older. Ash and buddleia have reclaimed the lawns, ivy's climbed to the gutters and giant fireweed masks the ground floor windows. I'm looking at the holed roofs, pitted brickwork, and broken window panes, and to me it seems more like deliberate damage than nature's work. Plus there's a lingering stink of decomposing bodies. Senses on max alert I head for our old camp site. First I spot the swings, then the bench hidden under a hill of brambles, and then I hear the stream; this is definitely the right place.

The first thing I do is set snares. Traps set I climb up to the broad branch of an ash tree and settle against the trunk for the night, listening to leaves rub and swish and the creak-grind of branch on branch. Slowly day sinks to evening and I speculate on what treasures I'll find in the ruins. A louder rustling wakes me from a light doze and I see below me a lithe, spotted hound pushing through the grass towards the stream. It pauses, ears pricked, front paws in the water, head up and sniffing. I tense, it growls and I feel for my knife, but the growl is answered by a high pitched whine and more canines push to the water and start lapping. I must be downwind, because these hounds show no signs of noticing me.

They're cautious as a pack of Rats and from the safety of my tree I salute them as brothers. All sizes, all colours and bearing the sleek health of successful hunters, they drink deeply. Soon as the scout laps his fill, the pack melts into the undergrowth taking my good wishes with them.

'Bout half hour on, more rustling. Not careful and furtive, loud and clumsy, made by a pair of scabby figures weighed down with backpacks. Once through the bushes they crouch by the stream and drink. Unlike the canines, they don't keep watch.

I hold still, not wanting to be noticed. Can't see any weapons, but that don't mean a thing. A sudden *crack-crack, crack-crack* rips through the silence. Heart revs up, my whole body twitches, but I'm not the target, cos below me the scabby pair have pitched headfirst into the stream, blood leaking from holes punched into their backs. I stifle my gasp as four strangers break cover. The leader, a stocky grey-beard with a pigtail, hefts a hi-tech trooper rifle. His three companions carry low-tech hand guns. All of them pack hunting knives and wear remnants of trooper uniforms.

The leader with the vari-shell gooses the others into stripping the deaders and searching their packs. Then he stands sentry, watchful as a dog scout. I fasten on their faces, the leader's an oldster, the three youngers share his likeness—his get, no doubt. Like him they braid their hair; two with a brace of plaits falling either side of the face, the third with a Medusa mass of Dreads. All four are full fleshed, healthy looking and wearing genuine trooper boots that spark my envy. Task done they fill their water flasks upstream of the shooting and start dragging the bodies out of sight.

Their trail is easy to follow and it doesn't lead far, just to the ramshackle group of dwells. They dump the deaders in a pit which they cover with a fence panel and weight with stones, before disappearing into a dwell with a half-flattened roof. A short time later they appear on the flat part; a fine lookout post, offering shelter plus an all-round view.

The older guy keeps lookout while the young ones kindle a fire and spit a cow haunch.

'Madoc,' says the old guy, speaking loud, unafraid of being heard. 'Don't you put that meat on till the fire burns low.'

'Wasn't gonna,' says the boy with the Dreadlocks. One of the others laughs and hands out bottles of booze. The oldster drinks, trooper gun on his shoulder, eyes on the fire. I creep closer trying to think of a way to liberate those well made trooper boots. How sound do these killers sleep?

Takes a while for the fire to burn down enough for Madoc to place the spitted joint on the uprights set either side of the glowing embers. That done he looks to the grey-beard.

'Leave it cook now, boy.' Grey-beard says. 'But keep an eye on it while you and your brothers sort out the backpacks.'

They sort, I watch. And as the joint cooks so the burning fat spirals up, then drifts down in a tantalizing cloud setting my belly rumbling. I circle closer, thinking to seize my chance of liberating some loot, should an opportunity arise. The dwell nearest the killers' seems a likely roost. The roof is completely flattened, so on the one hand I'll be a sitting duck up there, while on the other it'll be easier to get to, because the rubble piled against the far wall makes for an easy climb-up. Turns out it's not all that easy, my worn boots don't grip well and I'm forced to move real slow and stop every time a chunk of rubble slips out of place. Only hunger for a pair of genuine all-weather super cleated trooper boots, keeps me going. In the end I shuck off my lousy boots, string 'em round my neck and finish the climb in my stocking feet.

Night falls and the sky is clear and bright with stars as I reach a top floor window. A big stretch and a silent, toe hurting scrabble and I'm on the roof. I plan to crawl along the wall, take a couple of rights and get within spitting distance of the killers' roost. I start well, but half way round I spear a knee on a pointed stone, miss a fall-down by a whisker and make a noise a tribe of deaf cats could hear. Dropping flat I hug the wall and pray.

'What's that?'

I squint ahead and it's the old guy, rifle to shoulder and aiming in my direction. 'Cy, go see what's up,' he says and a two-plaiter leaves the fire and walks to the edge of the roof.

I close my eyes to slits, and stay frozen still.

'Anything out there, Cy?' calls the oldster.

'Nothing,' Cy yells back, but I don't start breathing till he turns back to the roasting meat.

'It's always happening, Dad. The place is falling to bits. Isn't it about time we moved on?'

Grey-beard walks around, rifle at port, 'We move on my say so, not a day before. The troopers ain't made it out this far, son. Soon as we spot their flying spies we'll be off.'

'If these shacks don't fall down first.' Cy mutters.

Ignoring the mumbles the oldster talks on. 'Curse of the world, poor housing stock. Back when I was a boy they sold well-seasoned wood and good Welsh slate. Then came afford-able housing. Cheap tack I called it, and I was right. New stuff's collapsing about our ears while the old is standing proud.'

'Till Templeton sends his bombers, Dad. Won't rest, that old mizzer, till he flattens the damn country. Says he's gonna build a New Britain.'

'If you believe that Cy, you'll believe anything. Templeton ain't no builder, son, 'less he's building himself a kingdom.'

Fresh bottles pass and I crawl closer, peeping from behind an abandoned water cistern. The oldster abandons his patrol and sits with his sons around the cook fire.

'Madoc, I reckon that joint's about done. Get it down and start cutting, and remember I likes mine bloody. And Cy, stick more wood on the fire, looks like it's gonna be a cold night.'

My mouth waters as Madoc lays the beef on a plank and starts cutting great slices onto tin plates. My belly grumbles louder as

I watch all four of them tuck in.

After a second helping the two double-plaiters swig deep and start singing. The others add their voices to the tuneless choir. With the cook-fire replenished it blazes high and crackles loud, and with the rooftop ringing with the sound of drunken voices I quit worrying over making noise. These guys have had their own way for too long. Confidence kills as fast as bullets, Rats know that all too well.

I watch as they take turns in tossing empties off the roof and cheering at every smash and crash. Then the youngers with two plaits crawl into the shelter offered by the half-roof, leaving Grey-Beard and Madoc drinking by the fire.

'Feed the fire, son,' says the oldster.

'Sure,' says Madoc and piles floorboards onto the flames, before sitting his father to watch the blaze. After a time the old guy says, 'I'll take first watch. Get some sleep, I'll wake you later.'

Madoc wraps himself in a blanket and curls up by the fire. Grey Beard stands, dawdling round the roof before joining his boy. It's not long before he puts his rifle down and pokes idly at the fire with a piece of wood. Next thing he's sitting slumped. Yeah, but is he sleeping? Might this be my chance? I wait, ready to move and watching him close. Soon as he starts snoring I know it's time to make my play.

I'm up and on the move, when I hear a sound. I freeze. The old man? I take a careful look, he's still slumped and snoring.

The sound repeats. A dog howl! More follow. Grey-Beard still doesn't stir, but I prick up. Could it be the pack I saw at stream? And like a knife stab, an idea spikes into my brain—an idea so sharp it'd earn a sharky grin from One Eye. Slipping down from my vantage point, I don my boots and head for a sycamore poking high above the rest. Once there I climb as high as I can, find a firm perch and start howling like a bitch in heat, a skill I learned from One Eye. He used the ruse to lure enough canines to line his clothes with a coupla layers of dog fur. 'Ain't felt cold since I insulated my duds,' he said. 'Dog fur's better than cat and you don't need so many of 'em.'

I cease my howls when the pack howls back, and I scoot back to my roof perch to wait on events. Moving a tad too fast I lose my balance, noisily.

Grey Beard grabs his rifle, staggers to his feet and looks in my direction. Half asleep he may be but I reckon I been spotted. I hold still, he raises his rifle, but he's distracted by a wave of dogs leaping up from inside the house. Before he does more than yell, they're on him and he's down. More dogs pour in and over Madoc who's struggling to free himself from his blanket.

I marvel at the hounds, at their fitness, their speed. The oldster tries to raise the rifle but fails and a black mastiff rips it from his hands. The meat smell excites the pack and a good half dozen spring at the two guys staggering drink-slowed from the shelter. Dragged down they're lost under yipping hounds.

Grey Beard fights to his feet, kicks the mastiff and fends off two patchy terriers, before sinking to his knees. I think he's done for, but he seizes the rifle and fires on automatic. The blast shocks the pack to silence. Dogs are downed, ripped apart by the explosive rounds, but more pour from inside the house. A German Shepherd bites through Grey Beard's throat, the gun falls silent, the man lost beneath the slavering dog.

Madoc gets free of the blanket and grabs the rifle, taking out the Shepherd and several of its pack mates, but an Afghan springs, fangs his arm and the boy's shots go wild, hitting one of his struggling bros. Snatching his knife Madoc takes out the Afghan, but slips on a bottle and is lost beneath a fresh wave of snarling curs.

One guy heaves up from the dog pile—Cy. He fires a hand gun, one arm dangling useless and bloody. I join the fight, hefting bricks and tiles at him. I make a hit and he drops the gun and lurches for the shelter. Might be more guns there, so I hurl my knife. It spins true, thunking into the guy's back. The dogs take over and I watch, savouring the efficiency of teeth and claws.

Fight over, the pack cleans up. Dead pack mates and prey traveling the self same route. They melt away at sun rise and I go check, retrieving my knife from under the pile of marrow-emptied bones and pulling the boots from Madoc's feet. They're a tad nibbled, but serviceable and only a shade too large. After assessing the spoils I choose the stuff to carry back to camp and stash the rest for a later pick-up.

Don't think I'll venture the ruins today, found enough treasure here. Before setting out for the new camp I collect my snares. Waste not want not is a damn fine motto, for me as well as the dog pack. I've made a good haul, two brace of plump conies. I don't cook them till I'm out of the dog pack's range, though I figure they'll be belly-full and sleeping sound after the night's success. Next morning *my* belly's full of rabbit and I'm perked by a prime night's sleep. It's time to hunt for the markers that lead home.

And don't I go in big! Got my new trooper boots on, with three more pairs hanging from my pack, and I'm toting Grey Beard's fancy rifle. Two grinning sentries escort me to Man Ear, and I preen. Why shouldn't I? I came off top dog.

I hand the rifle and spare boots to the chief, informing him where I stashed the rest and he sends a round-up party straightaway. At the naming feast I tell the tale, giving my version of the mating call of a bitch on heat to loud applause.

At feast end Man Ear gets up. 'Stand, no name,' he says into the rapt silence. One Eye hands him a knife. 'Present yourself and receive a name well earned.'

I kneel, my eyes on his. I stay focused as a cold-hot line scores my cheek, blood flows but the pain melts in the blasting Rat roar. Man Ear holds the knife high for all to see its reddened blade. Silence falls.

'I, Man Ear, dub you Bitch Singer of the Whip Tail tribe of Rats. Have you chosen your first tattoo?'

I stand and answer my leader. 'A howling dog,' I say amid approving shouts.

'One Eye, take this Rat and mark her so.'

I walk with One Eye to the fire and stand in the heat as he needles the ink into my arm. I am so proud, I'm flying to the sun.

Rooted, at last. I've found home.

6

Eighteen months and a few camp moves later two strangers turn up, 'riving the day we cairned Venner Grace in the ruins. A greatly respected venner, Grace. One of the few Rats who survived to old age to lend their wisdom to the tribe.

'I was born in the city,' she said to One Eye 'fore she died. 'Bury me as far into the ruins as you dare venture.' He promised to do what she wanted and when she'd breathed her last he asked for volunteers to carry her into the ruins. I volunteered, as did Dex and four others. Venner Grace had always been kind to low-rank nameless Rats, unlike some oldsters who lorded over the un-named.

Man Ear tasks One Eye with saying the Words over Venner Grace, and awards the volunteers the honour of expressing our loss by wailing the ceremonial death howl of the Rat tribes.

Duty done, One Eye leads us home to give witness that all was carried out as the venner wished. Reaching camp we head to Man Ear and find him deep in conversation with stranger Rats, young looking but bearing several honour scars incised on their cheeks. Man Ear calls One Eye to the pow-wow, but waves us volunteers away.

The rest leave, but me and Dex hang around, sprucing up the cook-fire while eyeing the newcomers. The black-haired, sweet looking one does most of the talking, the other, a spiky-haired redhead is more watcher than talker. His eyes are everywhere, he clocks me and Dex clocking *him* pretty quick. We inch closer to get in earshot, but Man Ear orders us away with a glower.

We slope off, but glancing back I meet the redhead's watchful gaze.

'Think they're gonna stay?' I ask Dex when we're well clear.

'Hope so,' she grins 'Fight you for the looker?'

'Which one's that, you reckon?'

'The smooth talker, him with the black curls.'

'He ain't *that* pretty, Dex. Not worth tussling over.'

'So, you like the redhead?'

'That colour? Frink, no. And did you see the way he sneered when he saw me looking back? 'Sides, they might just be passing through.'

Turns out Striker and Pinch are here to stay.

On the quiet I watch Striker. He in his turn watches everybody, but keeps his council. Careful, I like that. I'm also getting to appreciate red hair and amber eyes.

One Eye gives me the griff. How the pair's clan was smashed in a trooper blitz. Seems the BuzRats stayed in one place a tad too long, giving the Troopers a chance to ferret them out, bursting over the rubble in tracked carriers accompanied by air machines. The handful of Rats that escaped were the ones out foraging or a few like Striker who had an escape route already in mind.

Yeah, One Eye's sure taken to Striker. 'What have I always told you?' he says after giving me the story. 'Forethought and planning never lets you down. Mark my words, Striker is a Rat to watch. Got a brain, that boy. Uses it well. Sharp, he is. Watch and learn, young Bit, watch and learn.'

Dex makes her play for Pinch and catches him sweet and easy. Course she crowed—won the prize didn't she? But I'm not so sure. The red-head has something about him, a quiet watchfulness that piques my interest. Mindful of One Eye's words I put my tracking skills to the test. Takes Striker half a day to map the camp and find all the ins and outs, another day getting pally with the venners and learning the tribe's history. Shadowing him I get to know more about the WhipTails than I ever thought to ask. And Jeez, can that guy sweet-talk when he wants to. Suck info from the hardest of hardened troopers, him.

Striker's an early riser. Up before dawn he makes a tour of the camp border, walking ghostlike, sniffing the air like a predator, ears cocked and listening hard. Since I been tracking him I've had to up my game, don't want to be caught stalking.

So I'm up and out in the pre-dawn grey, and he's ahead of me walking a path he's trod before. He drops to his knees like he's found something. I ease closer … and he's up and on me fast as a sprung-boxed monkey.

I fight him. Course I do. Been taught by the best, me, and I don't go down easy. Time we're done we're both breathing fast and loud, there's blood dripping from his nose and he's developing a real neat shiner. Me, I'm battered and bruised, but lost in his amber stare I feel no pain.

'Ah, my cat-eyed stalker. Think you're clever? Think I've never spotted you?'

I keep shtum.

'What is it? Think I'm fifth column? You reckon I'm a snitch for the troopers? Come on, say.' And then he only goes and *grins*, like I'm some punk kid.

I'll teach him to laugh at me. 'Okay,' I say. 'Let me up and I'll *say*.'

He leaves go of my shoulders and gets up, freeing my legs. So I kick him where it hurts and run back to camp, leaving him groaning. That'll teach him.

No more following, I vow. No more glimming for red hair in a crowd of dull browns and blacks. No more pining over glowing amber eyes, and I'll put a *definite* nix on heated daydreams.

Jeez, but that's easier said than done.

Now I've sworn off even thinking of the guy, I see him everywhere. Nights he sits across the camp fire staring at me. I go hunting and he's out same time, making sure I see he's holding a better catch than mine. Been getting the feeling of being followed, but when I look around no one's there. Could be my imagination, but I doubt it. Could be he's just proving a point.

Today's the day I help train the ratlings in tracking. Soon after I get started Striker strolls up and starts working with a second group. It's like I'm some magic-maker conjuring him out of thin air.

About an hour later, class finishes and he walks over. Okay, so what's he gonna say? What's he gonna do? He gets to me and I look him in the eyes and wait. Frink me if I'm gonna speak first.

'Seems we got off on the wrong foot,' he says.

I keep shtum.

'Think we could start over?' he says with a wrinkly-eyed smile.

I'm tempted. He looks sincere, like he really means it. So I shrug an okay.

Thing is I kinda like this newcomer and One Eye's right, he *is* sharp. Even on first sight I knew there was something about him. He's tall, fair skinned and wears his rust red hair glued into spikes threaded with hollow bones and found-beads. So yeah, I'm willing to give it a re-boot.

Seven days later we're an item and I'm learning more about him by the day. F'rinstance I know how he makes his hair stiffener—by boiling bones. No way am I gonna glue my hair, but I liked cosying up to the teacher. Some nights when I'm too tired, too brain-active to rest, I count the beads on his hair spikes till I sleep. Always been a counter, me. It's a habit, I tell Striker, and he grins his hunter's grin.

I love the way he dresses, the leather trews and waistcoat he made from pieced animal skins, fit him like they bin moulded I love the way his fierce smile turns gentle when he looks at me a certain way, and how his amber eyes warm when he kisses me. Truth is, I don't know what he sees in a runtish, black haired nothing like me. Says he likes my green eyes, reminds him of a cat he knew. Oh, and he says I'm a doughty fighter—brave, he means. That kind of talk always ends in a roughhouse and as I never pull my punches there's usually a few hot minutes before we settle to loving. Wonder if our kids'll have Striker's red hair?

Could life be sweeter?

7

Spring. Two years past my naming day and six months glued to Striker, I'm about to lead my first patrol on an info hunt for Man Ear. A scout reported that troopers have been spotted pushing out from the nearest NOP compounds and moving into Rat territory.

Man Ear wants intel, wants to know 'xactly what's up. Whatever's happening is well north of us, but even here, in the south, we've noticed an increase in trooper aircraft, and a ramping up of ground patrols carrying some pretty weird gear. Fr'instance, I been chased by a shell that followed me round two corners before it ran out of whatever gave it zip.

The WhipTails lost a good quarter of the clan last winter. Some taken by dog packs, some shot by troopers, but most … just disappeared. Other Rat tribes tell the same tale. Could be some Rats are following Throat Tearer into the Wilderness but that's best not broadcast. Man Ear's convinced Templeton's brewing something nasty. Me and Striker think along the same lines.

Me, Dex and Pinch are not the only patrol venturing out, Striker's taking one. Man Ear's sending scouts in all directions. Preparing for another move the chief wants rock-hard intel 'fore he stirs the tribe.

Lately, it's like we're always shifting camp. Sometimes I wish me and Striker could settle somewhere and live *steadier* lives. P'raps one day the world will turn and peace will come again. Yeah, and One Eye's gonna grow a brand new glim! Nah, this is *it*. We gotta make the best of it—least I got Striker.

Before we set out on patrol, I go hunting with him—the send-outs need to be well stocked. Patrols can last far longer than expected so it pays to be well prepared. Patrols leave at darkfall, we don't aim to stay out long but it's wise to be well prepared.

We hunt late morning and catch a brace of skinny dogs and some kind of big bird before we turn back to camp. I shot the bird with the hand gun I brought back from my Trial jaunt. It's a good gun, but not a patch on the hi-tech vari shell that Man Ear claimed. But, hey, that's the way it goes.

Half way back to camp a small machine swoops out of the sky and hovers over us, gabbing. It's a while before I realise it's gabbing words. '*NOP cant*,' I sign to Striker. He signs back with a finger to his ear, and we listen till it starts repeating; then Striker shoots it down. We get back to camp and One Eye tells us he's seen one but killed it before it messaged. We tell him what ours said and watch him boil.

'Lay down our arms? Turn ourselves over to the stinking troopers? That's crazy talk, no one's gonna do that. Committing suicide, that is. What else did it say?'

'It said troopers are the arm of the rightful government of New Britain. A government headed by that craphead Templeton. It didn't call him craphead, natch, gave his full name, General Julius Templeton. Said insurgents should surrender their weapons and work for the good of the state.'

'*Work?* For that narding frink?'

'Don't shout, One Eye, I'm just the tale teller. Templeton wants us Rats to give up fighting, become citizens of the New Order and reap the rewards of a new era of peace and prosperity.'

'Yeah, like that'll turn our minds! Templeton's got a different idea of peace to us Rats. He wants a thumb placed heavy on every man woman and child in the country. Do this, do that or get squashed, that's his idea.'

'That's the carrot, One Eye, be good and prosper.'

'And the stick? Come on, there has to be a hitting stick!'

'Yeah, there is. Rebels who don't hand themselves in and continue to resist will be caught, chipped and reclaimed.'

'Chipped? What the hell does that mean?'

Striker answers. 'Templeton's into new tech. Dex told me they put info about folk on a small bead and insert this *chip* under the skin. How? I don't know. Look, I just heard talk, thought it fantasy till that flying machine started spieling shit at me.'

'So what did it say after that?'

'One Eye, if you'd listened to your machine before you killed it,' I say, 'then you'd know that Rats caught 'resisting the lawful government' will be regarded as feral and be neutered.'

'Neutered? That mean what I think it means?

'If you think cutting, sterilization, then I reckon you'd be right,' Striker says. And as he says those words I shiver, the blood running cold in my veins.

One Eye takes his rage into the ruins with a box of refills and comes back with a tally of ten dead fly-bys and a pocketful of twisted metal to prove it.

When time comes for the patrols to set out, Man Ear tells me to approach the NOP compound from the west, make a quick recce, cause no disturbance and return to base with the info. He tells Striker to go east. We walk together till we get to the crippled high-rise then split. I'm sorry to see him go. This is my first taste of command and I feel strange, not scared exactly, more like unsettled.

The night is quiet, can't hear no howls and only the occasional fly-by whizzing in the distance. Dex, the girl I 'helped out' with the heavy rock, is my second. She brought a net with her, wants to catch a fly-by because she thinks they're capable of much more than spieling cant. We work well together, me and Dex and I believe she's right. Pinch's my third, a brill sketch artist and a trusted map maker; and Dex's main man.

We take a break from trekking after a couple of hours, eat a jerked meat bar, slake our thirst, then walk on. I call halt after a few miles and we listen to the sound of hunting dogs and a vixen crying for a mate. I hear the feathery rush of owl wings and the death squeak of some small mammal. A Rat's existence in three words: death and hunting.

We travel on, reading Rat signs telling of trooper sightings, tribal losses and the like. We add our own marks to the record, dated by the current slashtag. Some time later, say two or three in the morning we get to the troopers' post, lit in bright arrogance at the end of a new-made road.

We circle the post committing everything we see to memory and sketch pad. Post's a blocky building circled by a plas-met fence. Inside the fence and linked to the block is smaller fenced area holding tracked vehicles. The whole area's lit with powerful Mag-Beams and lousy with sentries. Dex points to red light-spots winking along the plas-met fencing and signs their purpose.

'Eyes. Auto cams that react to temperature and movement.' We move back and she points to ripples of sparkling light waving above the mesh, and whispers, 'A fringe of sound seekers attached to plaswire filaments on the top of the fence.' She'd know, having escaped from serfdom in a city compound. 'Those little seekers pick up sounds a dog'd miss. Bit, this place is serious business. Looks to me like they'll be making their push sooner rather than later.'

Satisfied we know enough we set off with the info, not stopping to collate the information till we're well away from the fort. Pinch adds our input to his map while I enter the estimation of troop numbers and Dex's knowledge of the fence alarms, into my notebook. After a meat bar and a stim-tab we trot for home.

Half hour later and we're off the home trail, making a dog-leg to avoid a trio of fly-bys. 'I swear there's more of them every time we go out,' Dex says. I agree, though Pinch expresses doubts.

We're walking through crumbling high-density housing, Pinch on point, Dex tail-ender. My eyes are glued to the skyline, looking for fly-bys, but my mind's on the hi-tech fort behind us. The NOP is on the up and spreading fast. Too narding fast.

Warned by a moon-glint, I watch a fly-by cross the street and disappear through a gap between two houses. We drop, holding motionless a few beats before running to a ruined house and squatting behind a wall. In minutes the machine returns. We watch it crossing and re-crossing, sometimes disappearing into a building for minutes on end. It moves with no hint of engine noise. Dex is right, these machines are more than dreck spreaders.

A nudge from Pinch alerts me to a second machine coming straight for us. We're in shadow. How the? Hell, can it smell us? This one's bigger than the first and covered in weird bumps. Dex fires at the first one, Pinch and I aim for the big bastard. Dex's blows up while ours banks and weaves, firing like some mini fighter plane, and we miss with every shot. Dex joins in and with three of us blasting we take it down, but before it crashes I take a hit. The noise dies and I feel blood dripping down my arm. All too soon the hurting starts.

'We'd best get going,' I say. 'I'm betting troopers will turn up pretty soon.'

'Let me tie a bandage, fore we go,' Pinch says.

Once my arm's bound we head away, eyes on the skyline. It's not long before we spot another flier.

'Reckon it's one of the talkers. Right shape, right size,' Pinch whispers.

Ducking under a leaning wall, I do some fast thinking before giving the sign for silence. Using my good hand, I sign, 'You two, take the info back. I'll be the lure. I'll take the fly-by as far as I can. Dex, here's my notebook.'

She takes it, but Pinch shakes his head and points to my arm signing that I should go with Dex. *He*'d be the lure.

I shake *my* head, I'm wounded, weakened, they have best

chance of getting home. My patrol, my responsibility.

Before Pinch tries another sign I lob a shot at the hovering machine and run, snatching a quick look to check it's following. It is. I chew a handful of stim-tabs and settle to a steady run. An overdose of stims is the least of my worries.

I head in the opposite direction to Dex and Pinch, running till I'm out of breath, my sleeve stiff with blood. Pausing for a breather I check on the fly-by. It's hovering just out of range, an eyeless watcher moving when I move, stilling when I still.

Right now I'm tucked into a doorway. Doorway's wide, tiled green and white and blocked by a rusty gate. The words on the arch above my head read City Line. Between the hoverer and the shut gate I'm stuck. I'm going nowhere.

Arm throbbing, pain drilling, I sag against the grill, sip a mouthful of water and contemplate tightening the bandage. A closer look changes my mind; bandage, sleeve and skin being fused in red-brown varnish. I reload my handgun, look up and, hell, now there's three flying machines. I fire, they dodge and I take it as a bad sign when they don't fire back. Frink it, they must want me alive.

What if I take a chance on them not wanting to off me? I step forward. Good, they're moving back, keeping the same distance between us. Do I run? There's an alley opposite. I could dive in there. It's narrow, perhaps I could pick them off as they come at me one by one. Worth a try. I get ready, but the fly-bys start firing, all three shots hitting the ground at my feet. I back up to the gate. They want me penned. Soon as I hear vehicles approaching, I know Dex is right, fly-bys *are* more than they seem. I'm betting these ones messaged the troopers. My guess is confirmed when all three light up like year-end bonfires, all sparkles and beams, showing me clear against the grating – pinpointing me for the narding troopers.

I do something I should have done first off—investigate the barrier. The gaps in the metal grill are grunged with a mix of shredded paper, plastic and twining weeds. Behind the grating there's a blockage, rubble from a ceiling collapse. In the light from the fly-bys I see a hole in the top of the grating, a squeeze-way, near the door arch. Can I get through? Gotta try. I climb the grill, my bad arm hurting like it's being pulled off. Now the fly-bys are warbling, the vehicle noise louder, and some gruff voice shouts, 'Don't fire, take her alive.'

No one's taking *me* alive, I'll dig a gate spike in my throat before some trooper lays hands on me. Anger fuels my stretch to the squeeze-way and I bull through the rusted hole, spikes tearing my clothes and ripping my skin same time as a trooper shouts 'Halt and surrender'.

Cop that. Another heave and I'm through and falling on top the rubble. Daren't stop, they'll blast the gate to come after me. The rubble shifts, gives way and I'm sliding, and rolling free-style. Heavy lumps smash into me, then comes a head crack, and I blink out.

I blink back, coughing dust and rolling in an avalanche of stone and sharpness. There's no light. The roof's falling. Buried, I'm being buried, being suffocated. Another head crack and the fear flows away, taking me with it.

8

I wake in black stinking darkness with a mouthful of grit, and I'm lying on my side with my arm hurting like hell. Where's Dad? Got to move, got to find him. Don't faint, Cass, or you'll never find him. Keep breathing.

Dad?

God, I remember; he's dead. I covered him with stones. Am I dead too? Who's covered me with stones?

Stop. Think. I'm not Cass any more. I'm Bitch Singer of the Whip Tails and the fly-bys are onto me. I climbed through a hole and the roof fell on me. It's quiet, the troopers must have gone … for now.

Gotta get up, get away. So what if it's dark and your arm hurts? You're still alive aren't you? Suck it up and move on. You want to get back to Striker, don't you? Then *move*.

I make myself get up. Thinking of Striker gives me the strength to fight the pain. Everything hurts. Even moving like a trod-on snail costs. I stick my arm into my jacket and button up. Good as a sling, that. Lucky it's my right arm seeing as I'm a lefty. My head spins, I bite my cheek to keep focused, put my hand out and find wall tiles. Can't stay here to be bagged by the troopers. Nah, Rats chase death, they don't get chased. Forward Bit, into the dark.

I check my gear: gun—missing, knife—sheathed. My pack's

on my back so I've a few dried meat strips, some hardbread and a food bar. The water flask's in my pocket, about half full. I feel in my pocket for a stim-tab, find two and swallow one. Soon as the arm pain eases I head into the black, thankful for cleated boots. Even with them it's slow going; feeling for potholes and rubble, scared to fall on my injured arm. Worst thing is the dust. My throat hurts, it's so dry, but I have to eke out the water. Reckon I've a long road ahead of me.

A few yards on and I hit a stretch of crunchy stuff. Shells? Next minute I hit something that rolls with a hollow sound. Frink, it's a bone-field. Fear spurts me to a faster pace. Don't want to leave *my* skull for some future stumbler to kick.

It's easy to lose track of time in the dark, and far easier to lose control of your thoughts. Blackness isn't just the absence of light, it's a real force, a real … place. I keep going, kicking more skulls and treading through a swathe of brittle bones. How many dead folk are here in the black with me? How'd they get to be dead? Sickness? Tunnel blockage? Some crazy, running amok? Does it matter, dead is dead. Comes to us all.

I'll just sit a while, Dad. Five minutes and I'll be fine. Just five minutes, please, Dad. My arm's hurting so bad.

Get up. Gotta get up. Can't, it's too dark.

What am I doing here? Who am I?

I'm Cass, let me rest.

No. I'm Bit. GET UP.

I'm up. My good hand touches the wall tiles and I follow the curve. I'm not alone, the pain walks with me. Don't want it to leave. Pain is life.

I walk and rest and walk again, and the blackness gradually fades to grey. When the pathway starts sloping upwards the light separates into shiny diamond shapes. I get there and find a barrier between me and the light—a rusty expanding gate. I rest my head against it and grip the flaking metal. Outside the barrier is a sun-bright street, empty of troopers and fly-bys. I've reached the end of the tunnel. Beyond lies freedom. I take a tiny sip of water, chew the last stim-tab and psyche up. One kick downs the rusty gate, and I'm free.

Nothing stirs outside, my adrenaline high fades, balance lost I fall on my injured arm. Out gusts my breath and the world greys. A sudden spat of rain shocks the colour back. Can't stay in the open for fear of fly-bys. Dizzy, unable to stand, I crawl into the shadows of the gateway and wait for my eyes to work properly.

I count the seconds, my fear of fly-bys rising with every breath. After a hundred million years I get to see across the rubble strewn road, to a line of fire-blackened shopfronts and a half-demolished office block. The end wall is kept from falling by the skeleton girders of the nearby burned-out building. The gap between them looks promising, deep and black-dark. A good hiding place? Now all I have to do is get there and check it out.

Time I do, I got scraped knees, my arm's on fire and there's precious little in my water flask. I got no choice but wriggle deep into the cleft. I keep going for as long as I can, before exhaustion takes hold and I crash out.

I open my eyes, feverish and parched, and moisten my lips with a smear of water. Next time I surface I'm cooler and manage to sit up and look through a gap in the girders. The light's changed to the crepuscular glow that comes with dawn or dusk. Which, I wonder? I lay down, too tired to think. Each time I wake the light is brighter and my mind is clearer.

Turns out that from the mouth of the cleft I can see the rusty gate lying on the pavement. There's no sign of troopers. Why haven't they bulled through after me? 'Spose it's time to consider my options.

I'm considering and getting nowhere fast when I hear something. Troopers? No, dogs barking. Gotta move back into the cleft.

The barking gets louder—dogs onto a scent. My scent? Cleft's narrowing, no way out. Go higher. How? Climb the girders. With this useless arm? Hell, they're coming, start climbing.

I grab a girder and haul up. Stretch for the next, and haul again. God, how it hurts. I wedge my neck against a cross girder reach one handed and, *pull,* ignoring the sick feeling. Forget fainting, Bit. *Haul up.* Wedge and haul, wedge and haul. My neck's bleeding, I'm quivering weak, but the howling spurs me on.

What's that ahead? A basket of twisted metal. Burned out lift car? Got to be, look at the cables and half-melted number panel. I squeeze inside the cage and watch the pack of scrawny mix-breeds loping towards the cleft.

One leggy cur climbs the leaning wall, reaches a girder and looks up. Others scrabble after it, jostling for position. Long Legs rears up. Feet on a cross-girder snout raised, hackles proud. It sees me. My nest's too high for it to reach, isn't it?

The dog stares, panting and drooling. Deep hacking barks break out and the pack turns. Long Legs follows, scrambling down the wall and running the street, nose down, leaving me trembling like a youngling Rat.

Got to eat. Sweat breaks by the time I retrieve a food bar, trooper made, chewy, bland but energy giving. It's too heavy to lift to my mouth. I'm thirsty, but can't summon the will to get the flask. I leave the bar lie, and sag against the crisscross bars.

What's that? Scrabbling, getting louder, getting closer. Dogs?

Craning I see a creature half cat, half rat skittering towards me along a girder. It has a long body, stubby legs a short tail, and it's furred in shades of brown; chocolate body, milk underneath and bitter dark legs and tail. Rounded ears and a pointed snout complete the picture. With the creature comes an odour, distinct yet not unpleasant and strengthening as it gets nearer. It looks at me with bead-black eyes, bright and knowing, and I don't want to scare this beautiful, quirky thing. I breathe light and steady and with a chirrup it springs to my lap, squirming inside my jacket, its wiry body quivery and hot. A picture flashes to me from one of my father's books; it's a ferret. I relax, we settle. Crouched together in the lift cage, the ferret and I fall asleep.

It's with me when I wake, poking a nose from my jacket when I stir and sniffing at the squashed food bar on my lap. We share the bar and what's left of the water and I brighten. The sun is shining and I can just about move my arm. I catch a glimpse of something glinting in the garden of the house backing on to the ruined shops. A reflection? By craning and twisting I get a better view, and it could be a pond. The only way to find out for definite is to climb down and investigate. Easy to say, but doable?

Soon as I move the hurt fires up. My chest tightens and I'm fighting for breath. I *know* if I try climbing, something bad's gonna happen. The dogs'll be waiting, or my legs'll give out and I'll fall. If I move, I'll die.

The ferret saves me. She, and it has to be a she, being so pretty and delicate, climbs up and licks my tears. I rub the top of her head and she creels. I'm not alone. The battering wave of panic withdraws and the shaking ebbs.

Stroking the ferret's shining coat, a name comes to mind. 'Come on, Brown, let's go find that water.' And pulling wide my pocket I invite her company. She accepts.

Time I touch ground I'm all ashiver. Not from panic, from exhaustion. Getting over the wall into the garden is a labour of Hercules. Hope there's water on the other side.

I drop into a jungle of big leafed weeds, snaking brambles, ivy draped trees and wild sprouting shrubs. The sound of trickling water draws me to a weed edged pond. The water is sweet and well worth the fight to get to it. My arm could do with some attention, but it'll take a long soaking to free up the sleeve and bindings. It'll hurt, and I'll need clean bandages to bind the wound. Could be I'll find some in the house at the top of the garden.

I turn towards the house and Brown jumps ship, disappearing into the greenery. Well, why *would* she stay with me?

I get there to find the house in a mess, doors down, windows shattered—must have hosted squads of squatters. Ground floor trashed, staircase dicey but worth a try if I stick close to the wall.

Bathroom's unspeakable, bedrooms likewise. Nothing useful here, might as well go back to the pond. Wait on, is that a cupboard? No, a door, half-hid by a bookcase. A quick shove reveals a winding staircase.

Yay! An attic; untouched as far as I can tell. The small window is unbroken, the gingham curtains hanging neat above a narrow bed. It's gloomy because outside there's a well grown ash tree. The window opens after a hefty push and I'm in easy reach of a stout branch. Great place, water close by and the means for a quick exit.

I take the curtains, washed they'll make good bandages, and head back to the pond. There's light enough and little excuse to hang fire so I rip one of the curtains into strips and dunk them in the pond. Then after taking a good long drink I plunge my arm right in.

It's all I thought and then some. Takes I don't know how long to soften the sleeve, drag off the jacket and remove Pinch's bandage. Takes a further age to clear the mucky wound and bind it with the wrung out rags. I'm shivering cold time I'm done and head back to the attic. I get there, wedge the door and it's all I can do to get to the bed.

Something nips me and I open my eyes. Brown's sitting on my chest grooming her whiskers, her belly bulging and her breath smelling of fish.

I move and my arm doesn't shout, merely grumbles. I feel stronger, try gripping my knife and my fingers do my bidding. Okay so I don't see me cutting a throat any time soon, but I look as if I can. Time to head for camp.

By the smell, Brown's been fishing. Think I'll do the same. I drag the jacket on and the ferret springs to her pocket. Downstairs I spot a screw-topped bottle under the stairs. It'll hold an extra day's drinking water, so I grab it.

I'm almost at the pond when I hear splashing. Creeping

closer I see the duck weed swirled by something big. After a few secs I make out an odd looking fish, then more ripples and more fish; big orange and white patchy things, like something from a comic book. Catch a few of these beauties and I won't have to worry about short rations. Takes a while but I come up with a beaut idea.

I turn the spare curtain into a catch net, threading it on two long sticks and dragging it scoop-wise through the water. Brown watches my every move. First scoop reveals leaves and weed and snails. Brown seizes the snails while I clean the scoop for another go. This time I net a red and white fish and dump it on the grass before hitting its head with the haft of my knife. Brown tackles the head while I move further along for my next try. This time I net a bigger, orange coloured fish.

Building a fire using floorboards from the house I use my knife and flint to spark a small pile of dust, fluff and wood shavings into a fire. As the flames take hold I add more dry wood and gut the fish. Brown goes into ecstasies over the leavings and begs more.

'You eat much more and you'll burst, madam,' I say, and it feels good to talk again. Another slice satisfies, and she curls into a ring and watches me skewer chunks of fish on greenwood sprigs to toast near the flames.

The hot sweet flaky flesh tastes better than wonderful, bringing to mind childhood feasts; my mother's Christmas banquets and her delicious birthday treats.

Full to the gills and listening to the gentle snores of my new friend, I wrap the larger fish in leaves, coat the parcel in mud and push it under the embers to cook. That done I hunt more unwary fish. These I cut in strips to smoke so they'll last till I get back to camp.

I clean my flask and the plastic screw top and fill them with clear pond water. Tomorrow I'll take my direction from the sun, find the locating signs and take Brown to New Camp.

Yay! I'm heading home.

9

A month on and Brown's a fixture. Striker's used to her smell and Brown's stopped nipping him when he nestles close, so all's sweet and cosy—family-like. Summer's in the offing and I should be feeling chipper, but the coming raid weighs heavy. The WhipTails are joining forces with the Carrion Crows to attack the new trooper post. Dex and Pinch made it back well before me and delivered the info to Man Ear. When I got back I said that I agreed with them; the new fort was too big and too busy for a single clan to take. One Eye told me Man Ear and the Crow's leader, Talon, had got together and agreed a plan.

The Crows were well up for the attack. They'd caught a wounded trooper and got him to spill some hot info while 'conferring' with Talon. Apparently Talon's famed for his 'little talks' with prisoners, using the bladed gauntlets that gave him his name.

'Know this Talon?' I asked One Eye one night when we were sitting by the camp fire.

'Of old; since they used to call him gotch-eye.'

'Gotch-eye?'

'Old name for a guy with bi-coloured eyes. Talon's got one blue and one hazel.' He took a sip of boiled acorn water, spat into the flames and said. 'Knew an old venner once, who told me never to trust a gotch-eye.'

The Crows' informant swore the post had been hit by sickness and was seriously undermanned. He also said that reinforcements would be late arriving, due to trouble of some sort in one of the compounds. So Talon convinced Man Ear to act fast before the extras showed up and that's why we're trekking in the peeing rain towards a trooper post that's got more tech than even *two* clans can safely handle; leastways that's what *this* Rat thinks.

Who listens? Only Striker. He says I'm right, says the fort won't be the push over Talon thinks, even if it is man-poor. We're sticking close to One Eye—he's come back safe from a fair few raids. Hope his luck rubs off on us. Mind, he's done nothing but gripe since we left camp: cursing the weather, the route and most of all the Talon-influenced attack plan. Not that he's been carping behind Man Ear's back, nah, he told Man Ear 'xactly what he thinks. Yesterday he stood in front of the whole pack at vote time, listing his misgivings with particular emphasis on how powerful the trooper technology had become. Reminding us of the sensors plastered to the fence wall and the fly-bys that don't just spit propaganda but communicate with troopers and are armed to kill. He finished by questioning if it was prudent to risk so much relying on tainted information.

He knew and I knew that when it came to voting, the tribe would vote to fight. No Rat wants to be judged timid.

Every pack member fit to fight is with us. The young of both tribes have gone with the venners to hiding sites to await the outcome. None went happily, all the older ones volunteered to fight. Staying with lore givers and nursing mothers didn't sit well, but they obeyed. Main camp was dismantled last evening and anything too heavy to tote was buried for later retrieval.

Striker and I made damn sure we travel light, taking only dried food, water, ammunition and in my case Brown. The rest we cached. Brown's in the pocket I sewed inside my new weatherproof coat. She doesn't mind where she goes as long as it's dry and she's with me. Besides she's attracted to the bloodstains left by the coat's previous owner.

Time we reach the fort it's dark and raining hard, but the Mag-Beams show bright through the driving rain. Taking position we wait for the off. When the signal comes I'm almost too stiff to move and it takes a combined shove from Striker and One Eye and a timely nip from Brown to get me going. The fort is quiet, all I hear above the footfalls is my pounding heart. A barrage of Rat-aimed shots outs the lights, and then we're at the fence.

Striker hurls his hook-rope over the plas-met, jerks it tight and he's climbing. I follow, One Eye close behind. We're over and there's gunfire and close up knife work. The fighting peters out as the gates go down.

It stops raining, and out of breath I sit against the fence and watch the packs loot. As is my habit, I start looking for things to count, beginning with the trooper dead. When I'm done I'm surprised how few there are. This place is *seriously* under strength. Striker's close by, mooching by a half-track, so I go join him.

'Bit,' he says, 'look here.' He points at a caterpillar track. 'Wrecked, same as the one next to it and the one over there. I checked the fuel tanks, they're dry and the fuel store's filled with empty drums.'

'Yeah well, I've been counting corpses and there're too narding few. It's adding up wrong.'

'Where's One Eye? I lost sight of him after I climbed the fence.'

I look around. 'There he is, coming fast.'

Soon as he's close he shouts. 'Bit, Striker, move. Talon's knifed Man Ear. It's a sell out.'

As we start for the downed gates, I hear the unmistakable noise of trooper craft and hi-vee rifle fire. We're across the gates and just as I'm thinking we'll make it there's thunder directly above me: a troop carrier. Next thing there's a slamming bang and I'm wrapped in the sticky web of a trooper stretch-net. I go down glued and tangled. Striker's caught same as me but I can't see One Eye.

Now there's a pile of us on the ground in the muck and slime, all wrapped in trooper webbing like a bunch of sucked out flies. A trooper holding a bloody knife checks me out then moves to Striker who's lying next to me, unconscious. The trooper stares down at him, contempt marked clearly on his face. My heart thumps, my breathing's ragged; web-trapped and powerless I can't do anything but watch.

The trooper frowns, leans forward and my heart stops. But it's not Striker he reaches for, but Dex, lying next to him and bleeding bad. Knife held steady the trooper rips off her bead necklace, and I tense. He's gonna slit her throat—kill my first friend, my bonded sister. I steel myself to make record of her dying, and as the knife comes down I take breath and sing the ululating death cry of the Rat tribes. She won't die unseen and she'll know a Rat cries vengeance. Her eyes open, they gleam in the Trooper's helm light and as he draws his knife across her throat she bares her teeth in a snarl.

We're loaded into the carrier, the dead Rats left behind … plus a living one. Talon, the traitor, sits in the parked flyer next to the carrier, beside a grinning trooper. He assays a grin, more rictus than smile, and as the carrier door slides shut I stare into the lighted cab—the fortunate watcher who sees the smiling trooper put a bullet into Talon's treacherous brain.

The carrier engine fires up and I breathe in, loosing the net enough to let Brown squeeze from her pocket. I manage a foot wriggle and she chews a few strands, freeing my legs enough for me to crawl. I count heads: fifteen live Rats and two fresh dead and still warm. I get back to Striker. Brown's on his chest and he's stirring, bones and beads trembling on their spikes. The relief I feel is so strong it hurts. Wouldn't want to go on if Striker had gone the same way as Dex. I snuggle close to him, feeling his warmth. He's alive and for now that's enough for me. Then the questions form. How many carriers? How many Rats survived?

It's a fair old ride, and when we stop Striker's open-eyed, but still muzzy, the lump on his temple risen large and red. The door rolls up showing a structure like no other I've encountered; a gigantic balloon-like building made of what looks to be stiffened cloth.

Troopers drag us onto flatbed trolleys, then wheel us inside the rounded fabrication, past rows of troop carriers and half tracks illuminated by an eerie glow emitted from the walls.

Brown's in her pocket and Striker's slung next to me, fully alert. He ghosts a smile and relieved, I grin back. The troopers push the trolleys through heavy see-through swing doors onto a smooth floored corridor and along to a narrow roll-up door. Once through the door we're in a square, grey room. The pushers decant us onto the floor and wheel out. A trio of black clad fully armed troopers enter. One guy wearing two silver bars on each shoulder douses us with a sharp smelling spray. The netting shrivels and we rub life into our limbs. My legs are fine and it doesn't take much effort to get the blood flowing in my arms so I help the others, signing the same simple message: keep shtum and expect the worst. Pinch looks worn-down devastated. He's lost Dex, I know how he must feel. But he bares his teeth in a poor attempt at a smile. He's down but not defeated.

By the time all fifteen of us are standing, two additional figures enter, not troopers, these guys. No black helmets, no guns, no killer boots, these freaks are garbed in grey all-in-ones fitting tight and showing their sex clearly—one male, one fem. They got no hair and their foreheads are tattooed with indigo snakes twining round staffs of paler blue.

The male addresses the trooper with the silver bars, who prods us into three rows. Both greys unclip black oblong boxes from their belts and walk the lines, passing the boxes up and down our arms.

The fem stops in front of me. The box has a thick needle sticking out of one end and she's gripping it tight, and with the troopers eyeing my every move, there's no way I can jump the bitch. Concentrating on the needle I don't notice her other hand till she's slashed my sleeve with a blade, exposing my skin. Moving ultra-fast she presses the needle into the fleshy part of my arm and it's worse than the worst bee sting ever. I lurch, rifles point and stay aimed even when I get my balance. Striker's next. Soon as we're all stung, the grey male addresses us.

'The implants you have been given will update us regularly on your current status. Attempts to remove the implant triggers an alarm and will be punished severely.'

Chipped! We been chipped. What next?

'Troop Leader?'

The trooper with the shoulder bars snaps a salute. 'Med-Tech?'

'Get them clean.'

At a signal from the troop leader we're prodded from the grey room into a grey corridor. Is everything in this frinking place grey? One side of the corridor is blank, the other lined with roll-up doors. Door four is our destination and we're shoved into a grey room far bigger than the last, with a low ceiling half peppered with holes.

A trooper orders us remove our clothes. I don't want to; none of us want to, Rats rarely undress. But they're the ones holding the guns. We comply. Striker stands close and we shield Brown as she burrows into the heap of discarded clothes.

A pair of female med-techs enter and they shave our heads with powered razors. I keep my face blank. It doesn't hurt half as bad as that first shaving when I joined the tribe. My hair falls softly to the floor and the black strands mingle with Striker's rusty red. Naked, spike free and bead-less he looks different, then he smiles, his amber eyes glowing with warmth. Nah, still the same old Striker.

Sheared we stand under the colander ceiling. A med-tech slams the wall and cold water spears from the holes. The guards hoot as the water hits and we shiver.

'Silence,' snaps the tech and the hooting stops.

The water's replaced by thick foul tasting goo that squirms between my shuttered lips and down my throat in a burning trickle of filth. A guard shouts, 'Look at them jump. Bet they'll miss their fleas.' Another joins in, 'Never been so clean in their whole mizzing lives.'

A harsh shout, this time from the silver-barred troop leader, silences opinions on the mating habits of Rats. I endure the cleansing in silence, as do my pack mates. The goo is washed away with another burst of water followed by a blast of drying air. I keep an eye on the pile of clothes, Brown's hiding place.

A bulging soft-sided cart is wheeled in. 'Dress,' a med-tech orders. The cart contains mud-brown coveralls and ridged pull-ons for our feet. The foot-stretches fit, the coveralls don't, no matter how I tighten the wrist and ankle grips or cinch the belt. Same with Striker. Same with all of us.

A guard points, 'You,' he shouts. 'Clear those stinking rotten rags.'

I wouldn't obey, if not for Brown. I sign my excuses to the pack, loosen a wrist band and start loading the discarded coveralls into the cart. Brown slips inside the sleeve, runs up my arm and settles at against the tight cinched belt. She's safe, just one lump among the many. Job done I'm ordered to push the cart out of the room and into the corridor. As I push I imagine what One Eye would say and what he'd do. I didn't see him netted, guess his luck is holding strong. The med-tech in charge springs a roll-up and points, 'The cart, in there.'

I push into a narrow galley where three circular covers, waist high and mounted proud, are fixed to the wall. A guard pulls a lever which opens one of the covers and out comes a roaring blast of heat. I jump and the guard swears, then words me slowly, miming what he wants as if I've only half a brain. 'Dump, the clothes, moron.'

I load the clothes into the chute, smell the burning and watch the leaping flames. Brown is warm against my skin, she scratches gently and I shudder to think what might have been. When I join the others we walk the corridor, signing. No one notices.

There's still only fifteen of us. I expected more to be added. Looks like we're the only survivors. I tell about the furnace and Striker makes it a definite order that we continue to stay shtum.

'*What next?*' I sign to him.

'*Cutting,*' he says in a sharp two fingered move.

I remember the fly-by telling how us Rats would be chipped, neutered and re-educated. Striker's right, we've been chipped, it's cutting next. I swallow the fear.

We arrive at a bench set next to a pair of double doors. Eight Rats and the bench is full, the rest take the floor. I'm last on the bench and Striker's two ahead.

The pair of tattooed techs push through the doors, leaving us with silent guards, fingers tensed on rifle triggers. It's a long wait till a musical chime sings out and a guard prods the first in line to enter. It's Owl Hunt, one of the Carrion Crows. He stands, showing no fear. He's been mute since capture, no sounds, no signs—shamed by Talon's treachery. Now I catch his eye and sign, '*Luck*'. I want him to know he's ours. He acknowledges with a nod and I'm glad he knows he's not alone.

He's not inside long and when he comes out he's grey as dirty slush and shaking like he's adder-bit. More is hustled in next. She looks long at me before signing a swivelling one-fingered salute at the troopers and striding into the room, head held high. I expect her to be out as quick as Owl Hunt, but she ain't. Time moves on and she doesn't emerge. I think back to how she got her name.

She won through Trial, bringing back a huge sack of real coffee beans, much to the tribe's delight. Man Ear as leader had first dibs, then the Rats with the most scars took theirs, and so on down the line. The finder and the other nameless Rats got nothing. I asked her how it felt to lose her prize and she smiled hugely and told me 'There's more; much, much more. A stonking great van full.'

When she does emerge she looks real sick, sliding to her

place on the floor by Owl Hunt, biting her blooded lips. Sitting hunched she leans against Owl Hunt who takes her hand in comfort. It looks like females suffer most inside that room.

When Striker stands I sign a quick pattern and when he comes out he fakes a stumble. The guards laugh at the weak Rat and allow me to give him a hand. It's Pinch's turn and he makes the most of it, snarling at the guard and drawing twitchy eyes, allowing me pass Brown to Striker. Dex'd be proud of him.

My turn comes and I enter a room that's grey and stark and polished shiny. The two med-techs wait by a piece of strange equipment; a thick, coal-black column with a metal shelf sticking out mid-way.

'Hurry up,' calls the taller grey.

The machine hums like a purring cat and under its dark surface lights flicker. The grey holds a glowing wand connected to the black column by a snaking cable.

My feet won't move, 'cos once these soulless butchers get me on that slab, they'll put my dreams to death. I'll bear no children, raise no family … because of what they'll do.

'On the table,' the tall grey growls, and gestures to the other one, who takes my arm in pincer grip and drags me forward.

I climb onto the vibrating shelf and it's as cold as clay. The shorter one digs a needle into my neck with casual disdain, ignoring my yelp. Straightaway coldness spreads and I can't move my limbs. Nausea attacks and I heave. The needler grunts her displeasure and unzips my overall, squirting cold jelly from waist to pubes. The other steps closer, holding the glowing wand. 'Step back,' she says, and the first retreats. The wand is held to my body, smearing the jelly over the lower half. The machine noise alters, the hum giving way to a penetrating whine. The noise increases bringing excruciating pain, and I black out.

I'm wakened by a slap. The machine has resumed its gentle purring and I'm ordered off the table and out of the room. Weakness hits as I struggle to stand. I'm woozy, and the grey slaps me again. I pull my coveralls together and stumble to join the line of sitters. Striker manoeuvers next to me as I do up the overall, then holds my hand as the pain drags through me. Brown creeps back to my sleeve and we sit like that till the last Rat leaves the pain room and we're ordered to our feet. Striker looses my hand, and that's as great a pain as the other, if not greater.

Walking under the eyes of twitchy guards we exit the corridor by way of a scratched and battered swing door, into the massive vehicle store and onwards to an open roll-up and a waiting carrier. Ordered inside the tracked vehicle, we're shackled to floor rings listening to trooper laughter and the words of the silver ranker.

'There they go, lads. Neutered animals off to their cages. Hey Rats, you have fun, you hear?'

The carrier door slams and one of the new guards speaks to his partner. 'These poor sods don't know what they're in for, do they? CRCs? Grinding places, just grinding places, spitting out slaves to build the General's empire.'

The second guard hushes him, 'Shut it, Clancy. You want to get ground up with 'em?'

Soon as they test our shackles the troopers go up front to the driver's cab and the carrier rocks away. Me and Striker clutch the bolt rings one handed and take turns to draw signs on the other's hand, signing love, and our fears of separation.

By the time the carrier stops, the dragging pain in my belly has settled to a deep physical ache that ignites raw hate as I think of the kids those murderous creeches robbed from me, and the future they stole not just from me but from every one of us Rats.

Taken outside and we're marched to another giant prefab. Inside it's cold, crowded with figures wearing the same ill-fitting mud-coloured coveralls as us. Keen eyed troopers line the walls and tattooed med-techs move through the crowd as if they're inspecting machine parts or meat animals.

We stick together as a group. A mix of two tribes—fifteen in total … all that's left.

A med-tech approaches and waves a flat box of lights over

my arm, studies it then does the same to Striker and the rest. The tech's grey coveralls fit snugly, defining every muscle and every bone ridge. I fantasize stabbing him in the heart or cutting the tattoos from his blank face, line by hurting line.

The tech moves on and Striker signs, *'Go walkabout. Each of us take a different path and we'll meet back here to compare findings.'*

Here, is a tall scratched metal pylon reaching to the ceiling and about twenty paces from the door. A quick glance tells me there's about fifty captives all told. Like us they have shaved heads and wear muddy all-in-ones. I move into the crowd and the strong chemical smell makes me cough.

Time I get back to add my knowledge to the whole, our group has swelled by five more Rats. One by one the group signs their findings. When the hands stop moving. I sit against the pillar to get things sorted in my mind.

The troopers aren't just collecting Rats. We only fished a handful from that crowd. The rest are law breakers, the brain sick or those born damaged. Word is we're to be shipped off to one of the CRCs. Finally I get to know what the initials stand for—Citizen Reclamation Centre. Templeton's store houses for malcontents. In a CRC we get to be re-educated, reclaimed and made into valuable workers fit to serve the Party.

More comes to sit by me. *'Reclaimed,'* she signs, and adds a filthy finger motion. *'Slaved, more like.'*

We wait till the carriers arrive. Our twenty strong group stand together determined not to be separated. I link arms with Striker. We *have* to get into the same CRC, can't do this without him.

All goes well till we approach the three carriers, then a scuffle breaks out, halted by gun shots. In the hustle I'm ripped from Striker's side. When things quieten there's a host of muddy bodies lying bloody on the floor. One of them's Pinch

I look up and see troopers herding muddies towards the carriers. I spot Striker, but can't reach him. He's being pushed toward the tattooed techs standing at the ramps leading into the carriers. I try keeping all three ramps in sight, frantically going from one to the other in hopes of seeing which one he enters. He's not in the first five of us that go into the largest carrier, nor in the second five, but, yes, I see him now, walking up the ramp to the second carrier along with four more of our group. Fifteen of us accounted for. Sixteen, if you count Pinch.

Striker looks around, I wave and wave and before a trooper beats my arm down with his baton, he sees me and waves back before he's pushed into the carrier.

Now I'm moving forward. Please let me be loaded into his carrier. Please, please, please

Someone shouts my name. Who? There! Three faces I recognise, looking round. Looking for me. I wave and shout but they don't hear, don't see. They're shunted up the ramp and into Striker's carrier, and the ramp retracts. The carrier's fully loaded and the doors slam shut.

One of us killed, nineteen loaded into carriers, and one left—me. I watch the carriers leave and the dead scraped into wheeled bins like so much rubbish, and mourn in silence, my face stone still, my eyes desert dry.

Hours later I'm taken into the third and smallest carrier, and the door is slammed. I sit against the carrier wall summoning the strength to keep on living. I'm Bitch Singer of the Whip Tails. I'm Rat, and I will not give in.

But deep inside, I'm crying bloody tears.

10

Time moves in a silent wave. With no way to measure its passing I can't tell how long I've been held in this prison place, this CRC. Don't know when I'll be freed; could be months or years, could be I'll age to death in here. There is no light at the end of my dark tunnel. Without Brown I'd have given up; many do. As a dumb nil I've buried these lost-hopers, or loaded their tech-tortured bodies into incinerators.

Nil: my designation in this cruel place. A label I use as camouflage, to sink from notice. A nil has the lowest of low profiles.

The med-techs use their brain-machines to train detainees to work for the betterment of the state. The true nils, brain-injured insurgents or those born damaged are ruled unteachable, without value. Most become drudges, while others are subjected to the med-techs' experiments, in order to 'to advance the frontiers of scientific knowledge'.

I choose to be a *useful* nil, doing what I'm told with a vacant smile, and working my fingers to the bone without complaint. When called for burial duty I see all and say nothing, but inside I pray that both victim and perpetrator get their just deserts.

How to become a nil? First be scared as hell, then use your use your sense and a good serving of imagination.

Wrenched from my clan and crammed into a carrier shackled with a bunch of strangers I studied my fellows. I supposed most were doing same as me, keeping shtum and working the angles. All 'sept a couple of wrinkled oldsters and a guy who was too brain-slow to understand orders, a guy who reminded me of Slinger, a Rat who recovered from a head shot, but lost most of himself in the process. When he wandered into the ruins, no one searched.

It was a long trip in that rattle-trap carrier. Time we stopped the air was rank, the deck slick with pee and spew. It halted outside a spiked ring-fence heavy with eye-cams. Around the fence a forest of prickthorn stretched far as the eye could see. Inside it was a massive silo marked CRC 1 in orange day-glow lettering; my home for the foreseeable.

Waiting outside the silo was a lumpy figure wearing trooper black, tapping a meaty thigh with a silver-topped ebony cane. The figure fronted a line of muddies dressed same style as me. Wasn't till we got up close that I saw the thigh tapper was fem; large of feature, wearing shoulder bars of shiny gold and a perky cap topping her frizz of silver-gilt hair. Her thick-lipped mouth was painted a startling baby pink.

'My name is Chief Mont,' she said, her voice a miss-tuned cello. 'This is my facility, run by my rules. Follow them to the letter and you *might* make it through your term … however long that may be.'

And that was it. She strode away, leaving me and my fellow detainees staring at the line of muddies, wearing black arm-bands, trooper-issue boots and toting trooper-style truncheons. A wiry, brown-skinned redhead stepped forward. Her hair was a rich mahogany, not fire-bright like … Striker's. Picturing my mate brought on a wave of sorrow that almost broke me down.

'Listen up!' Red shouted, and pointed to the armband. 'See this? It means Authority. A black bander gives an order, you obey without thought. I'll make it clearer; us banders run this hell-hole, got it?

'Chief Mont and her reclaimers might be the gods, but we're

the hands-on angels. And don't think you can take us.' She stamped her heavy boots and patted the baton hanging at her waist. 'Like for you to try, though.' She grinned. 'Welcome to CRC 1, losers.'

I glanced over my shoulder and saw our trooper guards hot footing it to the carrier. Can't say as I blamed them.

Our entry into the windowless silo that was CRC 1 was through a bank vault door. Shackles removed, urged on by banders, the door hissed shut behind us, severing us detainees from the living world.

The banders vanished through a slide-door, leaving us in a metal walled cube. We stood quiet and afraid, beans in a metal mouth, waiting to be chewed.

Something flickered behind a grill on one of the grey-paint walls. Watchers? All heads turned to the grill, and the fem next to me started shaking like she was gonna fall to pieces. A flat voice called, 'Hold still!' and blue light-beams spear from the walls, rippling over us one by one. It felt like invisible ants marching over my skin. My implant stung and my shaking neighbour screeched high and wild. A siren shrieked, I thought of Brown and said a prayer.

'Unknown metal found,' the voice declared.

The blue beams winked off, a door rolled up and the voice instructed us leave. All of us walked out, 'sept the shaker. We left her stuck to the wall.

One down. Who's next?

We moved into a long grey room where a trio of banders waited; Red, a mouse-haired fem and a pock-faced guy. Red held a gun and shouted words so fast I couldn't catch their meaning. She headed for me, scattering detainees right and left. 'The rodent first,' she spat. The other banders grabbed my arms and Red pushed the gun barrel to my cheek. Instead of the expected bullet I got a white-hot line drawn along my scars, one by hurting one. 'No Rat scars allowed here,' she crowed. 'Neat piece of laser work, that. Pity it didn't hurt more.'

Released, I fingered the faint lines, all that remained of my hard won scars.

Mouse-Hair took over, a slim, muscular fem with a done-it-all expression, 'Strip for inspection, you turds.'

I went cold, couldn't move, because Brown was tucked into the folds of my coveralls. Mouse-Hair strode over, boots smacking the floor. 'Strip!' she ordered. I stayed motionless. 'Jeez, not another dummy!' she said, 'We got us another useless nil! Took one hit too many. Jeez, damn troopers don't know when to stop.'

She mimed the removal of my coveralls and dropping them on the floor. 'Do. It,' she said, loud and slow.

Another dummy, she'd said, and I was back in the carrier again, seeing the brain-slow guy that reminded me of Slinger. A dummy? Maybe that was the path to tread. Adopting Slinger's inane grin I stayed where I was. When Mouse-Hair repeated the mime, I began to undress, slowly, all fingers and thumbs. She lost patience, fast. Mumbling 'Dumb nil,' she hared off to shout at some other poor muddy, while Brown did her vanishing trick, eeling into my discarded clothes like water through a pavement crack.

My path was set, from now on I'd play dumb. For the first time since I was separated from my clan I felt I was doing something positive, doing something *I* chose, not what others chose for me. I remembered I was Rat. And what did Rats do? They fought. So that's what I'd do, fight back the only way I could. I'd be no slave. I'd be my own master—live or die, Rat through and through.

What did Striker say, when he caught me following him? That I thought him a fifth columnist? He wasn't, but I damn well would be. Never surrender; a good strong motto.

11

A year or so on I'm an accepted nil, with Brown my undiscovered ace in the hole. Without her I'd be mind-broke like the rest. Brown tells me that I'm alive, that I'm real not painted into Picasso's Charnel House like the hateful print in Dad's study. It's Brown that keeps me from being a grey-black twisted body, mouth fixed open in a silent scream, trapped inside an art book. Sometimes, on a bad, bad day when the techs call on me to take a 'test subject' to the burner, I think I'd be better off in that book. Painted people don't feel pain, know loss.

That first day in CRC 1, with Brown burrowed into my pile of shucked off coveralls, I *knew* they'd find her and knew they'd kill on sight. When Pock-Face headed towards me, calling for Mouse-Hair to come look, I got so scared I peed my self. Straightaway Pock-Face sheered off, ordering Mouse-Hair to do the job.

I readied myself to die. 'Cos I'd use all I had to keep them from her; teeth, nails, kicks and gouges, everything. Time she came up to me I was tensed and ready.

'Stand still, you stinking nil,' she spat. 'Gonna burn of those pretty tatts of yours. Brace yourself, it's gonna hurt,' and she grinned as she waved her pocket-sized laser gun in my face.

I almost grinned back. They weren't after Brown!

The pain of the lasering was bad. I coped but I gave 'em a

show-stopping performance of squeals and sobs that drew all eyes to me, not my pile of coveralls.

'Get dressed, nil,' Pock-Face yelled. 'Inspection's over.'

I tried but my arm muscles locked and I couldn't pretend to be more helpless than I was. He made an over-the-top sigh, 'You're right, she's just another brain-shook mizzer. Why don't the troopers finish 'em off? No, it's patch 'em up and ship 'em on to us.'

'Waste of time and effort,' agreed Mouse-Hair. 'She'll do for a trooper joy-house. Take anything, troopers.' She pointed to the coveralls and then to me. I nodded, they walked away and I began the slow painful process of dressing while keeping Brown hidden from sight.

Chip up-dated, I was informed of my new name. I'd be Dor from then on. After a squirt of foul smelling head-scrub, Red led us detainees into a grey corridor and up a flight of open steps fixed to the curving silo wall. She ordered Pock-Face take us to our quarters. 'Make the rules clear,' she said. To Mouse-Hair she added, 'Make sure there's no laggers.'

The treads didn't look strong enough to bear our weight. The guy behind me hesitated, and Mouse-Hair clouted him with her truncheon. 'Up, slug,' she yelled. The line moved upwards. Several sets of ill-lit stairs and many landings later we arrived at our sleeping quarters.

First time Brown did her escape act was a coupla days after that. Sleep time I unrolled my mattress … no Brown. My first thought? She's left me. My second, what if she's been caught? By then I was breathing fast and my eyes were stinging. But I plugged into the sleep-teach and lay down. In a CRC you followed the rules or suffered the consequences. Head covered I let the hot tears fall. How could I survive without Brown? She was all I had left.

The plug spoke its endless scribble but worry eclipsed the words. Later something woke me, not the klaxon but the smell and touch of warm wriggling ferret. Brown was back and full-bellied by the feel. She nudged me with her cold nose and I smelled blood. She'd been hunting. Where? Inside the ducting or outside? Who cared; she'd come back to me.

A year on nothing's changed. I still hate the sleep-teach as much as I hate Mont and the Banders. Every narding night detainees bed down in their sleep rooms next to the black pillar that recognises their chip-ident. Each pillar has ear-buds attached by an elastic cord and we sleep with those buds stuck into our ears, listening to the gems of wisdom spouted by our glorious leader, General Julius Templeton. Forget once, and you're punished with a truncheon hit. Forget twice and you disappear. Try hooking to the wrong sleep-teach and the same rules apply. The banders made this clear on that very first night. And when they told us the reclaimers would know, because they knew *everything*, they were right on the money.

That very first night, back in the sleep room after eating in the mess hall, Pock-Face made sure we were plugged in before he left. I was flat on the mattress lying under the blanket, listening to the General, with Brown on my chest nibbling the meat I'd shoved up my sleeve. Seemed Templeton was the only man with the strength to haul humanity from the brink, the only man with the vision to see the onward path. And guess what, I was one of the chosen few who was gonna help build a glowing future for the citizens of New Britain. My labour would construct new cities, erect manufactories and build the laboratories that would make the country great again. Over and over the same damn cant. Well, I thought, hallelujah and bring on the dancing girls!

When the morning klaxon moaned I woke nauseous, sickened by the night-long drivel. Leaving Brown tucked into the rolled-up mattress I joined the rest of the muddies helter-skeltering down six flights of open treaded stairs to the half moon shaped mess hall to eat a meal of thick, seedy porridge followed by two yellow, chalky-tasting tabs and a mug of tainted water.

Meal eaten we waited for orders, and in marched the head honch, Mont, tapping the ebony cane against a black trouser leg. A pair of troopers walked behind her. She had no need to call order.

'Assignments,' she snapped. 'Group 1—Assessment. Groups 2 through 10—the Training levels. Groups 11 to 15 outside labour. Groups 16 to 20, it's your lucky day—Ship-out.'

The muffled gasps as she said those final words told me more than I wanted to know. Pock-Face appeared, Mouse-Hair in tow, 'You're Group 1,' he says. 'Follow us.'

We left the food hall and passed a big G painted on the wall outside, took a stairway down one level to –1, and down again to –2 .There we stopped and followed the banders along a corridor to another grey room and a guy wearing trooper black with the snake and staff emblem of the med-techs tattooed on his forehead.

'Sit!' he barked, gesturing to the seats in front of square glass panels set flush to the wall. I made sure I was last to find a seat.

'Watch the screens and do as instructed,' he ordered.

Pictures appeared, coloured circles accompanied by a voice like the sleep teacher which told me to press certain certain buttons on the pad before me. I obeyed slowly, made mistakes, got flustered. The instructions grew more complicated. I was told to move arrows, follow routes, match objects and I started to whimper, scratch my face, and sob. At session end I'd not succeeded in completing one single task, and my cheeks dripped blood. The tech hauled me from the stool.

'Another useless, brain damaged moron, fit only for grunt work. Bander?'

'Yes, Senior Tech?'

'Get this one out, can't assess what's not there. Leave the rest.'

Jeez, this is it, I thought. What'll they do to me now?

12

Pock-Face walked me back to Level G and ran a chip reader over my arm, pressing various buttons. 'Right,' he said.

Been scared before, me. But never as scared as this. Been used to fighting troopers, using guns and knives, used to giving as good as I got, but now I was weaponless. Where was he gonna take me? And what'd happen to Brown?

I took a deep breath, and steeled myself to hear the worst.

'You're to clean the mess hall.'

Shock combined with relief rendered me catatonic. He sighed and dragged me through the mess hall to the serving hatch and banged it with his fist. The hatch slid part way open to show a thin-faced scowler.

'Med-tech outed another one. Find her scut work, Arbie.'

Arbie shook his head, 'Another nil? What those troopers do to 'em?'

'Think I care? Get her working.' And Pock-Face stomped away.

Working? I closed my eyes and said thanks to whoever or whatever was watching over me.

The hatch slammed, feet stamped and Arbie entered the hall through a side door. A small man, Arbie, dressed like me in Muddy coveralls, but with an orange band on the sleeve. He grinned, lopsided, took me through the side door into a utility room and demonstrated how to fill a bucket with hot water and add a soap tab. Then he handed me a cloth and pointed to a mess of convoluted pipework. 'Get that lot clear of grease. Keep at it till I come back.'

Soon as he left I started scrubbing the pipes. Grease cleared I took on the filthy vent grills and rubbed till my nails ripped and my skin blistered. After a time he called halt and inspected every twist and turn. 'Not bad. Dumb you may be, but by damn, you're thorough. Right, chow time.' He took me into another room, filled with steam and cooking smells, and handed me a wedge of dark bread and a thick slice of cheese. Then he patted my head like I was some 'bandoned pup, before sitting at a table near the serving hatch where three orange banders were eating something hot and hearty. I sat close to the wall trying for invisibility, watching them eat and listening to them talk. Wasn't long before a klaxon sounded and the mess hall started filling with hungry muddies. I was directed back to the pipe room to scrub more grease.

Soon as the hall cleared Arbie sent me and a new arrival, a blank-eyed guy, into the empty hall and bade us stand tight against the wall. A strong smelling rain sprinkled from the ceiling, washing down the tables before sinking through holes in the floor. When the rain stopped we were given mops, buckets and wipes and told to start cleaning. Arbie watched from the hatch for a time, then shouted a cheerful, 'That's the style, carry on.' I kept mopping, slow and regular making sure one square was clean before starting a new one, but the other muddy had no system, wandering here and there and sometimes going over the same bit again and again. When the hall was clean Arbie smiled and gave me a nod. 'You done well, girl. I'll inform the black bander.' But when he looked at my companion he shook his head. 'Getting worse. Pity.' Then he frowned, and spoke more to himself than to the blank-eyed guy, 'Given up. Lost the will.' And he called over his shoulder, 'Beatty, call the med-techs.'

At sleep time Arbie sent me back to my quarters with a

handful of meaty treats and a pat on the shoulder. I smiled an inner grin, Brown was gonna love 'em.

End of my first week I'd sussed my sleep-group: a third were destined for the manufactories, a third for the labour fields, and rest, like the fool with the loose mouth, were rushing towards the lime pits. The other inmates of CRC were the same mongrel mix, worst off were the nils, the piss-poor brain-sick, brain-hurt feebs who disappeared without a ripple, like the cleaner from the mess hall and the squint-eyed guy who forgot how to feed himself.

I played it canny, doing the dirtiest of jobs with a smile and keeping my ears open for useful nuggets. I cottoned fast that it wasn't the troopers you had to watch for, but the banders. The reclaimers? They might be the organisers and order givers, but the banders made narding sure the orders were carried out.

The detainees are isolated by the frinking rules. They don't talk or play and I doubt they dare dream. Nah, they keep their heads down, do as they're told and try to keep breathing. But me, I got Brown with me live and real, and Striker living in my head. Nights I dream of past times, days I plan our future, his and mine *together*. Because me and Striker are Rat through and through. We *will* survive. We *will* find each other. We *will* beat the narding system.

Trustees earn their bands by following every rule, never ever speaking out of turn and snitching on those who step a tad out of line. Course if you're aiming to be a black bander it helps to be turned on by violence and have a desire to lord it over others, and yeah, it pays to be on Chief Mont's good side. A Trustee *stays* banded by being brutal, ruthless and treading heavy on those keen to take your place. Laxity, a failure to carry out orders promptly, and the slightest show of weakness brings demotion. Stripped, a bander disappears into the population faster than a failing nil. On the surface the place runs smooth as a wayward wink, but underneath it's boots and blood.

Troopers rank low on my worry list. They have the cushiest

time, seeing as how the banders do their dirty work and keep the lid screwed tight. Seems a trooper's job is to strut and preen and stick it to the muddies in the dark. Nice work if you can get it.

The techs are the scary ones, even the banders give them a wide berth. Techs oversee A&T, assessment and training sessions. They also conduct 'experiments vital to the state'. I've seen the spark burns, the wire welts, and heard the cries of those not 'giving their utmost for the General.' I also help drag the corpses of feeble nils and battered muddies to the lime pits. Like the banders I steer well clear of the techy freaks.

One morning, early on I got slammed by a bander. He hoiked me out of the line heading to the mess hall. 'You,' he yelled 'You're out of step. Who's your group bander?'

I looked at him blank faced and he backhanded me. I didn't go down but I tasted blood where I bit my lip. Took all my willpower to keep from jumping him, setting my teeth against his jugular and biting, hard. Outside, I'd have eaten this guy for dinner.

'Answer,' he screamed, kicking my shin, till I fell down in a wave of pain. He kept on shouting while the line of muddies watched terrified. I curled up, blackness swooped and I woke in the sleep room with Brown licking the blood off my face. She wormed under the blanket when boots approached—Pock-Face and the rough that booted me.

'She's a nil, man, look at her.' I heard Pock-Face say. 'She's not stubborn, she's brain-shook. Got dented hard before she got here. It didn't go down well, that beating. You're a new bander, save the kicking for the *real* troublemakers, yeah?'

Word spread to lay off dumb Dor—a nil too stupid to be any fun. Turns out I'm ignored by banded and un-banded alike. Suits this dummy just fine.

13

Mont and four other reclaimers run this pleasure palace; strutting around in their nil-spruced uniforms, wearing nil-polished boots, their New Order Party badges all shiny, peaked caps all jaunty—monarchs of all they survey. They're the top of the pyramid, standing on a bunch of troopers who in their turn stand on the trustee banders.

Comes a day when I'm working on the top floor—reclaimer territory. Been leased from the techs by officer Trant who wanted a reliable nil to clean his stink-hole sleep room and scrub his putrid san-unit till it gleamed. I put a rush on, and in an hour I was near the finish line. I've learned it pays to work double quick in reclaimer territory. I wanted to be done before Trant came back. That cold-eyed creep scares me worse than a pack of rabid dogs. He's not the only one, all reclaimers come from the same frinking mould.

Mont's suite is up the far end—never bin there, never want to. Heard what goes on.

All done. The room's as neat as a new combed beard and there's a half-chewed meat bar up my sleeve, a treat for Brown. Time to go. I'm two steps from the stairs when a voice calls, 'You!' Narding hell, it's Mont. Know that frog-croak anywhere. I turn, slowly, inch by halting inch.

'Oh, Trant's little nil. No, don't move, don't scurry away. I want to see how well you work.'

She steps into Trant's room, putting fingers on ledges, testing the tautness of the bed covers and visiting san cubicle to sniff loudly. 'Remarkable,' she murmurs and steps up close to me. Without her cap her hair is a frizzy wildness. She leans down and pokes her lumpy blackhead-crowded nose into my face. She smiles, her glossed lips crack, and I shiver. The smile broadens, her pupils widen, she huffs a laugh and her booze-laden breath near chokes me. 'So quick, so thorough, so … bijoux,' she says, and beckons me to follow. Crap, guess I know how this is gonna turn out.

Mont's suite is all I've heard and more, two rooms furnished ultra luxe. The sit-and-eat kitchen's filled with hi-tech doodads, and the bedroom's flashier than a high-priced whorehouse. A quick look-round shows me a mirrored ceiling, gold painted walls and a kingsize bed smothered in a purple throw and plastered with eye-dazzling multi-coloured cushions. Mont pushes, I fall amongst the cushions and close my eyes against what's coming.

When it's over she showers, 'Be here tomorrow,' she says, 'I will inform the med-techs.'

Jeez, and just like that I'm the new joy-toy.

Though I'm Mont's new acquisition I still sleep nights with my group, plugged into the canting sleep-teach. Days I'm her little playmate, what she wants she gets, but slack times I been learning how to operate her comp. She don't mind me watching her work, why should she? I'm a dumb nil, for godsake. Right, so it don't balance out, but I take what I can, like getting access to news sheets and the use of her cook-room. I even know the year date's 2040. And I find out stuff other folk don't. F'rinstance I knew before Mont's reclaimers that half the troopers assigned to CRC 1 were to be sent to Venture City Compound to help quell an 'outbreak of civil disobedience'. Reading that gave me such a boost.

When Mont chucks me out nights, I go back to my group's

cheese-wedge sleep room—two straight walls abutting the curved frame of the silo. First thing I do is check Brown's safe. It's habit, she won't be disturbed. All detainees know not to touch another's mattress. We're told that from the get-go. It's a rule, and *no one* breaks a rule in a Citizen Reclamation Centre, not if they want to keep breathing. Brown enjoys the titbits I filch, even though she's not dependent on me for food, having her own ways in and out. Most nights she spends some time outside, coming back with muddy paws and weed burrs in her coat. Often her muzzle is wet from a kill.

Being pet to a psycho, I learn to take what comes. Mont likes pain. Mine, hers, it's immaterial. Today she taught me to make real coffee from actual beans and laughed when I spat out the burning spoonful forced into my mouth. Soon stopped laughing when I sprayed the second mouthful on her.

'You wasted it,' she snarls. 'Know how much that cost?'

Next thing she tips a boiling kettle on my feet, and laughs like it's the best joke ever as I hobble to the wash room to soak the scald. Told me I'd better not be late in the morning. She likes it when I'm hurting.

I do get some days off, like when Mont visits other facilities, or when she falls 'sick'. The sick days are my favourite because they are wholly mine, Mont either too hung over or too insensible to remember where she is or where I'm 'sposed to be. Some of her sick days are not entirely self-inflicted. Some days she eats something that disagrees with her; little offerings Brown finds outside, delivered to Mont by way of an omelette, or a fiery curry. Sometimes those sickies last two or maybe three days, if I work the dose right.

Read a mailing on Mont's comp, today—the names of the next load to be shipped off to the Work Hall. My name and number's on that list. I'm getting out! Excitement spurts. If I keep alert I might spot a chance to escape. But what if I do take that chance?

I'm twenty years old and the only thing I'm good at is killing troopers. Odds on, my future's in a cat-house, or in the labs. But being Mont's sweety has its plus points, without the heads-up I'd have lost Brown for sure.

Forewarned I slip into the sleep room and tuck her into my coveralls before reporting to the med-techs. I get there as the meal horn sounds, and as we file to the mess hall a trooper sprints up to the pockmarked bander and mutters something. Straightaway we're led away from the food room to a passage that takes us to the bank vault door, the entry point to CRC 1. It's go-time. I get ice-chills thinking how close I was to losing Brown.

Outside there's a winged carrier: we're flying out. Pock-Face stands silent, watching troopers shackle us to floor rings, before he heads back inside. My group's not the only one leaving today. Two more emerge from the silo and are shackled with us. It's tight, two muddies to a floor bolt and the takeoff is jerky. The trip lasts forever, but eventually we land.

14

I step out of the carrier into fog, the landing beacons haloed, our destination hidden. A long march later and another balloon-type fabrication looms. We shuffle into a long narrow room and our escorts order us undress. I see the sprinklers straightaway and know what's coming. Like before, Brown hides in a pile of discarded clothing while the med-techs shave us and shove us under an icy shower.

The new coveralls are bright orange and as ill-fitting as the old. Instead of stretches we're directed to a wheeler filled with worn leather work boots with fresh studs and toe caps. I ferret through the footwear and surprise, surprise I find a pair that fit. I suppose crippling workers is counterproductive.

'Trooper,' a tech calls, 'take them to the hiring hall and send in the next batch.'

The hiring hall is awash with orange. Line upon line of blank faces, shaven heads, all dressed in vivid coveralls. My group is added to the lines, our implants checked by grey-clad med-techs. They limit their checking to our implants, just as well for Brown.

The hall is thick with troopers and they line the mezzanine floor that rings the hall. All of them carry stun-guns. As well as troopers I see citizens carrying chip readers searching the lines for likely workers.

'This one?' a high voice queries, it's a blue-coveralled fem who looks me up and down. Her coveralls are finer than mine and fit perfectly. Her companion, a man dressed entirely in mauve from hair to boots, sniffs disparagingly, 'Dear Heaven, no. A skinny shrimp like that! Owner Hetherington would think you've lost your mind. Besides, she stinks.'

It's not me that smells, just my nervous ferret. They stand there discussing my shortcomings halfheartedly, their eyes everywhere but on me, both of them fingering the steel bracelets soldered to their wrists. Were they remembering what it felt like to be up for grabs?

My next viewer runs his checker over my arm, snorts in disgust and says to his companion, 'Says here she's a good worker, but she's a nil if ever I saw one. What the hell's she doing in a work hall? Should have been shipped straight to a joy house.'

'Oh I don't know, some patrons like them quiet. How about General Cummings' wife?' They move away but not before the second speaker tweaks my cheek, hard. I stand straight faced, fighting my urge to gouge his eyes out.

Time passes as do folk, some with steel bracelets, some without. Only a few stop to check my chip before moving on. As the day wears on a steady stream of orange clad souls leave the hall; workers under bond. Gradually the number of seekers lessens, and the lines of orange shorten.

A trio dressed in identical livery stop in front of me. One runs his reader along my arm.

'Simeon, are you really looking at that runt? Are you serious?' This from the fey figure with blonde frou-frou curls.

'Sir wants a handmaid for her ladyship.' The one holding the chip reader says.

'That's what he *says*. Get a dwarf, at least they've got some muscle on them.'

The third, a dark faced giggler, tugs them onward. It's hard to keep from gobbing on their shiny, high heeled shoes.

After a long gap two fems wearing steel arm rings stop and stare. The one dressed entirely in red waves her reader at me.

'You're right, Lucia,' she says to her companion, a woman in blue. 'It is female. I suppose you could breed from it. No, wait a moment, there's something else. She's a reclaimed Rat. No hopes of breeding there.'

Blue butts in. 'Dear, I wouldn't take it even if it was fertile. My employer wouldn't thank me for diluting his gene pool with such floor scrapings. They say even reconditioned Rats can't be trusted. Most end up in the arena or consigned to the labs.' They both shudder and walk on leaving me in the shadow of their dread.

A fem in muddy brown walks the line handing out concentrates and offering a pipe of water. I shake my head but she insists. 'Drink your fill,' she whispers. 'You don't know how long you'll be here.' She speaks carefully and with practiced skill, barely moving her lips. 'You'll stay in the hall till you're chosen. If you're still here at day end, you'll sleep on the benches till viewing begins again at first light. If you *are* left behind tonight it's a bad look out. It'll be marked on your chip. Listen, there'll be a fresh batch of hirelings in tomorrow and if you're not chosen, you'll be trooper meat come day's end.' The muddy moves on, nodding at the closed stalls at the far end of the hall. 'Latrines, for when the guards permit.'

I eat the food bars, saving some for Brown. It's not long before a bell signals close of play and the few hirers that remain disappear. A guard climbs down from the mezzanine and calls to us leftovers, pointing to the latrines. 'Use the heads but don't waste time in there.'

I wait my turn and once behind the swing doors I free Brown to drink at the flushing water before I sit down to empty my bowels. Sitting there with Brown on my lap I feed her the concentrate, then leave the cubicle.

'Show's over till tomorrow, so get what rest you can.' With these unexpectedly civil words the trooper heads back to the open-tread stairs to the observation gallery.

15

I estimate twenty-five of us leftovers stand in the dimming light, and only a handful of benches remain illuminated. We drift to them, autumn leaves in the gloom, while troopers lean on the rail above, watching.

Where do I sit? By the one-armed giant or the mousy woman with weak legs and a twitch? Easy to guess why these are rejects. Most of the others look to be nil, or bear the scars of disobedience. Some wear the constant smile of the permanently deranged and a couple have the flicking eyes and wandering fingers of perverts.

A brace of troopers stamp down the stairs. One holds a chip-reader, the other a bundle of restraint tape. One checks my chip. 'First day for this one. A treat for tomorrow, looks like.' They grin and check the rest. For the giant, the weak legged woman and a nil, it's the second day. They're cuffed with the tape and led away to a chorus of trooper catcalls and whistles.

Be me tomorrow.

Sickened, I choose an unlit bench well away from the rest. Brown slips from my sleeve and scampers into the shadows, glad to be free. I wonder about tomorrow, who'll want an undersized weakling—an obvious nil?

Someone is crying, a woman with no evident faults. Wonder what's on her chip? I look away as two figures detach from the group and saunter towards me. Even a snatched glance tells me they're bad news. I look up at the observation deck where the guards watch with interest. No help there. I shouldn't have moved so far from the herd. These jackals are hunting. Bet I know what's on *their* chips.

They halt near me chatting like I wasn't there. I look from under my lashes. The tall one is fair skinned and muscular with blond stubble. He's marked patterns on his skull with dirt and rolled up his sleeves and trouser legs to display pumped muscles. Hell, even this guy's coveralls fit like they were made special. But as I look further I spot the sores on his ears, neck and hands.

His sidekick, a head shorter, thickset and dark-skinned, has rolled up sleeves showing muscled arms shiny with grease. He's posturing like a beauty king, trouble is his good looks are ruined by the worst case of squint-eye that I ever met.

'Yeah, you're right man, it is female,' says walleye to the blond. 'But only just. You think she's fem enough for the two of us?'

They step closer and the blond leers. 'I'm always right, Sterry. You should know that by now. Spotted her as fem straight off. A fem heading for a trooper crib.'

The walleye, Sterry, answers, 'But tonight she's ours, Track, yeah?'

Track nods, 'Yeah,' he grins.

I've locked my hands tight to the bench top. Suddenly and with all the force I can muster I heave my work boot into blondy's balls. He collapses, mewing.

Sterry makes the mistake of squinting down at his writhing pal. I undo my belt and swing it buckle first toward his eyes, Striker's voice in my ears, 'Go for the weak point, Bit, and never show mercy. The metal prong drags across his eye, snags on the socket and the belt's almost wrenched from my hand as he joins his oppo on the floor.

I hiss for Brown, belt up and step over the moaning duo to join the rejects sitting in the light. A pair of hands beats lonely applause. On the observation gallery one of the guards, a sergeant, claps appreciation.

Morning starts early in the work hall. The doors open to admit fresh orange-wearers and the muddy brings food and water to us remnants. The guard nods us towards the latrines, and once our chips are updated the new round begins.

I mingle with the newbies, putting distance between me and the two scabs I'd cold-cocked last night. The lines snake up and down the hall and the prospective takers swoop forward to bag the best. Some merely use their readers, some make more physical examinations, handling and in some cases fondling, the merchandise. I stand mum-chance watching neighbours selected and removed, or rejected out of hand. The lines shrink faster today, more takers, bigger hauls. One guy dressed garishly in vibrant patterns minces away with two handfuls of good looking youths, another dressed in liveried red walks away with a string of comely fems.

The lines condense, bringing me to a familiar figure. Lightning blazes from my head to my toes and back again. He's taller, his face fuller but his eyes still have the same watchful, guarded expression. A familiar fiery stubble hazes his skin. Like last night's jackals he's used dirt and grease as decoration, redrawing the scars lasered from his cheeks. I whistle the double notes of a Rat alert and Striker turns to find the source. His face doesn't change but when our eyes meet they *burn*. We stare, disbelief and longing roil and twist inside me. I tap a signal on my cheek. Slowly we drift together until we touch. The hall fades, the throng disappears and it's just the two of us speaking, touching and loving like before. I remember my first sight of him, the quirky rufous hair all decked with beads and bones, the confident stride, the heart-fluttering grin, and feel the surge of heart-pounding, forever love.

I sketch my months of silence in the CRC and tell him I'll be trooper meat at close of day. He tells me he'd been banded early, and asks about Brown. He's shocked when I pat my waist. The conversation ends with a sudden influx of hirers. The troopers push the straggling lines into new configurations and as the lines alter I see the two jackals I bested the night before.

A glum faced man-mountain is examining their chip readings. His bald skull, greasy and gleaming under the strong illumination, appears dinted and battered. His face is a mass of random scars, his misshaped ears bright with jeweled studs. He pulls the jackals out of line, checks them over with businesslike hands, his eyes cold and calculating—assessing livestock. He nods, calls a trooper to update their chips and walks towards the doors, his hirelings in tow.

Watching them go I'm relieved to be spared their company in the brothel. I drag a smile from somewhere. Striker shakes a finger, 'What?'

I sign back, 'Later.' Then smile again at the stupidity of signing such a thing. There'll be no later. The smile dies.

I look back to Sterry and Track and don't notice the pair approaching me until a dig from Striker's elbow draws my attention. It's the applauding sergeant alongside someone very different, a statuesque woman who over-tops the trooper by a mile. Her hair is cut super short and is black as a moonless night, framing one of the hardest faces I've ever looked on. The eyes are pale roundels of ice-rime, the gaze painfully intent and when she looks at me it's like she's digging in my brain to see 'xactly how it works. Her nose, jutting like the beak of some giant eagle, is balanced between the blood red dagger tattooed on her left temple and the matching arc of scarlet brilliants studding her right ear. Dressed entirely in figure hugging black she looms like a midnight iceberg. The short hooded cape swinging from her shoulders and high glossed boots complete the ensemble. She leans towards me, grinning like a feral cat. 'Well, Sergeant, what have we here? Undersized, certainly, but not stunted. Deceptively strong I'd say. Bright, you think?'

'Cunning, certainly Ma'am,' the silver striper answered. 'Intelligent, possibly. Keeps her head, that's all I know.'

'Her chip?'

'Well, now, wouldn't be relying too much on what that says, ma'am. Says she's of low-grade intelligence and has minimal communication skills, but she acted cute enough last night. I reckon she'd suit your purpose. If I'm wrong you can take back my squeeze. Can't say fairer than that, now can I?'

'You've picked me winners in the past, Sergeant, so I'm inclined to go with you on this one. By all means record her as mine.'

Looking straight at me she says. 'I claim you, girl. Follow close.'

I make as if to follow, but fake a stumble so I can sign to Striker one last time; the thrill of finding him choked by my despair. I flick a few words and fast as a snake the black clad fem turns and grabs my hand in an unbreakable grip. 'Rat signs, eh? Talking to this one?' she says, her other hand flashing out and gripping Striker's arm.

Both of us snared in seconds. What the hell is this fem?

16

Our tableau turns heads and that pisses off the giantess. 'Mark them both as mine, sergeant,' she growls. 'And no, I don't want to see any more, not with all eyes on us. I'll be back tomorrow and don't worry, you'll be credited with both finds.' She smiles, viper-like, and the sergeant disappears.

She frees us and we follow. I'll not cross a fem who moves that fast and smiles that way. Stone killer, this one. My hand's numb and even Striker's cheeks have paled. I rub my wrist as we track her striding form through the crowd and out to the sky-cruiser parked outside. The driver's alert, starting the motor soon as we exit. She pushes us into the cab then springs aboard as the driver speeds away. We fly over the guard fence and I swear I hear the scrape and twang of eye-posts. I swallow, hard.

We're crammed onto the driving bench. I'm next to the pilot and he's a rare sight; glow-black skin with a face seamed and chipped with scars. Not deliberate cuts like a Rat's, more like fight scars. Guy looks tough as jerked meat. Old though. Fortyish? Gotta be, though his tight stretches show more muscle than any oldster has a right to and he pilots the speedster with casual ease. He's missing the little finger of his right hand, cut off cleanly, unlike the ear which is hacked to a mangled stub. Don't know what he is, but he doesn't smell Rat.

We fly over ruins, first climbing then swooping, zigzagging

along narrow street canyons and over pinnacled high rises. Striker's squashed beside me and he tenses as we scream towards a hill of debris. I hold my breath, my heart fluttering out of sync. This guy's out to kill us!

I'm reaching for the driver's arm as he pulls us back from crashing. We arrow up and over the rubble, revving towards a new built highway spearing through the ruins. Takes me a while to start breathing again. Now the madman's really zooping the juice and we're flying faster than a thought, leaving troop carriers and shiny speedsters in our wake. We're riding high and smooth and our pilot's smiling, relaxed. This guy knows exactly what he's doing.

Leaving behind the shattered urbs we fly over mile upon mile of empty land, before coming upon great circles of fenced ground. Most are centred by balloon buildings, the rest with half completed ones. I look at Striker and he signs NOP compounds. I shake my head, too small, too individual. One building, striped red and green is set inside a square fence, quartered by observation towers and surrounded by a jungle of vegetation, more trees and flowering plants than I've ever seen in one place. Soon as I glim the orange clad workers, I know how come. Hell, as a slave holder, nothing's impossible.

Some time and several estates later we're swooping towards a large complex and a clutch of bland grey balloon buildings. As we close in I see the ring wall's pierced by a heavy gate, both wall and gate are spiked and spotted with auto-guns. The air above the compound shimmers, like there's warm air rising. Some kind of defensive shield? We land, the aircraft wings fold, the gate opens and we drive through. I crane to look and the shimmer's still above. Striker points it out, signs *power shield* on my hand.

The craft enters one of the smaller balloons and comes to a smooth halt. We're here. Wherever here is.

Our hirer springs out and we hurry after. She palms a wall pad and a grey roll-up opens smooth as oiled skin. All four of us step into a plas-met box. I touch a wall, exciting an array of winking crimson lights. The owner laughs and the box drops down so fast my knees dissolve. Striker keeps me upright till it stops.

'Take them,' the woman orders and strides down the tunnel-like corridor, palms a winking wall and walks through another roll-up. The black skinned driver leads us to a hinged door with a lever handle. He operates the handle and slips through. The door closes as I reach for it, snapping like an axe chop, nearly trapping my fingers. I'm still staring at my hand when it opens again. 'Too slow,' the driver whispers hoarsely. 'Got to move fast if you're gonna survive in Spartax's Hold.' He lets go of the door and me and Striker manage to scrape inside before it slams shut.

We find ourselves in a low-ceilinged, dim-lit passage facing a pair of doors; one one green, one red, neither has handles. They show signs of frequent use, grey paint showing under numerous dints and scratches. The driver points to green, 'You, in there,' he says, disappearing through red.

I stick close to Striker as he pushes the door. It opens to deafening noise. Inside a frenetic mess of figures shout and laugh and move top speed. It's the laughter that shakes me, haven't heard sounds like that since before the CRC. Then the smell hits, jolting up my nose like a hit of fire powder: food, real, hot-cooked food.

A strident voice yells, 'Newbies.' Two warm dishes are pushed into our hands and we're nudged in the direction of a counter packed with plates and pots. The same voice yells 'Take what you want and make it quick, it's near change over.'

Bemused we scoop a ladle of colourful stew from a huge metal pot. It's full of meat chunks and the rich smell brings back memories of Rat hunts and festival feasts, and sets Brown squirming in anticipation. I snatch a bread slice, topped with sliced meat, from an almost empty platter. Someone pushes me to a rack of cutlery and then to a table with bench seats. We sit, eyes roving. Brown climbs onto my lap and grabs the meaty chunks I offer. She demands more and I filch Striker's cold meat slices.

I'm scraping the last glorious remnant from my bowl when a handsome round faced, brown skinned guy pushes in beside us. 'Hi. Name's Kai. Been told to show you round. It's change over time, next sitting's about to come in. Dump your dishes in the cleaner over there.' Then he's up on his feet and heading for a blue door so fast I gotta race to stuff a protesting ferret into a sleeve, dump my dish to catch up with Striker and our speedy guide. What are these people on?

The blue push-door leads to a square room, tiled floor to ceiling with blue squares and with full length mirrors stuck on the walls. The room's equipped with sinks and showers plus a line of shuttered jakes. Our guide waves a hand, 'Wash room,' he states before tanking towards black painted door. The next room is oblong, far bigger than the last and chock-full of beds, some at floor level and a load more on the wide ledge jutting from the walls, a mezzanine, like back at the work hall. The guide, Kai, weaves between the wooden supports with the ease of long practice. I can hardly keep up, slowed by my first good meal in an age and barely notice the room. I do catch sight of corner ladders and notice there's no barrier to stop sleepers falling off the mezzanine.

Kai speeds us through a green door and we're back at the food hall. Bodies are exiting while others push in and Kai's almost lost in the throng. I fix eyes to his bead-strung plaits and push through the crowd keeping close to Striker. A grey door opens and Kai slips through. I put on a spurt, catch up, and we're back where the driver left us, in the dim passage with green and red doors.

Fed up with the rushing I stop to catch my breath and call to the speed freak to stop. Kai hesitates and is lost as Striker lunges at him, speaking calmly into his face. 'We're staying put, until Bit and I get an idea of what the jack's going on.'

'Jehu skimped on the info, did he?'

'Skimped? If Jehu's the mad driver you're damn right. He gave us nothing and I, for one, am feeling a tad sore.'

By the look on Kai's face when Striker tightens his grip, he's got the message.

'Who was the fem who hired us and what exactly are we hired for?' Striker growls.

'Ease up, man. I'll tell you, I'll tell you. Come into the training hall and I'll set you straight.'

The training hall lies behind the red door. A massive L-shaped room, so high the ceiling's lost in shadow and with two walls pocked with protuberances. All sizes, all shapes and all colours stick out of the walls in an unfathomable pattern. Kai points, 'Climbing walls. Different colours, different grades.' He pauses for a couple of seconds, then continues the tour by pointing to the mats stacked in the corners. 'Fall mats.' Next he shows us weights and bars and ropes, 'Exercise gear. And here's the close combat weapons and …' He walks on but he's lost Striker at the knives.

'Wait, Kai,' he calls. 'Tell me about these.'

'Okay. That section is for bladed weapons. Axes, knives, swords, those are the most popular, but there's scythes, machetes and a heap of other stuff. You name it we got it.' He moves along, 'Bows, here: all kinds from horse bows to crossbows. You like knives? We got 'em all, and bolas, kendo staves, spears. That enough for now?'

I nod, dazed, and follow Kai, but Striker's mesmerised by the knives. I call and he breaks away his eyes glistening. 'Hell Bit, it's not much like a CRC is it?'

'Grab a mat,' says Kai, looking hard at Striker and me, as if he's testing us. I stare back. He's big and muscled, with a pleasant face topped with a mass of thin bead-threaded plaits. His brown eyes are merry and his mouth well used to smiling. I sign a few words, disappointed when he doesn't sign back. He's not Rat.

'Your hirer, Spartax is a fight proprietor who trains her teams in this ludus. The teams fight under the Raven banner as Spartax's Ravens. She trawls the work halls for talent. She got spotters in the military, and pays well for likely fighters.'

I hold up my hand. 'Wait up Kai, you've lost me. I don't understand you. For a start, what's a ludus?'

'A gladiatorial training ground.'

'That doesn't help.'

'Spartax trains fighters for the Games.' He stares at me and then at Striker. 'Come on. You can't tell me you don't know about the Games?' We shake our heads. 'Where have you two slash-brains been hiding?'

I feel a blood rush and spit out hot words, 'We been in the ruins killing troopers, then enslaved in a CRC. Can't think *how* these fancy games of yours have passed us by.'

He grimaces, shrugs and starts again. 'Yeah, well, okay. The Games are the latest craze. Since the Sickness, sport has been dead. No football or boxing, no horse or dog races. Nada. So, how are folk gonna forget their troubles? Enter the New Games, promoted by the General himself. Gladiatorial contests, he calls 'em. Rich pickings for team owners with gravy to spare for the cits.'

I remember my father spouting Roman history, 'Bread and circuses,' I say. 'Keep the people happy and they don't think revolution. Same old, same old.'

'What?' says Kai, but I shake my head.

'Nothing. Tell on.'

'In the New Games sponsors train teams to compete for big prizes in city arenas. Teams are six strong, and the citizens watch and wager. They can bet on anything: whole teams, two on two bouts, one on one; any and every combination you can think of.' He pauses to see if we're keeping up. We nod.

'Spartax's teams are moving up the ranks, fast. She picks her arena teams from the best in the ludus. The crew you've seen about the place? Teamers. We train non-stop and fight to win points, because the Arena teams are chosen from the top listers. You two bring our number to fifty. Competition's fierce and getting fiercer by the day.'

This time Striker halts Kai. 'Just what kind of events are you talking about?'

'Mortal combat, what else? We fight in the Arena, no holds barred, and we fight to the death.' He stands and hauls us up to face him. 'Welcome to the Gladiators of the New Order.'

17

A siren howls and Kai springs to his feet. 'Frink! We're late. We gotta meet with Spartax. Come on you two, *run*.' And he's off through the door with me and Striker speeding after him. We catch up as he enters a metal box and soon as we're in, the box shoots up so fast I'm rocked off my feet. 'What *is* this thing, Kai?'

'An up-and-downer, a riser. Come on, you gotta know it's a *lift*.'

Back in the vehicle store, Kai hurtles to a roll-up with a glo-panel on the wall beside it. He presses a sequence, the door rolls up and we're outside haring along a rough-crete path. I'm blown, Striker's out of breath, yet Kai's breathing easy. How come?

Skidding to another roll-up, he palms the panel, states his name and we enter another up-downer. This time I'm prepared, and when the box drops I stay on my feet. But I don't like hearing the nasty little clicks and hisses. It's like there's *things* living behind the shiny walls. The sounds get louder and Striker slams a neck lock on Kai.

'No harm, guys,' he wheezes. 'Swear to you, just Spartax's little checkers.' Striker loosens his enough to allow easy speech. 'Spartax is careful, s'all. Do I look worried?'

Not over the noises perhaps, but Striker certainly has him going. The noises stop, the wall behind Kai opens and there's Spartax. Striker releases Kai, eying our owner warily.

'Take warning,' Kai murmurs, 'Spartax asks, give her the truth. Lie and it's the labs. Talk straight, yeah?'

The room is bright lit but windowless. Spartax sits behind an uncluttered desk made of some shiny, reddish wood. She crooks a finger, we move and the roll door guillotines behind us. I stamp on the urge to run, concentrating on walking steady, same as Striker.

Spartax moves her head and a gleam from a light stand dances on the blood-brilliants studding her ear. She's dressed in black and behind her the wall is patched with screens and meters, raising memories of Mont's hi-tec 'quipment in the CRC. But Spartax's stuff looks to be streets ahead of Mont's.

The three of us line up in front of the desk. Spartax, the cat who's got us clawed, lets the silence stretch. Inside my coverall I feel Brown move and I'm comforted.

Spartax addresses Kai, her voice a whiplash. 'Your timekeeping leaves room for improvement, Kai. Deduct five points from your game score. Go wait outside.'

'Ma'am,' he nods and exits through a hinged door.

Spartax rises, slow and fluid, and I spot a Rat kill-knife at her waist. She glides forward, looking us up and down like she's choosing which joint to hack off first, then glares directly into my eyes.

'Sergeant Stow tells me you might suit requirements. However, the Sergeant is not infallible. Tell me what might be on your chip,' she purrs, her eyes wide and glinting like mica chips.

I look at the woman who owns me body and soul and, mindful of Kai's advice, I speak true. 'Before the CRC I was a free Rat. I won my name through Trial, had a mate and a bound friend. I used a range of powered weapons though I'm more familiar with hand to hand and knife work. I've killed my share of troopers. Taken by treachery I was chipped and cut by Templeton's med-techs. From the time the troopers took me I chose to be mute. Now I choose to speak.' I take a steadying breath and trusting Kai's assessment of her I shrug Brown from my sleeve.

'Here's the bound friend.'

Spartax's pupils widen, though her face stays blank. She stares at Brown, her eyes hardening and I tense. She goes for Brown I go for her, no matter what that brings me.

Striker butts in, 'And I'm the mate.' And her glims beam on Striker, full heat.

'Ah, my impulse buy.' She says, pursing her lips, 'Speak.'

'Like Bit, I won my name through Trial and have a tally of trooper kills. Caught by the same treachery I was chipped and cut. Sent to CRC2, I won a Band in the third week and kept it until the day I left.'

I'm impressed as hell that Striker earned a band so fast, and kept it for so long. I know how rare it is to hang on to authority for a whole term. Hope I get a chance to hear the story. We might have adapted differently to the CRCs, me choosing invisibility and Striker doing the opposite, but we both survived. Course we did, we're Rat.

We exchange looks and turn to Spartax. Maybe she'll offload us to the labs or pass us to a trooper joy-house. So be it, we'll take what comes.

'Survivors. That's what I look for. You two … and that creature, will stay until I see how you shape up. Jehu will ground you in the basics but before I make a final decision I'll observe you fight and see if you are worth persevering with or meant for lab meat.' She pauses, 'What names do you use? I take it you won't be using the ones recorded on your chips?' She points to me and I answer clearly.

'Born name's Cassandra but my Trial name's Bitch Singer, I answer to Bit.'

She nods, then looks at Striker, who states his. A touch to the desk with a probing finger summons Kai.

'Take Bit, Striker and that creature to Eily,' she orders, then turns to us. 'Eily will inform you how this compound is run and what she expects of you.' A pause, then, 'What *I* expect from my teams is dedication and loyalty. Fail me and I ship you elsewhere.

Most rejects take the Blood Road.'

I don't need ask what that means.

Outside, Kai stares at Brown proudly riding my shoulders in her old way, so I introduce them. 'Kai, meet my ferret, Brown. Brown, Kai.'

Kai holds his hand to Brown who sniffs and huffs a welcoming breath.

'Do I pass muster?'

'You'd know if you didn't. She's a good judge of character is Brown. I've learned to steer clear of those she spurns. You're in, Kai, don't fret.'

He leads back to the food hall and delivers us to Eily; a green-eyed blonde 'bout same age as Spartax and looking just as hard. Like Jehu and Spartax, Eily has the body of a fighter and a face that's taken punishment. 'Spartax says to show them the ropes,' Kai says before he leaves.

Eily stares at Brown, draped on my shoulder. 'Spartax seen that?' I nod and she smiles. 'Okay then, what does it eat?'

'She. Her name's Brown and her favourite is fresh meat.'

'Plenty of that here. She can have as much as she wants. Right then, I'm Eily, and you'd be?'

We tell our names and she frowns, 'Rats?' We nod, she smiles, 'I've fought Rats, worthy opponents all of them. I'm housekeeper and comp tech, I also teach Kalarippayattu.'

She sees our faces, 'Kala's an ancient martial art. Covers many disciplines.' She changes tack, 'Met Jehu yet?' she asks.

Guess she sees our expressions, because she smiles. 'Guess you have. As well as Spartax's driver he's a weapons master and the best fight teacher you'll ever have. Spartax teaches strategy, it's an art form with her and she'll have you using your brains as nimbly as your bodies.' She chuckles, 'Confused? You'll learn. First thing to remember is that from the moment you passed into Spartax's hands she owned you. From now on she'll feed you, clothe you and train you. You get the freedom of the compound and the freedom to arrange your love lives to suit yourselves, providing no one gets damaged. But, and it's a very big but, you obey her orders without thought, fight only when she orders you and *always* fight to win. Losses she'll tolerate only if you're outclassed. Just you make sure you never *do* get outclassed.'

We stay mute when she finishes. My mind's full to bursting with new input and I jump when she calls out Kai's name in an ear-shattering shout. He runs in like a fleet fox. 'I'm done, Kai. Show them the sleep room and find them something decent to wear, and Kai? Bin the convict gear.'

Kai nods and we follow him out. Before we exit she says, 'Don't forget to give them the meals rota and the training schedule.'

'Sure thing, Eily,' he sings back.

When we reach the two-tier sleep room all I want is to get to bed and get some sleep, but Kai says, no, clothes first.

'I'm not leaving this room. I'm dead on my feet.'

'Fine, the clothes are kept here.' Sliding back a wall panel, I glim a vast cavern full of clothes. 'Three sections, right? First, everyday wear. Middle, training gear. Last, Arena wear. Arena gear's black because Spartax's Ravens always wear black. Take anything that fits. Wear it, alter it, do what you want with it but if it goes back in, it goes back clean and mended. Okay?'

'Okay,' I say, 'but can we get some sleep now?'

Striker looks as creased as me and we're both relieved when Kai says it's okay.

'Sure. Use any of the stripped beds, covers in the drawer underneath. Don't worry about oversleeping, our morning wake-up could rouse a corpse. I'll give you your training schedule at breakfast. Sleep well, you'll find tomorrow tough.'

Striker and I choose a bed and cling together under the blankets. We fit together well as ever and the bed is roomy enough to sleep a pair of Rats and one contented ferret.

The future? Hell, as long as I got Striker, nothing's gonna faze me.

18

Kai was right about the wake-up. I peer through scrunched eyes at Kai yelling 'Get up, get dressed. You *can't* be late. I'll forfeit another point.'

'Clothes,' I mumble and he flings an armful on my face. Struggling up I see a maelstrom of rushing bodies.

'What's going on?' Striker groans.

'Siren's sounded. You got minutes to get clean, dressed and down to breakfast. You'll be in deep dreck if you're late and I'll be in it with you.'

'Why you?'

'I'm your guide till you get on your feet. Your mistakes are mine, so MOVE.'

I grab a stretch as Kai disappears into the washroom through the blue door. He's exaggerating, right?

I don't waste time glorying at the blasting shower because the steamy room empties fast. I drag the stretch over my damp skin and scoot after the crowd, Striker at my heels. The green door leads to the food hall. We grab the oatmeal and fruit on offer and sit at the nearest table. When the oatmeal's eaten I voice an idea. 'The doors are colour-coded.'

'No, really?' gasps Striker.

'Yeah, really. Green doors, food hall; blue, wash rooms; black, sleep rooms; red to the training hall.'

'Bit you're a genius.'

'Right, so you worked it out. When?'

'Last night. Wondered when you'd twig.'

Kai appears from nowhere. 'Come on you two, time for training,' he snaps, and darts away. Why's everything in this place done max-speed? They *trying* to confuse us?

Last into the training hall we're blasted by Jehu. Sluggard is the kindest word he uses.

'Join in,' he yells as we watch the class warm up. That I manage, but when they start on work-ups I'm soon out of my depth. After months in the CRC, I'm stripped of fitness and strength. Can't keep up; legs melting, gasping 'stead of breathing. I can barely stay upright.

Work-up over I collapse on a mat while everyone else, Striker included, runs and jumps and does other stuff I can't bear to watch. Instead I try rubbing my body back to life, aiming to join in soon as I'm human. Midday comes, Jehu calls rest and Striker lurches back to me. 'We're not going to make it, are we?' I say. He hasn't breath to answer.

After a cup of water and a dry food bar I stand with the others as Jehu gives instruction. It's then that I learn that these ultra fit, ultra hard youths are not the champion gamers I take them for, but tyros. Hell, if these are novices what are the real gamers like?

'Today you will observe a demonstration of how metal weapons are used in Kala. For newcomers I'll remind you that Kala's an ancient martial art from India. This is only one aspect of the weapons training you will receive in the ludus. A whole range of disciplines have been used and adapted in our aim to make Spartax's Ravens the most feared team in the New Games.'

The combatants are Jehu and Eily and they fight three short bouts, the first with curved daggers and the second with swords and shields. In the final and most terrifying bout they fight with flexible swords. I hold my breath for the duration of the electric match and when it ends both Eily and Jehu drip blood.

In the intervals between bouts Jehu demonstrates in slow

motion each strike and counter. But not after the final bout. Too fast, too instinctive for beginners, he says.

'Tomorrow, you will watch more experienced teamers fight with wooden weapons. Before you touch a metal weapon you must master wood. Same time as you practice with wood, you'll be taught the bare-handed techniques of attack and defence.' He held a hand up to still the murmurs. He looks at me and Striker as he says the rest, 'If you think you have an understanding of unarmed combat—think again.'

I've lost count of the days. All the hours of physical training, learning the moves of martial dance, meld together like a mess of cooked cheese. Evenings we study full-body oil massage with Eily, to increase flexibility, treat muscle injuries and stabilize bone tissue and nerves. She chooses one of us to demonstrate on, pouring warm scented oil on our skin and kneading, palpating skin and muscles till the tension flows away and the body sinks into stupor. Then we're partnered with more experienced teamers to learn the graded techniques under Eily's keen eyes.

When Jehu told us he was gonna teach us dance moves, Striker looked like he was about to cut and run, but Jehu did some fancy footwork and brought him down neat as a ninepin. 'That's the kind of dance physicality we teach. Training the body for the acquisition of the killing art. That okay by you?'

The days spin by and the nights are dreamless. Food is plentiful and tasty and the only spur is bettering ourselves and outperforming our companions.

My favourite's the climbing wall. On our very first attempt after we'd put on the harnesses, Jehu directed us to keep to the grey holds and pegs. 'Starter level,' he said. 'Don't worry about falling, the harness will keep you from the floor.'

So I start up going from grey to grey, me and Striker neck and neck. I know slow and steady's my best bet, not so Striker. I look up and he's ahead, changed from grey pegs to yellow, moving up a steep-jutting face; going strong and making it look easy. I'm thinking of trying for yellow same as him, but before I make the move he stops dead, his hand reaching for a peg that's sinking into the wall. Stymied he feels around for another hold and can't locate one. Now he lowers a leg, backtracking to the peg below. That one's gone as well. I whistle a two-tone warning and he freezes. Same time his yellow handhold starts retracting and he's swinging from his harness against a sheer, blank wall.

He needs help so I abandon the grey route and take the black, the quickest way to reach him, only to find my pegs shrinking same as his. And there we are, two fool danglers waiting for rescue. Have to wait a damn long time amid the hoots and catcalls of the training class. Jehu let us down after class is ended and long after food has vanished from the food hall. 'Take warning,' was all he says. We shower and go to bed, stomachs empty and minds too full for talk.

Since then we've got acquainted with the rest of the trainees, making firm friends with Kai. He gave thumbnail sketches of our fellows that fleshed out our first impressions. We learned from him in detail how the place is run and how Spartax, Jehu and Eily's time in the arena informs their training methods. When he talks of Spartax's Ravens he almost bursts with pride. 'The Ravens are *the* hot prospect.'

Every seventh day, training is suspended; the day set aside for bouts between teamers to vie for the points that'll win a place in an arena team.

'See, fight season's almost on us,' Kai said as we watch a bout. 'This season Spartax is pushing hard. Word is she's entering a Raven team in every one of the smaller venues. She wants max exposure; wants as many Ravens as possible to get a real taste of action. This is her second season and she'll want to be well up the points table come season end.'

'So when do we get a turn in one of these weekly bouts?'

Hell, Striker's keen, keener than me, by a long walk.

'Next seven-day,' Kai answered calm as lukewarm water.

'*Next* seven-day?' I say, my voice too high. 'We'll be creamed. Been watching close, so I know.'

'Calm it Bit. You won't be fighting them,' he points into the hall, 'you'll be fighting him,' he grins, pointing at Striker.

19

'Don't worry,' Kai says. 'You've seven more days' training till you fight. And it won't be a killing bout. They want to see how you move, your reactions, your determination.'

'Funny, but that doesn't comfort me one tiny bit,' I say back.

Kai stands and Striker grabs his hand. 'Wait up. Don't go running off before telling us more.'

The boy pulls free, 'Got to go. I'm on next. I'll send someone.' He's edgy, eager for the bout, eyes fixed on the scoreboard. 'Name's up. Gotta go.'

He jogs to a bench down the hall, stops and points at us. A fem stands, she's using a crutch and favours her right leg. She's also got a bandage around her head. 'Bit and Striker?' she says and eases to the bench at my nod.

She's taller than me, but not by much, with short white-blonde hair slicked back to show her face. Her eyes are grey … and angry. She aims them at me, then turns them on Striker. 'You're Rats,' she states, and starts signing fast and neat. *Nab, me. Of the Silent Killers. You?*

'Bitch Singer. WhipTails.' I sign. Striker signs his ident, plus his CRC number. She gives hers and Striker informs her that he met Silent Killers in there. He names them and Nab's expression softens.

I give two short finger flicks asking how long she's been with

Spartax. Four months, she signs.

'Hurt, how?'

'Quilla,' she finger spells, then drops her hands to her lap and starts to speak, as if signing grieves her. 'Quilla, and a faulty staff. She lunged, I vaulted and the staff snapped. I got KO'd and that fox stole the point.'

Nab curls her lip at a tall ginger haired fem wearing multi-coloured stretches. 'She knew the staff would break. A cheat she'll regret next time we fight.'

Quilla, the fox, bares her teeth at Nab and points to the score-board. Her name is high on the list with an impressive number of points. Nab looks at me and there's blood on her lips. She files her teeth like One Eye and the familiar sight makes me smile. Nab smiles back licking her lips, her anger fading.

'What else you want to know?'

Striker takes a breath, about to launch a question when Nab holds up a warding hand and whistles a two-tone trill. In seconds two guys appear. They also bear the shadowed scars of lasering. They're alike, thin faced and brown eyed, but the one with darker skin is a few inches taller. They both shave their heads. The taller, browner one is Gard. The other, a smiler with filed teeth, is Manas. They stand shoulder to shoulder and it's clear they're paired. Nab says all three of them choose to sleep on the mezzanine platform. I give my name, Striker his, and the pair hunker down in front of us.

'Confused?' smiles Manas. 'I remember what it was like when I first got here.' Gard, nods, unsmiling so I don't get to see if he files his teeth.

'These bouts are ruled same as arena bouts, but no killing allowed.'

Gard takes up the tale and, no, he doesn't file. 'Start of day the fighters are entered on the score board. When your name's highlighted you fight. Until then you won't know if you're fighting solo or in combination. More importantly you won't know if you'll fight bare-handed or weaponed; same as in the arena.

The arena board is run by the gaming-comp. Soon as your name lights up you grab what you need and go fight. Manas tell 'em the combinations.'

Manas offers another grin while Gard remains straight faced. 'First off there's a solo, that's one on one. Then there's a doubler, two on two, and so on to a whole team bout, six on six. The board tells you exactly what weapons to use. In the arena it's just the two teams fighting. Here,' he said indicating the melee in the hall behind him. 'The whole ludus fights on the same day, that's why it looks chaotic. Keep your eyes on the board and you'll learn what's going on.'

'What about our bout? Mine and Striker's? We're still on basic moves, haven't even started weapons training yet. What will they expect?'

'It's an assessment, that's all. If it's weaponed they won't expect finesse. Spartax is after a base line. You know powered weapons are banned from the arena? So are long range weapons like bows and arrows.' We nod. 'It's all close quarter fighting.'

Gard's turn, 'When you enter the arena, remember you're part of a team. You'll fight till the board says quit. No one leaves the fight-ground till the board allows.

'A practice bout isn't deadly, it stops for a bad injury. In an *arena* bout you don't hold back, you do what it takes to win and fight till you drop. This fight of yours next week? Just remember it's serious and you should fight to win. Spartax gets real narked if you hold back, and you *don't* want to risk that.'

The trio leaves and I watch board and bouts very carefully. I'll be fighting on that floor all too soon, and like Manas said, it's not the muddle it appears. There's only three serious bouts happening at one time and they take place in clearly defined circles. The other tussles are tone-up fights and warm ups played outside the circles. Striker points to Spartax, Jehu and Eily as they move about the hall studying the match bouts and taking glances at the warm ups. Everyone's being rated and they know it. As far as I can see they're all maxing out, not holding back at all.

I fix on the unarmed bouts and the raw power and grace of movement, the sheer skill of the combatants fills me with envy. Striker's watching the knife fighters like a snake following a music pipe. They're fighting so fierce I switch to watching. Bout ends and the guy gets the point and that surprises him. Near thing, then. The fem just smiles as they shake hands.

Fight day and I'm wired. Today's the day I fight Striker with the trainers watching every move. What'll happen if we don't come up to scratch? Hell, what'll to happen if *I* don't make the cut? Been exercising, doing the moves, running the katas every chance I get. Hope I've done enough.

In the training hall benches flank the walls, but only the injured use them, everyone else stands to clock the score board. It's blank so far. I start to warm up trying to block the thought of fighting with Spartax's cold eyes assessing my every move. Fifteen minutes later the board flashes the first names. It's like Rat Trial, word comes and you go. Tension grips, I stumble, my mind full of the coming bout.

I sit against the wall and relax, shoulders loose, hands resting on the floor, breathing slow and regular. In …out. In … out. Course it doesn't work, not with my head filled with Kai's rumour talk. According to him, me and Striker are top gossip and bets are mounting—on who'll win and how fast. Seems the big money's on Striker. General opinion says I'm heading for a joy-house. Reckon that'll be better that than given to the frinking Greys. I asked him but he wouldn't tell me what and who he'd bet on.

Can't stop the thoughts so I get up and walk around. Gard's name flashes. He and a tall fem are pitched against two squat guys

Can't stop the thoughts so I get up and walk around. Gard's name flashes He and a tall fem are pitched against two squat guys—staves and nets. Fight's fast and hard, over too quick to see the moves, just flashing staves, flung nets and two spider parcels on the sand. Gard winks at me when his winning point flashes on the board.

The bouts proceed. Kai loses, as does Manas, Nab wins her point after a long draining struggle. I watch a three on three, a couple of fours, a sixer then and hell and damnation, it's us. The board reads Striker v Bitch Singer. One on one: knives. Knives? Wasn't expecting that.

Eily, Spartax and Jehu wait under the board. Jehu points to a pair of identical knives, I take the left, Striker, the right, then we walk to the crimson edged fight circle and step in. Kai, Nab and the others push to the front of the growing crowd.

So it's the two of us in the circle and the hall's gone hush-quiet. Are we the only fight playing? The signal sounds. Game on.

It's got to be real, got to be fierce, full on. Anything less means ship-out. We talked last night, max effort we said. We're Rat, the weakest goes to the wall.

We circle. I'm a lefty and used to rucking with right handers. Trouble is Striker knows that, knows my tricks. Hell, but we've been apart a good long while and I might just have learned some new ones.

I switch hands, lunge overarm and cut him before he knows it. He replies with the 'xact same tactic, swapping his knife and slicing me. Okay, one for one. The dance speeds up. Feint follows feint. I'm faster than I was, and taller by a tad and my reach has changed. Reflex kicks in as we cut and parry, I'm nicked, he's nicked, but his strength tells. The bout ends and I'm down. We're both blooded, breathing hard, but ready for more. I class him to be the stronger, though I'm faster. All in all, I'm satisfied I've held my end up. I don't even mind when he's given the point.

We hand back the knives, I'm figuring if we've done enough to be kept on and Spartax walks off to view a bout just starting. I look at the approaching Jehu, and can't read him. Eily's already slipped away, and I got this doomy feeling.

Jehu's grim as he takes us aside and starts analysing the bout, move by move. He takes my hand and shows that holding the knife *this* way my third hit would have been more successful. He does the same with Striker. It's all there in his head, every move and every missed opportunity. When he eventually quits assessing us I venture a question, thinking it was worth asking seeing how he was wasting too much time on throw-outs. 'Say Jehu, this mean we're in?'

He pauses, and I wish I hadn't opened my mouth. Then he gives a micro-smile. 'No ship-offs. Spartax wants you both, go shower.'

Kai joins us on the way to the wash room. 'Knew Spartax wouldn't dump you. I watched her eye the bout and she was well satisfied. Besides, Jehu put a fistful on you.'

Nab catches up with us bringing Gard and Manas. 'Did all right for a pair of babes,' she says. 'Drink's on me tonight.'

After showering we push their three beds together up on the platform and sit drinking and talking. Nab donated the liquor and Kai wheedled the eats from Eily. Brown clambers over us all in search of titbits, allowing a certain amount of hand contact in return for her favourite smoked meat slices.

Talk turns to the past, stories of life in the tribes flood out and we slip into signing which ticks Kai off. 'Aw, come on, I'm no Rat, remember? Just a kid nabbed for stealing food. You cutting me out?'

'No,' Striker says. 'Just enjoying being Rat again. Want to learn Rat-speak?'

20

Kai's a natural, picking up signing fast as sand sucks water. Next morning I wake from a tangle of sleepers stinking of ferret musk, eager for the new day.

We work well as a group in the exercise session and aim to make it a regular thing—all Rats together, kind of style. Well, five and an honorary. Kai's eager to be fluent in signing, says he'd rather sign than vocalize, says he feels like he's found a new family. Says he feels good. Yeah, well so do I.

Instead of just competing we plan on overall improvement; strengthening weak points, sharing skills. We're in the training hall before general wake-up sounds and devote time before sleep to work on strategy.

Next fight-day Kai's name comes up early. 'Blood and piss, they've teamed me with Chun Lee against M'tan and Lialle, free choice of weapons. Fat chance Lee and I have got against those two. We'll be creamed.'

'*Will* he be creamed?' I sign to Nab.

She waggles a hand, 'Depends. Our Kai works too much on instinct. He was too good, too soon. I've told him; hell, we've all told him to work on his technique. He needs to plan ahead. Watch him, if he's backed into a corner he'll rely on pulling something out of the air. Fine if it works, but when it doesn't … Rely on that trick too often and you're on the blood road.'

'He ever fought an Arena bout?'

Nab shook her head. 'None of us have.'

'Let's get to the front,' I say, thrusting through the crowd. Kai and Lee make a well matched pair. Same height, well-muscled and eager. Nab slides a look at me, 'Look strong don't they? Top class? Can't count on looks. Lee does too much mirror time, has too many meets with adoring fems. Jehu's making a point teaming those two.'

'What point?'

'That they're lazy. Jehu's showing how far they've slipped. M'tan and Lialle aren't as talented but they *are* grafters.'

Gard pushes close and points to the guy holding an axe. 'M'tan. Lialle's the spear carrier. She's real feisty, doesn't know how to hold back.'

M'tan is thick-set, dark visaged and scowling, Lialle has short wiry curls, an ash-pale face, and eyes as hard as plas-met.

Kai's gripping a curved sword with his right hand and there's a small round shield on his other arm. Lee's got a double-edged dagger and a net.

'Chances, Gard?'

'So-so. Have to use their heads, though.'

Signal sounds and the fight starts … and is over in a blink—the losers, Kai and Lee.

'What just happened?' I ask Gard.

'Lialle trounced Kai and Lee got shoulder hit with M'tan's axe. Game over. And look at that, a bonus point for a fast win. Talk about rubbing it in!'

Kai creeps up like a slapped pup. 'Hi, Bit. Not one of my best performances, that. Dreck here comes Jehu.'

Hoiked away by Jehu he disappears till sleep time, appearing as we tote our gear to the platform having decided to move nearer to Nab.

'Where are you two going?'

'Moving up.'

His face falls even lower. 'Want to come?' I say. So now there's six of us sleeping close and that's when we become The Clan.

For the next few weeks we all work extra hard and it's not just our performance that improves, but our spirits.

Kai's been at the ludus longest, taken from the work halls eight months back, he was a wilder from the compounds and a small time thief till the troopers lifted him. The other three arrived later, all from the same CRC, and spotted by the same sergeant as me and Striker.

All of us Arena virgins.

A week later Nab shares a shower with me. She's worried.

'Lee's gone,' she says.'

'Gone? Thought he was in sick bay.'

'No, gone. Shipped out.'

'Where?'

'Who knows: another trainer, the troopers? The labs? And Kai's on notice.'

'That means?'

'Means he's next.'

'You serious?'

'Sure am.'

Hauled from the shower by impatient queuers we talk as we dress.

'Okay, Nab, what can we do?'

'Work him. Work him so hard he can't tell up from down, day from night. He needs safety plays, needs to think ahead, and be aware of pitfalls. Most of all he needs to realise he's not as good as he thinks he is.'

'I'll get Striker on to it.'

Striker calls a Meet, 'Have to sort you out, Kai. We're not going to lose you. This Clan sticks together; from now it's nose to the grindstone. Agreed?'

Kai, faced by such determined help, knuckles down. It pays off because at next Fight Day he wins his point easily. That night we skip the strategy session in favour of celebration.

Another fight-day and I'm looking at the board, my belly clenched to a fist. My name's just blinked up and my opponent's Quilla. Next to the names comes the symbol for an unarmed contest. I swallow spittle, wipe damp palms and walk to the circle. Quilla's taller, heavier, and an arena veteran. Nab gives me a poke, 'Remember, Foxy cheats.'

Foxy's smiling, ready for an easy win. She's got on her fave stretches—all sick greens and 'lectric yellows, meant to dazzle, and there's razor wire twined in her hair. Soon as Eily triggers the starter she's out with the taunts and insults. I wall off the distractions, eyeing her writhing snake walk. She gonna spring left, jink right? She's grinning like the bout's already won. Yeah, well, she's a head taller, fought more bouts, but I'm scared, and to my way of thinking fear adds an extra-sharp edge. I keep my face blank. Keep 'em guessing, a lesson learned in CRC 1.

Her left thigh tenses. Expecting a kick I drop and roll, knocking her off balance. She steadies, but I'm up and pivoting behind her, punching stiff fingers in her kidney. She turns … into a kick to the knee. She's down and a head kick sends her out. The end-fight buzzer sounds and my point flashes to the board. I don't caper or punch the air, I keep a straight face, hiding the relief and surprise that rages through me.

Then it's back to a bench and an examination of the bout with the rest of the Clan till Striker's name appears on the board. He's fighting Dace, weapon—épée.

'Pleased?' I sign because I know he prefers this heavy bladed duelling sword to the lighter foil. He winks.

I'm in the front as the bout begins, standing next to Manas, another lover of blade-work. Striker, like the rest of the Clan fights in grey. Bare foot, they don padded jerkins and transparent face masks. A dusting of chalk and they're ready for the off.

Dace is a tested arena combatant, known to be a stone killer. He's not worried over fighting a tyro. Bout starts, and it's 'Here pretty Rat, come to me, come take a bite, see what you get.'

Striker lunges, Dace parries, Striker retreats.

'That's it, fall back red-boy. Come again and I'll slash your rodent face.'

Striker assays a second lunge, Dace parries with ease. Striker's not as forceful as he should be. He backs off. Dace thrusts, Striker retreats, again. Frink! One step more and he'll be over the line, forfeiting the bout. Manas frowns. Striker's blown, breathing ragged. Dace is winning, and he knows it. He slashes wildly, Striker dodges, flinching. There's blood on his cheek, Dace shouts in triumph … but he's too quick to call victory, because Striker executes a perfect stop thrust and skewers Dace's sword arm below the padding, forcing him to drop his weapon. The victory buzzer halts the bout and a bleeding Dace is escorted to the med room while Striker sees his score increased by one glowing point.

Like me he leaves the ring without showing emotion. When he rejoins the Clan he allows just one quick smile.

Kai and Manas join with Asa and Wa'an, against four experienced arena fighters. They get the point in record time without Kai making one false move.

'He's going to be insufferable for days over this,' I tell Nab.

Her turn comes and she's to fight Eira with long-staffs. The fight with Quilla must have dented her confidence. She watches extra close as Jehu double checks the staffs. Soon as the signal sounds Nab forges forwards and wins the point with an aggressive display that surprises everyone including her opponent. Dented confidence? No way.

Gard fights in a six on six, unarmed, and he steals the show, downing one man in a flurry of kicks and chops, then wading into the rest. Bout won he gets back to us, bruised, glowing but unsmiling till he joins his clan.

Day's end, we celebrate, quietly and still manage an hour's training before sleep.

Day by day, hour by hour our bond grows ever stronger.

21

Brown loves the freedom of Spartax's; she's petted and fed and gaining weight. Nab says they keep ferrets in the NOP compounds. As high cost pets they bring status.

'I heard they're escape artists, Bit, that true?'

'Yeah, Brown's a free spirit. I'm betting the rest are, too.'

'How d'you find her?'

'She found *me*. In the Ruins.'

'Some did get free from the compounds, least wise that's what I heard. P'raps she was NOP.'

'NOP turned Rat, then. She knows which side to be on.'

Nab's an expert on the compounds, living in New London for a time after her tribe had been cut down in a trooper blitz. 'I was lucky, got singed by a heat-blast, fell into a scrape-hole and missed the round-up. Came to in time to watch the survivors loaded into carriers. I tailed them hoping for a chance to free them. Didn't get that chance. They were taken to a real fortress—fences, 'larms and more troopers than a dog has fleas. I hung round and stirred up as much trouble as I could before they bagged me.'

I scrape the last spoonful of thick flavoursome soup, remembering the weak slosh served in the CRC and listening to Nab talk of her days in New London.

'Days, I watched teen-brat cits parading their parents' gelt in the malls and markets. Used to follow them and steal what I could. Lots had expensive pets hung round 'em. Ferrets like Brown tethered to their shoulders; cats in walking harnesses; birds with clipped wings; even live snakes and lizards worn like jewellery. All tied tight so they couldn't get free and end up in some hungry cit's cook pot.'

'Hungry folks in the compounds? Thought it was all peaches and honey in those places.'

'For some. Not for all by a long mile. NOP high-ups live real easy on the backs of low-down plebs.'

'We're pampered, aren't we, Nab?'

'Yeah; pampered pooches, trained to bite.'

'It's not right, is it?'

'Right? Nothing's right any more. And what can we do about it?' She grinned at me like Dex when the trooper sliced her neck. 'Bloody nothing, save wait and be ready.'

'Ready for what?'

'To take any chance that offers.'

Meal over we head for the climbing wall.

The more we work, the more we practice, the closer we get. We're a tribe now, all six of us kin—a family. We'd all been trapped in reclamation centres, had our wings clipped, but like wild things we crave freedom.

Used to Rat ways we hold Meets. We voted Striker clan leader, then all six agreed the rules, a code to live by. Loyalty to the clan—top of the list.

As time goes on I get to understand how Striker'd been banded so fast and how he stayed banded. His pack is *all* to him. He devotes time to pinpointing individual weaknesses and works with us to improve. He also expects us to monitor him. Week by week we grow stronger. Fight season is upon us and all six off us are hovering top of the board.

Fight-Day's over. We did well, collecting points as well as

the usual dints and bruises. It's inquest time, examining bouts and commenting on good and bad practice. For once it isn't Kai getting flak, it's me.

'How could you have missed that jab, Bit? Wasn't it obvious?'

'May have been obvious to you, Gard, but it was a three on three, remember? And I was busy at the time 'cos it seemed like they were all after *me*.'

'That's because in that particular bout, you were the one to beat.' And there's Jehu, come up the steps so quiet none of us had noticed.

'Spartax wants you.' We stare at him, but nobody moves till he says, '*Now,* you slugs.'

We walk to Spartax's holt in silence. My heart's racing. Is it going to be bad? What have we done? But schooled to show nothing I walk with my wooden faced clan to our owner, the woman with God's own power over us.

She's sitting at the big desk. Her back's towards us and she's watching the silent flickering monitors with a com-plug in her ear. We stand waiting till she takes it out and swivels round.

'So … the Clan is top of the board.' She pauses looking from one to the other, ending with Striker. 'Eily and I wondered if you'd be able to keep up the extra sessions without your primary training suffering. It seems you have.' She smiles, a brief half twitch. 'You'll debut as Ravens in three days; fighting at one of the newer venues, a small arena at Spearhead. I'll be watching, fight well,' and we're dismissed and she spins back to the monitors.

Jehu leads us to a room I've not seen before. It's half the size of Spartax's and far messier, with hi-tech equipment scattered about amid black and silver boxes and tall light-studded columns. No wall monitors, instead shelf upon shelf of weaponry, from simple daggers to the latest long-sight rifles.

Jehu drags a leather chair from under a desk piled high with hard copy and comp-wafers. 'Sit,' he orders. There's only the floor, so we settle down and listen.

'In three days you'll be fighting for your lives. Spearhead is a new and highly rated venue. Teams go there to be noticed. The fighting—hot and strong; the audience—wild. The betting? Off the wall.'

He stares at us, one by one, like he's trawling through our thoughts.

'Watch your backs, every damn minute. With so much at stake some trainers encourage *shortcuts*.

'End of last season there was trouble over unexpected losses, fights being won by rank outsiders, favourites knocked out too narding quick. So we had the big betters insisting they'd been ripped off, and rumours of match rigging. This year the stewards will be hotter and keener and on the watch for fixes.' He shrugged, 'Best luck to them! A win at Spearhead means a crack at the big arenas. Take Caesar, he sends a team to every Game and he drills his teamsters in dirty play. I know, Spartax's filled you in, but it can't harm to hear it again. And keep in mind that the Game comps might be straight but nothing else will. Things happen in the arena that'd rock the steadiest teamster. Expect the worst and you might survive; expect fair play and you're on the blood road.

'Remember all fouls are fair if the judges don't see 'em.'

We're on the road well before dawn, Jehu driving the carrier, us in the back working through old fight scans. Brown's at the ludus, curled in a drawer in the food hall. Eily got hold of a case of high-qual cat food so Brown's in for a treat. She'll gross out and sleep till I get back. Before we left the ludus I told Eily that Brown was hers if none of us made it back.

Spearhead arena is built inside a new-built city compound, first of the way-stations reaching out from New London and built on the rubble of some blitzed-down city. I spend the journey from the ludus on the lookout for signs that might indicate surviving Rat tribes. Nada. Troopers had clearly been on the offensive, making the ruins safe for the builders. Rat-bands would have been rooted out. I hope some of them managed to find sanctuary beyond Templeton's reach. Jehu drives like a madcap, so we reach our destination well in time.

And there it is—Spearhead, a massive balloon structure dominating the surrounding NOP dwells and looking for all the world like a monstrous grey pumpkin from a fairy tale.

'Imagine what'd happen to *that* in a real high wind. I bet it'd roll a new six lane highway through those cheap-built dwells.'

'I'd give a deal of creds to be here watching when it does,' Striker says with a grin.

Jehu follows the arrows leading to a vast vehicle pound and finds a parking spot. Exiting the carrier we walk to the security fence and onto a gated entrance guarded by heavily armed troopers.

'That's not for us,' Jehu says. 'That's for VIPs; hi-rollers and NOP hi-ups, the ones who bag the pricy seats.'

The next gate is much smaller; the teamers entrance, also guarded by mil. Hard eyed types with twitchy trigger fingers who run our passes through hand-holds and run bleeping scanners over our bodies before giving grudging permission to enter the pumpkin vastness.

'Tight security. They expecting trouble?' I ask Jehu.

'The military is always careful.'

Inside we're confronted by more stone-faced guards and an arrowed direction board.

'What you want to see first?' Jehu asks.

'The fight-ground,' says Striker, speaking for all of us.

'Fight-ground it is,' Jehu says and leads us along a dim-lit curving passageway.

'In large venues like Spearhead, there's a main fight-arena placed central, with two or three smaller circles placed round it. Today you fight in Main Arena, and the smaller circles will host dog and cock fights and some try-out matches. The try-outs are staged to allow fledgling teams the chance to catch the eyes of the top-class trainers here for the Main bouts.'

We walk for what seems like miles before we get to a wooden staircase that creaks and groans as we ascend to a platform ringing the arena and get our first sight the killing field way below.

I look down and down past tiers of bench seats, and hold my breath as I take in that circle of sand surrounded by a shoulder high barrier. I get the shivers thinking of that smoothness scuffed up and stained with blood and guts.

'See behind that barrier, down there?' Jehu says. 'Those first few rows are the hi-priced seats. Best in house—padded soft and roomy, made real luxe for the high rollers. The seats above? Cheap rough-wood benches. The worse the seating, the less you pay.'

I look at circle after circle of bench seating and the top layers are already filling up with a motley crowd of cits and troopers, though the games are nowhere near starting.

'Cheap seats cost pennies. The ones close to the fighting are reserved days before the event and cost a fortune. S'where the big money's made, that and betting.'

'What's the smell?" queries Kai.

'Meat rolls and sweet-stuff.' Nab answers. 'Sold from first light to shut-down. Poisonous cack, made from who knows what and cooked up who knows where. Don't go near it.'

Jehu points to the circle. 'Forget everything else; that's where you fight. And remember that barrier's there for crowd protection, not yours. You climb it and the marshals hit you with power-prods. The two entry tunnels are gated shut soon as the bout starts, so there's no escape there.'

'It looks so small from up here,' Gard ventures.

'Big as the world when you're standing on that circle of sand.' Jehu answers thoughtfully. Then in a stronger tone he says he'll show us the rest of the layout. As we climb down the wooden stairway jangly music starts up, competing with the rising noise of eager spectators. Back in the dim passageway and the growing noise raises my excitement level sky high. We walk past door after door until Jehu stops at one labelled MED-SUITE. Inside there's med-techs rolling bandages, filling trolleys or just sitting and waiting for the wounded to arrive. Jehu doesn't point out the operating tables, but I see them *and* the shelves holding splints and saws and the stretchers used to carry the injured from the arena. So do the others. Guess I know what we're all thinking, but I for one refuse to dwell on what might happen and tread on. But I'll admit that I'm glad when we get to the armoury.

Centre stage, beneath hood and chimney, stands a forge attended by a sweating, leather-aproned giant beating at a dented shield, as immune to the scorching heat as he is to us. As we walk through we pass shelves and racks of weapons ready for use, before going through a door which leads into a large area containing stalls and cages and smelling of hay, dung and sweat. There's also a pungent whiff of something that stings my nose.

'What's that smell?' I ask Jehu.

'Mostly horse piss, but on occasion wilder beasts are housed here. The General's studied ancient Rome.' I nod, knowing what he means. Dad used to talk about bread and circuses and how they excited the citizens into forgetting hard times. Jeez, a coupla thousand years later and nothing's changed.

Soon as we get to the teamers' rooms my nerves kick in. Jehu locates ours and bids us prepare while he confers with other trainers. I don the Raven's uniform black stretches, my hands shaking, my mouth sand-pit dry. Nab and I grease our hair, in silence, listening to the scratch of Gard's razor scraping his scalp, watching Striker check his hair spikes and Kai plait another strand of razor wire into a braid. Then, grab-points greased and palms chalked, Nab and I begin the twisting turns of a kala warm up. Gradually my shakes subside.

Even when Jehu comes back he's not sure when our turn will come so in between warm ups we run scenarios. This arena only runs one-day events. As tyros, being stuck in this room for too long could fray nerves, affecting chances.

It's a fair sized room, equipped with drinking water, showers and jakes. There's pull-down rest shelves, but no windows and just the one door—and an armed trooper stationed on the other side.

'Why the trooper?' I ask. Jehu shrugs.

Above the door is a com-link that'll inform us when to leave for the ring and how we're required to fight. Jehu gives us a final run through.

'Okay. First, be assured that the system arena is absolutely fair. No human has a hand in choosing the fight combinations or selecting the weapons. The comp does it all. It's guaranteed tamper-proof by Templeton and his techs. Every team starts level. No team knows how it will have to fight until the very last minute. First time anyone knows is when the com-unit spits it out. That clear enough or do you want again?'

It's clear.

Our call comes mid-morning. 'First call Spartax's Ravens: Six-up: Own choice weapons.' Relief floods into me as the trooper opens the door and escorts us to the armoury—it's happening. No more waiting, it's *on*. Back in the armoury we know exactly what to do and chose without a thought.

I tie a belt round my waist, fitting a stabbing knife into it and easing a throw-knife into an arm-sheath. A rub of rosin on palms and soles and I'm done. I don't need to look at the others, I know Striker's gone for an épée and Nab for a pair of throwing stars. Gard joins me with his blade-edged staves and Manas comes with a shortened leaf-bladed spear. Kai nudges me to look at the short-range catapult he holds. 'Quality gear,' he signs. Tooled up, we move to the tunnel and await the call.

We don't wait long. 'Last call, Spartax's Ravens. Six-up: Own choice weapons.' It's go time!

We stride into the arena in the cruciform pattern that gives flexibility plus max protection. Striker leads, Gard second. Nab and Kai spread out to make the arms of the cross, then comes Manas, and last of all, me. Strongest in the centre, fleetest at the sides and rear. As fastest runner I'm tail ender.

We're quick off the mark and claim centre ground and there's a braying fanfare from trumpeters on the barrier. The crowd responds with a deafening outbreak of whistles and cheering. It's directed at us, first team in. The blast rocks me, though I was told to expect it, and the wide-eyed, wide mouthed screamers turn my stomach.

We're here, we're actually here and about to fight. So how do I feel? Scared, elated and ready to go, like I'm pulling on a rubber band and waiting for the snap.

A second brassy fanfare heralds our opponents and the crowd roar is less hearty. The trumpets fade and the com-system kicks in, announcing the teams.

'Cit-i-zens, first team in the ring is … Spartax's Ravens, their opponents … Caesar's Praetorians.' The crowd yells a full-throated howl and all twelve teamers lift arms in acknowledgment.

Caesar's six, dressed in multi-coloured stretches, stand in a circle, spearing spotlights dancing over the moiré patterns of their costumes, reflecting on mirrored inserts meant to dazzle. Their circle opens to a crescent, the crowd hushes and tension builds as we size each other up.

Their team comprises three males, three fems. Two faces spring out at me—Track and Sterry, the jackals from the Work Hall.

Striker signals a change of formation, to counter the Praetorians' half circle. The fight signal sounds and Manas and I slot into the arm of the cross next to Nab and Kai. Without pause Striker and Gard launch a silent dash to the centre pair, two tall and well-muscled fems bearing nets and short swords. The rest of us move to our positions.

I take the extreme right, towards the blond, Track. He's bigger than me and he's woven stranded rough-wire into his suit. Good for protection, but so lacking in flexibility that the Clan ruled it out. Track's packed more muscle since the Work Halls. Have to act super-quick if I'm gonna take him. I hunch, to make myself seem smaller, presenting as a nervous opponent. He snarls, preparing to counter a hesitant attack by stepping forward and raising the spiked chain mace in a leather-gloved hand. The other hand's covered with a spiked gauntlet, more hedgehog than glove, a complement to the spiked throat protector.

He yells, swinging the mace faster and faster. Inside I feel that rubber band give way and *snap*, I'm free to squat, dive, and dig my knife into his thigh muscle before rolling out of his reach. He's on the sand, bleeding and writhing. I creep back. My knife has forced strands of the rough-wire deep into the muscle; the more he writhes the worse it gets. I heel him hard, putting him out of his misery. He's out of the fight, but still breathing. I turn, ready for the next target.

Emerging from my fight trance the arena roar hits me anew. The crowd's howling like a pack of rabid dogs, the Praetorians yell curses and instructions back and forth, but I remain silent like the rest of my clan.

Judging Track out of play I look for Kai, as planned, but he doesn't need help, standing over an unconscious opponent, calmly reloading his sling and watching Gard finish his fight with a slashing cross-blow from his razored stave.

Nab's alert and ready to come to me, the next in line. I sign *no need* and she grins, filed teeth devilish as she holds her throwing stars at the ready. Blood-daubed Manas limps to me, leaving a rag-doll Sterry prostrate on the sand.

Last of all I see Striker, crouching over an obvious corpse, cleaning his sword with a handful of sand. He nods and we reform, watching the meds stretcher out the injured and drag away the dead. We stand thankful for survival, snowed by flower heads, jewellery and credit tokens thrown by an ecstatic, sexed-up crowd.

The din drowns the victory announcement, but the result board flashes informing us that we've downed the Praetorians in record time.

All's in my mind is Striker, Brown and bed.

22

That bout not only made our name, but fattened Spartax's money chest. A run of one-day contests followed and we cleared the board. Cits followed us from arena to arena and other trainers attempted to sleuth Spartax's training methods. We weren't the only winners in her stable, other Raven teams were doing good business because Spartax had capitalised on our training methods. Plainly a six-some, working together long term, achieved better results than six individuals, however talented, fighting a one-off. She and Jehu had taken to forming teams and training them as a unit. The wins racked up.

We're still cits' choice, despite the bookmakers raising our odds to an all time high, and Spartax is the trainer of the moment.

'Know something?'

'What?' I mumble, more than half asleep after a hard day's workout.

'M'Tan and Lialle asked me to set up a signing class. They want to communicate like the Clan.'

Fully awake, I sit up. 'You agreed?'

'Not without checking with the Clan.'

'You think it's a betrayal?'

'More like the beginnings of a bigger tribe.'

'So, call a Meet.'

The answer is a definite yes, and signing spreads through the ludus like fungus on damp wood. Even Jehu and Eily join in for fear of missing out. The ludus is changing, there's less enmity … we live as friends. We're becoming a tribe.

Fight season's almost over and I'm relieved. The Clan's fought hard, took its share of injuries and kept fighting. Maybe we're riding our luck too hard. Spartax feels the same. She called us in last night.

'You're not fighting next Games Day,' she said. 'It's the last of the season and I'm putting in Nena's six. They need blooding and no proprietor's going to put their best teams in for a last-time date. Go as observers this time. Do you good to be on the other side for a change. Mix with the crowd, lay a few bets, but stay away from food hawkers.'

Last Games Day will be held at the first arena to be built in Wales—at Cardiff Castle. The Castle Arena is meant to be a demonstration of Templeton's strength and power.

Thing is, Templeton's claiming the whole principality and its mineral wealth belongs to him But as the Romans and Normans discovered, Wales isn't easily settled by newcomers looking to pirate its wealth. Seems the Valleys have proved a prime location for guerilla fighters, and Templeton's feeling a tad miffed by the knock-back.

Eily's driving the Clan. Nena's six are travelling separate. When we arrive we stay seated till she registers. She comes back worried. 'Something's up. Caesar was registering and that's unusual. He only travels with his number one team and as far as I know there are no first-teams fighting here.'

'Scouting the young teams?' I suggest.

'Not him. He sends others to do that job. He only watches the A-Teams. So…'

'So you're not willing to risk Nena's team being slaughtered by the Praetorian A's. Am I right?' Striker asserts.

Eily nods. The Clan will fight today. Nena's six are heading homeward as we speak.

The com-link spits out an announcement; Ravens v Praetorians. Why am I not surprised? It's a 3-2-1, no weapons. Three against three, two against two and a solo bout. Each bout separate, no cross fighting.

'So, Eily, even if a bout finishes fast, we can't help a team mate in trouble?'

'Right, Bit. Odd choice for an end of season bout. Keep alert, I smell trouble.'

Walking the tunnel to the fight ring my mind's on the rematch. Last time we faced the Praetorians we walked all over them, ground their faces in the dirt. This time they'll be after payback. I rub my hands with rosin, thinking Eily was right to worry.

We enter the arena to a muted fanfare—and the Praetorians waiting centre stage. A glance at the wager board tells me the Ravens are favourite. There must be massive amounts laid on us. Another glance at the flickering board shows something new. Our 3-2-1 fight has been rated an accumulator. The crowd erupts in a paean so loud my ears go numb. What will they do if we disappoint such expectation? And what's more to the point, how will the bookies pay out if we win? Not that it's likely, with an accumulator we have to win all three bouts, before the punters collect.

I look at Striker, who shrugs.

Striker, Gard and Nab are fighting the three-up; Manas and Kai the pair. I'm the solo. We'll fight barehanded, officially weaponless, but hell, anything's possible.

I look at the six Praetorians, realising something's very wrong. For one thing I'm not scared—I'm not anything. I feel sleepy, dull, got no spark. Even the sight of the wolf-grinning Praetorians doesn't stir me. I look at Gard and his face is as dull as I feel. I slide to Striker, pull at his sleeve and sign 'Trouble', then 'Feeling bad. You?'

He blinks, shakes his head and whistles the double note that warns of treachery. I bite down on the double strength stim-tab fixed to my back tooth same time as the fight signal blasts. Striker's just-in-case idea. It kicks in as I walk to the solo-fight circle. I get there wide awake and ready, but keep this hidden from my Praetorian opponent. Guess what? It's Sterry, recovered from the drubbing Manas gave him.

I don my 'Dor' face and walk towards the grinning jackal and he comes at me with total confidence, expecting a walkover. He launches a kick, body open, arms theatrically wide demonstrating total assurance. I wait till the last moment to fall backwards putting him off balance. I land on braced arms and bounce back with a body slam. He makes a perfect pratfall and the crowd yells mightily as he hits the sand. My legs squeeze his neck in a scissor lock. Yeah, that stops his gallop. A tightening twist dims his lights, permanent. I don't dole mercy in a fouled match.

Upright and standing over his carcass I watch the other fights take their course. I can't help, can't even aid a pack-mate in distress.

In the three-up Gard's felled by a punch he'd normally shrug off. That fem has something in her fist. Striker bounces her, forcing her to drop whatever it is. He snatches it up and flings it at an invigilator. It hits his sleeve, hard enough to draw attention. He's got to have felt it. What's he gonna do? I watch as he brushes his white wand of office down the sleeve, dislodging whatever it is. No outcry? No holding up the wand and calling foul? Guy's dirty. How much is he getting paid to turn a blind eye? I study his maggot face, vowing to teach him the true cost of treachery.

In the two-on-two Kai's down and there's blood on his back. He's lying arm-locked about his opponent's neck. Manas ends his battle with a sudden twisting back breaker and sprints to Kai. He slams a heel into the temple of the guy Kai's gripping then stands over Kai till the meds appear. He's watching them close and don't they know it. They daren't try anything hinky.

Striker and Nab take the last three Praetorians down in a welter of kicks and gouges. Straightway they go to the fallen Gard. They get to him and though I can't see their faces, I can tell something's up, something dire. Nab feels for a pulse and shakes her head. They stand, fists tight clenched. Hell flames, it's too late.

Forced to take the salutes of the crowd, we stand arms raised, hearts bleeding, till they let us go.

Spartax is in the med-suite with Eily and Jehu, standing by Gard's lifeless body. Eily must have messaged them. They had to have come by flitter, only way to get here so quick.

I'm cold and way past anger; encased in icy hatred. Betrayal! Gard is dead because someone put the fix in. Why hadn't Spartax's informants sniffed it out? How come her ex-ring mates hadn't warned her? Hell, the Game Comp had to have been rigged, and wasn't that s'posed to be impossible? But there's another dog gnawing at my bones. The Clan hadn't been expected to fight today. Caesar expected *six* easy deaths.

Whose was the real fault? Ours for dropping our guard? Spartax's for not knowing? I'm ready to mouth off, but Jehu gets in first. 'In the rosin, Bit. An inhibitor, it slowed you down.'

I shut my mouth and smooth Gard's face. Then I look to Kai; unconscious with meds working on him, frantic.

'Let me see his back.' I say, remembering the blood.

'Can't do that. Can't move him, teamster.'

'I saw blood, a hole. Want to find the cause. Want it noted.'

The med stepped back at my tone, scribbling on Kai's chart. Spartax adds her name, with a glare at the med.

Another med checks the rest of us over. Nothing serious found. I take a breath and turn to Spartax.

'You still here? Not off racking up the creds? One dead, one on the brink and you with gelt up to your earlobes. Good call, *Boss.*'

The room quietens and in the distance the sound of

celebrating citizens comes clear. Spartax takes a step, as does Jehu, though Eily holds him back.

'Just who are you fighting, here, Bitch Singer of the Whip Tails? Me, the system, or your own sweet self? Shit happens, Rat. You know that. Why don't you work with me to clear it up?'

I'm looking into a pair of eyes cold as death and decide she's talking sense.

'Were do we start?' I say and Nab's held breath huffs out.

'First I hire extra guards at the ludus, second I source the rot, and third we get even.'

'Guess I can go with that,' I say and a mix of yesses and OKs signal the Clan's on board.

As we're preparing Kai for the journey back, I tell Spartax what I'd seen in the ring and she answers sotto voce. 'Had to be a long-range shot. That's why he's coming back with us, bad as he is.' I slide against the wall as they shroud Gard, and then slip out on a small errand.

I go straight to the wager board and smile at a skinny hang-about, and ask where the white-wanders hang out. He's only too pleased to talk to a fighter, shoots his mouth, and I'm off.

I got the maggot faced invigilator imprinted on my mind and I spot him right away. He's sitting easy on a bench outside the white-wanders' quarters, nursing a glass of something red. There's a smile on his face and his eyes are closed. Sizing up his pay-off pile, no doubt.

I cough, he looks up, recognition coming pleasing fast. Eyes wide he draws breath to scream, but loses it when I hit him on the bridge of his nose, hard so the bone presses in. I walk away leaving blood and wine to merge and pool on his pathetic corpse. A rat sent to join a Rat.

I walk to the carrier with Gard in my mind. The 'vigilator's dead, I made damn sure of that. Justice or vengeance? Either way it makes no difference; Gard's still dead and my heart's still broke. I've lost a brother.

Back in Spartax Hold we burn Gard with honour and I feel

like it's part of me burning. And Manas? He looks as if he's well on the blood road. It's up to the rest of us to convince him to step off.

Season's over and Spartax has sent out feelers, calling in favours and posting bribes, but nothing's turned up on the fix. As well as unofficial enquiries she's protested to the NOP Central Command over extreme rule breaches and possible match fixing. Jehu told us that she'd been assured that a thorough investigation had discovered no wrongdoing and proved conclusively that the Games Comp was tamper proof.

Two months later we're no further forward, no more information—stonewalled.

All that's been pushed into the background. Brown's missing, gone two days. Sure she skips off now and then, like back in the CRC, but never for so long. I've searched all the places I could think of, even asked Eily to authorize an outside search, but no one's seen her. I've asked everybody to check again.

'Have you asked Manas?' says Nab.

'Have you tried talking to him lately? Snaps your head off if you smile good morning.'

But I go look for Manas, he's in the training hall staring into nothing with a foil in his hand.

'Hey, Manas, you heard?'

'Heard what?'

'Can't find Brown.'

'So?' he says, and I can't stop myself, the words come pouring out and I'm shouting at him to get off his fat arse and find my ferret. He looks at me, really looks, for the first time in weeks, puts the foil back on the rack and walks out.

'I'm sorry, Manas,' I shout, but he's gone and I start cursing again.

'Wake up, Bit.'

Manas's voice drags me from a nasty dream, and he's smiling. 'I found her, come see.'

She's nesting at the back of one of Eily's crock cupboards, next to the cook stove in the food hall. And she's not alone, cuddled close are two sleeping kits. Brown creels, licks my hand and I hug Manas, hard, hard, hard.

'Go back to sleep, Bit. I'll watch over her till morning.'

I'd sooner stay, but one look at Manas tells me he's the one who needs it most. 'Right,' I say. 'You found her, you stay watching. She might want water.'

'I'll get it, and some meat scraps, case she's hungry. And don't worry I won't let anyone disturb them. They're safe with me.'

I wave good night and go back to bed smiling. Looks like Manas is backing off the blood road.

23

Manas is the self-appointed protector of ferrets, stationed near the cupboard he makes sure mother and kits are left in peace. He's been feeding Brown and keeping the bedding clean and taken to sleeping on a blanket laid next to the cupboard. I'm not jealous, not really, I'm glad he's alive again. But three weeks of having Manas as a permanent feature, Eily's ready to pop. Lucky for Manas the kits are venturing out. Eily's ordered the whole ferret family someplace, anyplace, else. I ready a box in the dorm and after a thorough inspection Brown settles in. Manas swapped beds with Nab to be next to them. He and Brown are tight, she lets him handle the kits whenever he wants.

The kits are five weeks old and swiping meat from Brown. Manas tells me she's far less protective. I could have told him that, because she's spending more time with me and leaving the kits with their nursemaid. Have to start vetting prospective guardians.

It's a long list. Soon as they know the kits are on offer I'm inundated. But they're only going to folk Brown and I vet. Course I know one's destined for Manas. I mean, Brown trusts him, so he's going to get her vote, yeah? Which one, though? Think I'll leave it to the kits.

No contest, the blonde female chooses him, pushing past her brother in her eagerness to get to him whenever he visits. He names her Silk.

Who's getting the male? I've asked the hopeful to drop in for a play session, while me and Brown watch tricks.

List's down to five. The little male liked them all, so no firm decision. Kai's fit again, and he's high on the list. He'd give his soul for ownership, but as I said to him, it's the kit's choice.

I'm playing with the three of them and Brown's getting nippy with the twins, so it's definitely near chuck-out time. We're disturbed by a shout from downstairs.

'Bit?' It's Jehu. Jeez, should I be meeting him somewhere else? Has he a job for me?

'Up on the platform, Jehu.'

It's not a job, he just wants to see the ferrets. Only he doesn't *say* that, he *says* he wants to ask my opinion on Manas, but his eyes are full of ferrets.

'Manas is fine. Can't wait to get Silk.'

'When's he getting her?'

'Soon as I find a mate for this one.' I lift up the wriggling male and Jehu smiles a rare smile.

He sits cross legged and stares from the male to the female.

'Why is he bigger than the other one?'

'Nab found me a book on ferrets. Generally males are bigger.'

Silk approaches him and he touches her fur with a gnarled finger. 'Beautiful fur. Like honeyed milk. And her eyes; polished amber. Can see why Manas is besotted. Think the little guy will come to me?'

'Try him.'

I hand the kit to Jehu and watch him relax on the ex-fighters cupped palms. I'm watching close and see a shocking thing— Jehu's stone face softening. I look away before he catches me. After a while he gently places the kit back with his sister.

'Why is he so much darker than Silk? She's all blonde while he's coal black.'

''Spect he's like the hob.'

'Hob?'

'Male's are hobs. Females, jills.'

'But Brown's the only ferret in the ludus.'

'I'm certain she's a runaway from an NOP compound. Where there's one there's bound to be more.'

Jehu isn't listening, he's play fighting with the dark-furred kit.

'I'd call him sable, rather than coal-coloured, wouldn't you? Fur's more silky and glossy. Hey look at them scrap. Will they hurt each other?'

'Haven't up to now.''

We sit back and watch as male jumps on his sister's short tail and they roll and twist in a scrappy ball.

'She may be smaller,' he says, 'but she's as fiery as her brother.'

Close up you can the difference. Silk has a narrow pointed head and golden eyes. The male's head is broader, flatter, his eyes obsidian. But what really sets him apart is the black bandit mask marked on his white face.

'What do they eat? How d'you get their coats so glossy? Is there anything they shouldn't eat?' Jehu pours questions at me. Never, ever heard him ripple on like this. I switch from watching ferrets to watching him.

Entranced by their antics, his face relaxes, a younger Jehu emerging. Next thing the male has abandoned dam and sibling, and pushed by Brown he's crawling up Jehu's arm, nose uplifted and sniffing. Now he's on Jehu's shoulder, now his lap and nosing pockets. He spots an opening in Jehu's shirt, crawls inside, curls against his chest and shuts his eyes.

'You want him?' I ask. From Brown's relaxed posture, she's fine with it.

'Hell, yes,' he says.

'Settled. What you going to call him?'

'That's easy. He's the Robber.'

Back in training I watch to see how Manas is performing and he's doing better than I thought. He's quieter, but as devious and vicious as ever. Kai's starting slowly, building up his muscle strength carefully before graduating to full blown, no holds barred sessions.

Since the Clan's success Spartax has instigated extra practice sessions, strategy reviews and having fixed training groups of six.

Our group is one member short, and though we've tried a whole host of volunteers, none fits right. Then Nab lays a name before me. 'Seen that new girl, Fee?'

'Which one? Spartax took on six didn't she?'

'Mid height, olive skinned. Hair like hedgehog quills.'

'Oh, that one. Ex-cit isn't she?'

'Thief, I heard. Watched her fight with Quilla. Good fight.'

'Quilla lost?'

Nab shakes her blonde head, 'No, she won, but Fee blacked her eye and split her nose. Best fight I've seen in weeks.'

'I'll mention her to Striker.'

Doesn't go down well with Striker. 'Fee? Nab wants us to consider *her*? She's a thief *and* a cit.'

Kai, ex-thief, fires up. 'And all you Rats are holy-pure, yeah? 'Spose a Rat'd never dream of taking something that didn't belong to him. Didn't someone tell me that Rats steal to live?' He's red in the face and breathing like a bellows. 'Have you any idea what it's like living in the compounds with no coin to buy food and all the handouts and all the jobs going to NOP cardholders? Listen to one who knows; not every cit is NOP.' And then he's gone, leaving me and Striker looking after him. Takes an hour to find Kai, apologize and call a Meet. At the Meet we decide to take an in-depth look at Fee before reporting back.

I spiel my findings first, 'I've watched her training and in practice bouts and I'll say this for her, she hates losing. I've seen three bouts where she won't admit it's over, and one time—you saw it Nab—she'd have kept going despite a dislocated elbow.'

Nab nodded agreement, 'She's tough and tenacious.'

'She's a fast learner,' Kai added. 'But I don't know if she'd fit with us, don't know as she'd want to.'

'I'd go along with that.' Striker says. 'Fem's got *attitude*. She fights well, but have you talked to anyone who likes her? She's surly, even growls at Jehu and that says stupid to me.'

'She don't like being bought,' defends Kai.

'Think I do, Kai?' I ask him. 'She goes on like this Spartax will get rid.'

'Told her that.'

'Didn't say it loud enough, did you? Look, you and Nab were cits so you've got something in common. Why not try getting to know her, and letting her know us?

'She'd turn her back.'

'Might not if you dangled some bait. Saw her watching Brown the other day, squinting through the door crack when I fed her.'

Fee agrees to visit.

We're all there when she comes, and Brown's running amok with Silk and Robber. I haul Brown off the kits and offer her to Fee. 'Want a hold?' Only her expressive eyes say yes. I rise slowly, stroll to Fee, let Brown sniff her and wait. Fee extends a hand and smoothes Brown's outstretched head, and the ferret jumps to the girl's shoulder. I wince, thinking she'll scream or hit out or even jump the platform, but she stands unmoving, letting Brown do as she wants. Then Fee reaches slowly into a pocket and offers Brown a titbit. Sighs of relief all round.

'What you think? I was going to kill it?'

'Her, not it. She's female and those are her kits. The dark one's Robber, he lives with Jehu and the light one's Silk.'

'Silk lives with me, says Manas. 'Hold her if you want, but gently. She's young and flighty.'

I retrieve Brown and Fee takes Silk from Manas and he starts telling her what she feeds on, where she sleeps. Fee sits next to him and drinks it in.

I study her. She's slim, mid-height, olive skinned, with jet-black stiff-straight hair, well slicked with grease. She catches me looking and stares right back. Her eyes are striking, large, dark and almond shaped. She'd be stunning if it wasn't for the scowl creasing her forehead and her permanent see-if-I-care expression.

'I came to see the creature, is all. I don't aim to stay slaved, don't want to make friends and I'm not interested in joining any damn team. Hell, it's bitten me.'

'You're shouting,' Manas says. 'You've upset her. Come back babe, come away from the nasty girl.'

'Look, what's-your-name, I ain't nasty.'

'Then quit acting like it. We're not the owners, we're in the stewpot same as you and getting along best we can.'

'Right, and there's the difference. I don't aim to *get along*. I aim on getting out.'

'No,' I say. 'You ain't. You're dead, girl, and you haven't the sense to realise it. Kai, tell her.'

'Word is, you're shipping out.'

'Great.'

'Not great. Spartax won't trust you to another trainer, not with your attitude. And you sure as hell wouldn't fit a trooper brothel. You're going to the labs.'

'Where?'

'The labs, where med-techs play with rejects like us. They'll stick things in you and cut bits off you. Freezing some folk, scalding others and infecting a whole lot more with the Sickness. Heard tell they're not too eager for a cure, just like making troublemakers suffer. And once they got you girl you stay got.'

'I don't believe you.'

But I see from her eyes that she does.

'This clan's on your side,' I say.

'What's a clan?' she asks. Interested?

'Never heard of Rat clans?'

'Crazy cannibals that live in the ruins?'

'Sit down and I'll tell you what Rats are. I finish and you want to go, you go, but if you choose to stay,' I pause and look at Striker then the rest, 'then you're welcome.'

She gets a quick run through of Rat history and how our particular clan came to be. Story over, she's quiet and thoughtful.

Striker breaks the silence. 'Got a proposition. You want to listen?'

She nods.

'How about this. Work with us for a time.'

'How long a time?'

'Till you find you *can* work with us … or you find an escape hatch.'

She looks up at him, he's smiling his best smile and she ghosts one back. 'Could give it a try, I s'pose. You seem straight enough.'

A week on and the Clan's up to six again and Fee's stopped searching for a way out.

24

How is it that when you think the way ahead's an easy stride, an earthquake tips you arse-up on the road? Yeah, and how come I was stupid enough to believe we were safe? Truth is I let my guard down, and pushed all the nasty 'what-ifs' right out of my mind. Stupid. Stupid. Stupid. Settled and safe with a new clan growing round me, I lost perspective, lost my fear of the future. I dropped the frinking ball!

Thing is, it started small. An accident, nothing more; an unlucky, unexpected happening. Leastways that's what we all thought.

Middle of the night a screaming fence-alarm tells of trouble; a whole section of the perimeter wall's flattened by a giant machine. Didn't know what it was till Kai enlightened me. 'It's a pulverizer. Troopers use them to mash rubble flat for the foundations of a new NOP compound.'

'What's it doing here?'

'Stolen for a drunken dare? A joy-ride? Who knows?'

There's no sign of the driver, and a thorough search of the ludus reveals nothing out of the ordinary, so it's put down as a freaky mishap. Takes the rest of the night and all next day to restore the wall. Spartax orders the night patrols beefed up as a precaution.

A day later the power fails. Jehu finds the remains of a slow release charge under the generator. Time the back-ups kick in we've lost some comp function. Takes Eily hours to re-boot.

A spitting mad Spartax wants answers.

'My best guess?' says Eily, sounding just as angry. 'Whoever jinxed the generator set the charge same night the fence came down. And I was too damn stupid to think past fluke!'

Spartax lays a heavy hand on her shoulder. 'My fault as much as yours. From now on we're on war footing. I'm ordering a thorough search of the ludus, inside and out. Every inch, Eily. Every misbegotten inch.'

Nothing untoward turns up, and things return to almost normal.

The second incident's the real wake-up call. First Game of the new season Eily takes Kevan's six to fight. Only two teamers survive, Mai and Kevan.

Eily swears illegal weapons were used. 'I'd stake my life that both N'go and Ger were blinded with a distance weapon as they advanced. I missed Ean and Link being downed but the crowd didn't like it, the whistling and stamping went on long after the ring was cleared. Held up the next tourney, and that never happens.'

'You protest?' asks Striker.

'I did, to deaf ears. No proof, no protest posted.'

Kevan and Mai are so badly beat up they can't give witness.

'Got a bad feeling, Bit,' says Striker.

'You and me both,' I say, remembering Talon's treachery.

The final straw comes when the Clan dons Raven black and fights at Brinkton Arena.

Despite scouring the comp, Eily's super careful. No carrier uses the same route twice. Today Jehu's driving, and he checks the carrier thoroughly before we leave. All's sweet—till the carrier veers and stalls a bare mile from the venue. We pile out, Jehu checks the track while rest of us stretch our legs. Soon as Jehu starts cursing, we go see what's up. The right-hand track's broken, lying twisted on the ground.

'Shouldn't have happened,' Jehu says. 'I checked the couplings before we left. They were good as new. ' He squats for a better look, then yells 'Down! This coupling's been lasered.' We're down before he says the second word.

I wait, cheek down on gritty soil waiting to be fried. Nothing happens. Few secs later Jehu says, 'Get up, sniper's gone.'

'How d'you know?' Manas whispers.

'Because we'd be dead had he stayed around. Sniper was top-rank, the track's was sliced neat as a neat sewn stitch. Bit, check the com-link, fast.'

Warned by his tone, the dead com-link comes as no surprise.

The jury-rigged track gets us to the check-in with minutes to spare. Jehu registers our arrival as we race to change. We hustle to the Gaming Board, only to find our team name's flashing red—we been disqualified.

'Back to the carrier, now. Come as you are, leave the rest.' Jehu orders. 'And watch your backs.'

First half of the journey he's silent, coaxing max speed from the damaged carrier.

Ludus in sight he vents his rage. 'Broken fence, a blown-up genny, the comp hack. A well-planned op meant to get us in range of that sniper. And that was the *easy* part. The hard part was fixing the Games Comp.'

'Fixed?' says Striker. 'Thought the games comp was sacrosanct.'

'Look, I registered inside the limit, yet the board said different.'

'Impossible.'

'Clever, that's what it frinking is. Clever, and ruinously expensive. Do you know the penalties for attempting to fix a Games-Comp?'

'Who the hell would risk it?' I say.

No one spits the name that jumps readily to mind. I know full well that a three-time hit rules out happenstance—Spartax is in trouble, real big trouble.

It's no surprise that Jehu and Eily go straight to the chief, and not long after a ludus-wide announcement is made. Everyone's to meet in the training hall at twenty-one hundred. No exceptions.

25

When the buzzer announces the evening meal, the Clan gets together on the sleeping platform. None of us are hungry.

We push the pallets together without speaking, and sit thoughtful till Striker breaks the silence.

'You know Templeton's behind it,' he says.

'But why's he doing it?' Nab queries.

'Word is Spartax is getting too popular. Her and her top of the table teams.'

'Yeah, and she's too popular to attack face on,' Kai says.

'That's underhand,' I say.

'That's politics, Bit.'

'So what's his next move?' Manas asks.

'Next?' Striker says. 'I doubt if we'll get armed troopers at the gates, if that's what you think. And I'm betting we won't be refused entry to the Arena. Stunts like that don't go down well with the punters. Reckon he'll start nibbling, undermining Spartax's support with the masses. Once he convinces *them* she's dirty, they'll drop her in a dead second. Templeton's a shark, single minded when he's after blood. And think on this, the Welsh are causing him trouble, playing dirty, using guerilla tactics—giving his troopers hell. A bust-up with Spartax would prove a great distraction.'

'She'll lose, won't she?' Kai whispers.

'He'll squash her like a maggot.'

'And us?'

Striker grunts, his face set hard, 'Fee? Your thoughts?'

She's surprised to be asked her opinion, but gives it straight. 'If Spartax is heading for the mangle, we'll be in it with her. I reckon she's worse off than she thinks, but she's not stupid she'll know who's after her. Jehu sure as hell will.'

Nab nods agreement, 'Yeah, they'll take her down and scatter the ludus. But they won't want her dead, she's too good a trainer. No, they'll give her a weaker team to train, or a locum role. She'll still be part of the Games but she won't be with one team long enough to get too popular. Cits'll be told she's 'sharing her expertise' or 'raising standards as a whole'. She'll be out of the spotlight but still working, that'll suit Templeton.'

'Be honest, what d'you think will happen to us teamers?' I ask.

'What do you think? We'll be sold off to other owners or sent to the labs. Those grey bastards are eager for bodies.'

'Been done before,' adds Manas.

'Ideas?' says Striker, looking from one to another.

'We're on a hiding to nothing,' I say. 'Remember what I told you about Throat Tearer?' He nods, so I tell the others. 'This Throat Tearer was a Rat, elected to leadership by touting the idea of decamping from the ruins, the compounds *and* the frinking NOP. Said Rats should start afresh in the Wilderness. I liked the idea… still do. Why can't we skip to the outlands, like Throat Tearer and his Questers?'

I know Striker's with me and by their faces I've tempted the others. Everyone's talking, sharing what they know or heard about the Wilderness. Nab says she heard there were places a great distance away blasted by the Sickness and not yet touched by the NOP. Kai says he's heard that too, but Fee scoffs. Kids tales, she says, 'Oh, there's a land far, far away where everyone can be happy. A tale my gran spun me when my empty belly griped. Yeah, one day we'll go there, my duck, she'd say. It's never gonna happen, Nab. I didn't believe her then, and I don't believe you now.'

But she wants to believe, I can tell. So I tell her how I longed to go with Throat Tearer and what I'd been told about the world beyond Templeton's reach. And as she listens she starts to smile.

Manas takes to the idea, no question. 'Silk would love the freedom ... so would I.'

'How 'bout we put it to the vote?' I say. 'Go or stay, majority decides.'

All hands shoot up—the Clan votes *go*.

'Right,' says Striker. 'The first thing to do is collect information, because we have to make a detailed plan. We need the location of any minefields, tox-drops and trooper outposts. A venture like this requires ample supplies and useful weapons—not hi-tech rechargeables. Stick to *basic* weapons. And, guys we start collecting straight after Spartax's meeting.'

It goes quiet so I say add my thoughts to the mix. 'I'm with Striker on this. We need to move double quick. If Templeton wants rid of Spartax he'll do the same. I say we go west, to the wilderness of Mid Wales—the Brecon Beacons and the Cambrian mountains.'

'Good plan, Bit,' Striker says, smiling wide. 'What say the rest of you? Wanna explore darkest Wales?'

'Good a place as any,' Kai says.

'And a damn sight better than most,' Nab adds. 'Bet Templeton's regretting his boast of an easy victory. Thought a coupla regiments would do the trick, did he? First Wales then the rest of Britain? Then where, France? The World?'

I get a thought and say, 'Remember Napoleon and Russia, Hitler and Stalingrad? Could be our great leader's eyes are too big for his belly. Could be the cits won't take well to failure.'

Silence falls and I know I can't be the only one daring to dream of Templeton's downfall.

'OK folks, show's over,' says Striker. 'If we want to be up front of the big Meet, we need go now.'

We're among the first to enter the training hall, and join Jehu standing by a pile of landing-mats. Well before time the room's filled. We got medics, drivers and off-time perimeter guards—the whole shebang. Even the the injured and the weak are there, propped in chairs or held by friends.

Spartax strides in with Eily and climbs onto the mat pile. With Eily on one side and Jehu on the other she waits till the hall quiets before nodding at Eily to begin.

'I've been fumigating the comps, found something; a worm giving access to all our programs and allowing them to be subverted. Our security's breached—we're open to a world of hurt.'

Now Spartax takes over, telling of her meet with the other team owners.

'They treated me as a leper, scared even to stand by me. Knew by the smell I'd been targeted. Just one of them showed grit, a guy I fought in the arena, I let him live when the crowd screamed for his blood. He reckoned he owed me. Told me the fix comes from way high.

'I'm too successful, the Ravens too popular. *Someone* has decreed that we're getting bigger than the Games themselves and we have to be knocked back.' She paused for a slow look round, then continued. 'I got an actual letter-drop today: un-signed, untraceable and drone-delivered. Letter told me that the *Party* has been convinced I'll use my popularity to go into politics, and the *Party* doesn't want any apple carts upset.'

We were right, Templeton *is* after Spartax—no room in his sky for more than one sun! Hell, I can almost *hear* the thoughts bubbling and fizzing as that message gets home to the ludus.

'I swear to you that I do not entertain such thoughts. I make it a point to steer well clear of politics. I'm a Games player. I follow the rules and win matches, that's all.'

She's red in the face, first time I've seen that. After a breath she goes on, 'I do not intend to be hounded from the Games, no matter who spurs the hounds. But we, and I mean every single one us, are entering shark-filled waters. Keep your eyes open. Dismiss.'

And that's it, she strides from the hall with no intention of being waylaid, leaving a shockwave of fear in her wake.

26

The training hall empties, but the Clan stay behind and Jehu motions us to join him and Eily. Striker speaks first. 'Think Spartax has a chance of beating this, Jehu?'

'Not a snowflake's chance in hell.'

'So … what's gonna happen?'

'She'll stand out for as long as she can, but she'll fold, she'll have to. No one beats the General.' He sighs. 'I expect she'll train again, but on a far smaller scale. She won't be made boss, though. I'm certainly not looking forward to starting over, but I might not have the opportunity. Too old; lab fodder with the rest of the chuck-outs.'

Striker turns to Eily.

'How about you?'

'I'll go along with Spartax, we go way back.'

I speak to Jehu. 'I got something to say, will you hear me out?'

'Sure, Bit.'

I dive straight in, giving the Clan's thoughts on the future, and my idea of moving west into deepest Wales, beyond Templeton's reach. I keep driving on, though he doesn't attempt to stem my flow. When I'm done and sucking in new breath, he stays mute, so I say 'What d'you think?'

He doesn't answer, his mind elsewhere. He takes Robber from his pocket, runs aimless fingers through the ferret's fur and earns a nip for taking liberties. The nip releases him from the trance. 'Well, Bit, I'll tell you. My mind's already loaded and now you've gone and added to that load.'

'Jehu, gotta tell you that Striker means to set our idea before the rest of the teamers. It's only fair they know there's another way out, instead of just waiting sheep-like to be sheared by the troopers. We're meeting in the eatery if you want to come.'

'Sure, Bit. Me and Robber'll come along.'

I look at Eily, she nods, but her expression's dour.

Time the word's delivered and the eatery full, it's an hour past midnight, and we're into tomorrow. Striker stands on a table, waiting. Silence gained he speaks.

'You all know there's trouble coming and you know where it's coming from.' He pauses till the muttering settles. 'The Clan have done some serious thinking and now's the time to spread those thoughts. The Clan is Rat, true tribesmen and initiates both. All of us follow Rat lore, and Rats never give in. Like teamers, like Ravens, we fight. But fighting the enemy facing us is suicide. The Clan chooses to fight for freedom, fight for a new life. Here's what *we* intend to do. Taste it, see if it's palatable.' And then he lays it on the line, word by startling word.

Time he's finished I'm prouder than proud. I'd follow him to Hades, even if he wasn't my man. He leaves the words to steep, before asking for questions. They come thick and fast and we do our best to answer.

Then Jehu stands like he wants to say his piece. On the nod he speaks, holding tight to Eily's hand.

'I spent some time before this gather, netting with some old comrades. I've been told that Spartax's time is up; the NOP is ready to pull the plug. Word's out she was paid to fix a bout, but her teamers rebelled and fought for the crowd instead. It's accepted they won the match against her direct orders.'

At this the hall erupts, but he flags quiet and speaks on. 'Yeah, it's crap, but believable crap and I don't doubt the compound will be rushed, and soon. It'll be staged. All the news-copters will see is a crowd of angry cits: troopers in cit clothing, ordered to cause max damage.'

Striker speaks, 'When?'

'Unknown. But it'll have to be soon if they want it to look genuine.'

Striker nods, 'So, time's short. We need to be clear on what we're going to do. Suggestions?

I raise a hand and Striker calls on me to stand.

'I say we get out quick. Find a safe route to the West, and just go.'

Lik and Beron request a voice, Lik gets the go, 'I say we take the carrier and pack as much baggage and rations as we can.'

Beron's next and he wants to stay and fight. More teamers want to speak and the babble grows. A double shout, 'Quiet,' from both Striker and Jehu, quells the noise.

Striker calls, 'One at a time folks, or no one gets heard. Quilla?'

'What about Mai and Kevan? They're nowhere near ready to travel. Do we leave them behind?'

Kai lifts a hand and Striker nods him speak.

'I've spoken to Mai and Kevan,' he says evenly. 'They're with us. I gave my word we'd see them safe.'

Striker speaks next, 'If we go, we go as Rats, and Rats don't leave clan-mates behind. And I'll make one thing clear; Rats run under one leader, and in this clan that leader's me.'

As a multitude of hands wave, as voices beg to be heard, my pride in Striker soars to the high heavens. But then a high-pitched voice shouts 'Spartax.' And the uproar dies instanter.

She marches in, boots loud in the expectant silence. She stands by Jehu and begins.

'You've heard Striker, now hear me.' Spartax isn't shouting, just talking normal. I guess, like me, everyone's holding their breath. It's so quiet that Robber's scratchy scrabble as he climbs to Jehu's shoulder sounds clear as clear.

'Jehu has the right of it. I've reached the end of my road.'

Pausing, she fingers a blood-red ear stud. 'But I'm not running.' She pauses again. The lull stretches on and on, but no one fidgets.

Then Striker stands and walks to her side. 'I call for a vote. Raise your hand if you wish to leave the ludus.'

A mass of raised hands signal the vote to leave is passed, but further questions reveal differing views on where to head. At the end it's decided that the Teamers will head west, on foot, and the drivers and guards will drive the carriers north-east, along a less rugged route.

When all's sorted we look to Spartax. 'I won't be harmed,' she says. 'I'm too valuable alive and training fighters.' She turns to Jehu and Eily. 'I'd advise the pair of you to stick with the teamers. Templeton will make you suffer in my stead.'

Eily's got tears in her eyes, but she'll obey. Jehu grasps her hand and bows his head. Yeah, so will he. Spartax hands Striker some rolls of plastic. 'Here are the safest routes I can come up with. This one's a road map, for those taking the carriers, and this one's for the walkers heading into the wilds. Take them with my blessing, and take all the supplies you need. Do not delay. Go now, before it's too late.' Then she turns to us all sitting there and staring at her, 'Move!' she shouts and we obey, as we always have.

In little over an hour the whole ludus is on the move. Us Teamers walk west, while the rest drive away in the carriers.

We leave Spartax alone in the compound, watching us go.

There's forty-four of us teamers leaving the ludus. I've counted. And if they feel same as me, then they know they're deserters running from the final battle, abandoning their leader to the mercy of the victors. It ain't a good feeling.

Striker's in the lead, taking the route he and Jehu figured after studying Spartax's map and the rest of us walk single file down the almost invisible path. Spartax is in my mind like an itching burr.

Brown's on my shoulder. She's not going to bolt even if we take fire, but Silk and Robber are wearing harnesses—they're young, they'll spook. So far all three are relishing the activity.

No one says a word we tote our packs and follow Striker—herd-sheep tagging a bellwether. Outside the compound we walk the scrubland till we reach no-man's land and have to negotiate the minefields. Nobody knows for sure who laid the mines. Some say Templeton, some say Templeton haters, even heard rumours of cross-sea invaders. I'd put my stake on the General, seeing as Eily filched the minefield plans from NOP files.

After the minefields we get to weapon-blasted rubbled areas and after that a forest of dead trees, wild weeds and skin-ripping brambles … and hills, ridge after ridge of ever steepening hills.

We halt at a clear-running stream to rest. Folk adjust backpacks, eat sugar bars and drink water from the stream. Nobody speaks, it's like we're all carrying a weight of misery, like we've done something unforgivable. I check the weakest, they're exhausted but claim to be strong enough to keep going. Mai and Kevan look bad, but supported by a team of helpers, they insist they can manage.

Thirst quenched, we follow the winding stream for a mile or so north. I'm tiring, fast. Since taken from the Whip Tails, and fit as I am, I've lost the way of walking on uneven ground, and the knack of forging through grabby brambles and mounding weed tracts. And, wouldn't you know it, the ground's getting steeper fast.

Up to now it's been cloudy, but the wind's freshening, scudding clouds racing across the sad faced moon. The pace increases when we hit clearer ground. The trees ahead seem miles away. Striker signals and we spread out and head for them.

My back's crawling, itched by invisible eyes, my ears hurt from straining for trooper noise and my damn neck's stiff from looking for fly-bys. It'll be better when we get under the trees.

Half way up the slope there's a maze of ancient brambles. By the time I get to the trees I've ripped both stretches and skin. The moonlight shows me other scratched faces.

Striker calls rest and it's good sitting under the cool shelter of full-grown trees, among a stand of half-grown saplings. Smelling the damp leaves and loamy soil I'm back again with Dad in our lonely shelter. Memories hurt, I go see how Mai and Kevan are holding up.

'We're fine,' Mai lies. 'We've had plenty of help.' Kevan says nothing, just lies back on the rabbit nibbled grass, eyes closed holding Mai's hand.

Rest over we go on, but slower, walking to higher ground through the thickening forest. When Striker orders Mai and Kevan sling carried, they don't protest.

The sun rises, the sky's bluing and I hear aircraft noise.

Asa climbs a tree, reporting smoke back at the ludus. His words are followed by the crumps and explosive whams. 'So much for the *no harm* ploy,' he says. 'Troopers are *harming* the ludus back to rubble.'

'Let's go,' calls Striker.

I look for Jehu, haven't heard or seen him since we left the ludus. I spot him and Eily. He's got his arms wrapped about her and he looks grim.

We set off northwest, Asa taking point, his black hair slick with sweat. We walk and keep on walking till we come to a defile leading down into a steep sided valley lined with ruins. The smell awakens my yesterdays, walking mouldering ruins with my father. Brown leaves my shoulder for my backpack. Manas comes to walk with me.

'Where's Silk?'

'In my pocket. She doesn't like it here.'

'Where's Jehu?'

'Here,' says the former weapons master. I turn, he and Eily are behind us and the Robber is lying cradled in Eily's arm, his head inside her jacket.

'You lived in the ruins, didn't you Bit?' Eily says. 'How did you stick it?'

'I got used to them a lot faster than I did the frinking CRC.'

27

A morning's walk and I'm feeling old as Noah. How far have we come? Greenstuff's a killer on the knees and ankles, my shoulders are aching from the carrisack and I'm sweating rivers 'neath stretches and waterproof. Got to keep shtum, Mai and Kevan are worse off. We need to build distance.

I stride out and catch up with Striker, he smiles and holds my hand.

'How you feeling, Bit?'

'All the better for seeing your grin,' I say. He hugs me to him, kissing my eyes, the tip of my nose and my smiling lips.

'I'll keep the rest for later,' he says and laughs when I blush.

We keep on till our path leads through a dead area; crushed stone, man bones, and withered vegetation. Jehu joins us.

'What d'you make of all this?' I ask him.

'Tox-blast. Could have been a dead township blasted free of infection. Who knows?'

'A solution to one of Templeton's little problems?'

'Yeah.'

'Jehu how you feeling about …?'

'Don't ask, Bit. I can't talk about … her.'

By late afternoon, even though Mai and Kevan have been sling-carried by a relay of helpers, they're hitting zero. Striker calls halt soon as we leave the toxic stretch, finding shelter in some ancient half-fallen castle. Asa climbs the battlement, trooper spotting. I sit by Striker in a scoop-out near a fallen wall, eating food bars and slaking my thirst.

Eily walks up, 'The injured can't go further. We should overnight here.'

'Too near that toxic site,' Striker says. 'Never know what'll drift up from it.'

Eily shivers, and we start trekking again. It's okay till it starts drizzling, before turning into a steady downpour. I'm soaked to the skin before we find shelter in a half wrecked barn—two sloping sides and a wonky corrugated roof. Place is packed with blown leaves and straw. Perfect.

I help Eily settle the unconscious Mai and Kevan on a pile of the soft stuff. Mai's feverish, so I go in search of a holly tree. It's not the berries I need, but the young leaves. Berries'll kill you, but chop and boil the soft leaves, leave to cool and it's good for fighting fever.

I hand the cooled potion to Eily and she grills me about Rat medications, writing down my recollections in a notebook.

I see a cold miserable night before me, before Striker comes to redeem his promise. He strips me of my damp underthings and warms me with his loving, and all in all it's a real sweet night. And to cap it all the morning dawns bright. Looks to be a good day for travelling.

Were up and out soon as we've broken fast, following the compass setting on Spartax's map. We walk slow but Striker urges speed when we reach scrubland, pointing to the dark treeline ahead.

I get the map out and he points to a big green patch—the National Parklands. 'See those trees ahead? We're on the edge, not far now. Pass the word.'

Night comes and we're still miles from the trees and don't find any convenient barns, so we cut brush and grass swathes to shelter under.

Mai coughs most of the night.

Morning brings lightning followed by thunder and pouring rain, but no troopers, so we walk and keep on walking. The promise of the green land ahead gives us heart.

Nights we sleep in Rat-type bashas made from branches layered with fern, and sleep comes hard. We grow ever more weary as day merges with miserable day.

Soon as we reach the woodland that coats the rising ground like an animal's hairy hide, there's a general lightening of spirits. Even Striker smiles when we move into the shelter of the trees. Hidden from sky patrols, we make camp.

Later, sitting by a shielded fire, breathing the scent of wood ash mingled with the scents of pine and fir and with Striker by my side I'm wrapped in peace. Watching Brown roll and play we talk.

'Think we'll be safe in the Wilderness?' I ask.

'Out of Templeton's reach, you mean.'

'Yeah.'

'We're fight-hardened Teamers. We're survivors. And don't you forget, I got you and you got me. Together we're invincible.'

Warm, comforted and loved, we sleep, but trouble comes with the morning light. Mai's real sick and Eily's worried, she wants Striker to halt the trek so she can try out some of my herbal remedies. 'If they prove as effective as that holly leaf mixture, we might not have to stay too long.'

Striker agrees to a day's rest and that suits the teamers. Suits me, too. We spend the day together, wandering, talking, loving. And strange to say I'm happy. The whole camp's quiet; pairs wandering off hand in hand, groups talking quiet but hopeful, and loners just relaxing into day-dreams. All of us, recovering.

After evening chow I sit with Jehu and Eily. I've Spartax on my mind, bet it's the same for them. Eily's feeding scraps to Robber. Jehu's sitting head down, shoulders bent, like he's carrying the weight of the world.

'Let me check Robber's harness, Jehu. If he skips to the trees we'll never get him back.'

He nods, his mind elsewhere. Eily looks up from Robber, eyes blank, face empty. Leaving Spartax cost them dear. Too dear?

Harness checked I wander among the teamers, testing the waters. The mood is good, despite everything. I get back to Striker and Kai's with him.

'The teamers are in good heart,' I say. 'Eager to go forwards, but glad of the R&R.'

'I've sent Asa, Fee and Nab to scout ahead. Kai's taken inventory. Tell her your findings, Kai.'

'We only brought a few rifles, because of ammo replacement. Plenty of blades and bows, and a good supply of dry food. And we've got the map, of course. Looks good, Bit. Reckon we'll be fine.'

'I think you could be right.'

'Optimism Bit?' Striker says, and smiles his old Rat grin.

We sleep early and well, tranced by the scent from the sheltering branches and with Brown curled up between us. A family.

Two mornings later births a sparkling day, Mai's brighter, Kevan's walking, and the scouts are back. We brave the forest, first off to cheery talk and laughter, but as the gloom deepens and the trees close ranks we tread lighter, watching for trail marks. The banter dies, giving way to frowns and dark mutterings. At night under the dripping canopy sleep doesn't come and black thoughts fester. The forest isn't quiet, even the rustling trees and water drips don't cover the screeches and howls of hunting creatures and their dying prey. Morning brings more wind and rain and a yearning to be quit of forestation.

I get the map from Striker and make a point of showing every single teamer that it won't be long before we're out of this damnable wood. Most ask if the Wilderness is all like this. I *say* no, but that's not what I been thinking.

The trees thin, exposing patches of grey-cloud sky. Then, joy of joys, I'm on the edge of a downward slope, looking on a great stretch of grassland and three dots that just have to be the scouts, Nab, Fee and Asa. Yay! We made it!

Suddenly the dots disappear and there's the sound of sky-craft. A pair of wingers glide into view and I shrink against a tree bole. Jehu crawls up with Robber poking from a pocket.

'Spotters, Bit. Hope they haven't spotted the scouts. They're flying grid pattern, could be they missed them. I think they probably missed us up here in the trees.'

'But did Nab and the others duck fast enough?'

'There's no sign those spotters saw 'em. Pattern's holding firm.'

'But they're searching for us, yeah?'

'Who else? I'll go back and check with the teamers. You all right, Bit?'

'Never better.'

Striker appears.

'What next, O Great Leader?'

'A nix on the sarcasm for a start, Bit. Look, we're aiming for the river, and it's down there. What do you think?'

'Thought you said nix the sarcasm?'

He unrolls the map, and points to a snaking river. 'Before we can cross we have to get through another ruined area. Map doesn't say how big. Could be the remains of a village or a small town.'

'Ruins I can take, if they're toxed that's a whole other story. Tox scares me.'

'You and me both,' he says, and nods to the returning Jehu. 'Hi, Jehu, how are the teamers doing?'

'Teamers are doing fine—raring to go. I told 'em not long now. Those spotters have a vast area to search, soon as they fly off we'll be heading downhill.'

It's tedious *and* terrifying watching the sky craft fly over and back, over and back. But slowly and surely they wing away and as soon as the engine noise fades the scouts give the go signal.

Nab tells us that they've located the ruins. 'Good news is they ain't toxic—bad news they stretch for miles along the river.'

We get there and she's right. She points directly at the ruins, 'Map says the fording place is there. Going the long way round could take days.' She looks up at the sky, 'We got days?'

Looking at the ruins I guess the dilapidation and decay's been hastened by fire, rain and weed attack, not by pulverizing machines or toxic blasts.

'Could be bomb damage,' I say. 'Templeton ordered bombings to clear Sickness-hit towns. I saw it happen.'

The crazed highways are lined with leaning buildings, some meeting mid way, some in collapsed piles and everywhere there's the rusty scribble of dead vehicles. Jehu's all for bulling straight through, 'We haven't time for caution.'

I point at a rising dust cloud, 'Jehu, every street's a deathtrap. That pile ahead's just fallen. We *have* to move slow.'

Then Striker sidles up to me, 'Think fly-bys, Bit.'

We press forward, past a rusty, half-broke sign—Llan, it reads. Just Llan.

Saying is a lot easier than doing. Sure I *know* we gotta cut the chances of spy machines spotting us and it's sensible to go before night falls. But sensible doesn't cut it when you're walking under tottery buildings on a surface that's all tilt and rock, not to mention the brick dust that clogs your nose. We come to a monster crack in the roadway, crooked as a lightning flash and far too wide to jump. We to cross it one by one by way of a broke-down pylon that bridges the gap.

'Don't cough,' Striker whispers before we pass a leaning building. 'And don't even think trod-on frogs.'

Building was a shop once upon a different time. Now charred and blistered plasto-graphs of smiling shoppers peel off the crumbling walls. Like Striker said I'm careful not to cough, even though my throat's thick with dust. Frink it, I don't even *breathe* as I cat-foot under a battered T..co sign that looks about ready to turn guillotine.

We make it through with just the one minor heart-quake when a rifle scraps against a wall and sets stuff crashing down. I'm shaking like a ferret's whiskers when I get to the water's edge. Jehu claps my shoulder, 'What did I say? A cinch.'

'One more word and I'll scrag you.'

'You and whose army?'

I laugh at the childhood taunt and pat his seamed cheek. 'I'll go check on Mai and Kevan.'

Kevan's fine, he's watching Mai who's pale and deep in sleep. Eily purses her lips when I ask how she's faring.

Sun goes down as we sit on the riverbank drinking fresh water under arching willow branches, all the Clan together. Manas watches Silk chase Brown's tail, Striker has his arm about my waist. Fee, Nab and Kai just loll.

Eily and Jehu stroll up and Robber springs down to attack his sister which earns him a nip from Brown. Eily settles with us, but Jehu goes off to arrange a Gather. He says we need to keep the teamers informed. Eily smiles, 'He's feeling better,' she whispers.

When he comes back he's followed by about half the teamers, the rest drift in as Striker climbs on a boulder. Everyone's ready and waiting as Jehu climbs up to join him.

Striker starts, 'Here's the plan. We'll cross the river here at the ford and then climb to the top of the ridge behind me.' He points across the water, then Jehu takes over.

'According to the map there's a range of hills beyond—'He's interrupted by heartfelt sighs and cries. 'But on the other side of that range lies mile upon mile of untouched Wilderness. And no we don't have to climb a mountain to get there, there's a way through.'

Everyone cheers, and he waits till it's quiet before saying on.

'It's a tunnel, built for coal and ore carrying rail cars. Map shows the track entering the tunnel and coming out the other side.'

More cheers, mine among them.

Kai waves a hand, 'What if the tunnel's blocked?' he shouts. 'We backtrack or start climbing mountains?'

Eily stands, 'Mai's worse. She needs rest. Staying by the river would help. She'll benefit from cold sponging and unlimited drinking water. I'm not saying all of us should stay here, a group, that's all. And when you reach safety, send back for us.'

'No splitting, Eily. We stay together,' Striker says, getting a nod from Jehu. 'How about we send scouts to check the route while the rest catch fish and hunt game for the journey. Dry food's palatable, but I for one wouldn't say no to a bite of fresh meat.'

This goes down well with the Gather. A vote is called and the plan's passed unanimously.

I'm one of the many volunteers who want to go scouting, Kai's another.

'Let me and Kai go, Striker. You've got things to do. You're needed *here*.'

'So are you. You're helping Eily, aren't you? And you look ready to drop.'

'And you're fresh as budding flower, I suppose? Eily's got other helpers, and I'm still Rat enough to be up and doing, and Rat enough that you can't stop me.'

He looks at me, hard, mutters 'Stubborn,' then shifts to Kai. 'Well, what you waiting for? Moon's up, get scouting the two of you.'

'Look after Brown,' I say as I hand the drowsy ferret to him and we're way. We don't wait to see who else is going, we just grab supplies and beetle off, aiming to be first across the river. I don't bother looking at the map, got it printed on my brain.

It's not an easy crossing, the river running high and spiteful, but we're teamers, trained and tuned, and we leap from one rock to the next without so much as a slip or slide. It's the climb ahead that tests our stamina, but when we reach the top it's well worth the sweat.

From the summit and in the glowing moonlight I see track lines in the winding glen below.

We start down easy enough, but the incline is steeper than it looks and we end up sliding down like we're on an ice sheet, landing on a built-up cinder track in a shower of earth and stones.

Track's a doubler—two sets of rails and it must have been doctored with some potion to repel weeds, 'cos the walking's easy. Round the second curve we're faced with a scrambled mess. Looks like the track's been missile hit. Rails lifted from the bedding track, curling and twisting in fantastic shapes, and there's a gaping hole to negotiate. Once we're across it, down comes a pour of hissing, spitting rain. Same time the moon turns shy and leaves us in the black, black dark. I got flint and candle in my pack, but they're useless. So we take what shelter's offered—a slanting lump of stone, and wait cursing till the moon shows its face again. Time it does the rain's done with and we're on the move. Fifty yards on it's pouring again. 'I'm feeling victimised.' I shout to Kai, but he hunches his shoulders and keeps his mouth tight shut.

Round the next curve there's a sight that'd hack off a saint—a bank of earth blocking the line. Right then I'm about ready to head back, but Kai climbs to the top of the slimy berm and waves at me to join him.

Seeing that I'm soaked to the skin, and a slime bath isn't gonna make me feel any worse, I join him. He points to a brick edged horseshoe on the side of the giant hill in front of us. Luckily the rain stops allowing me to see exactly what Kai's found.

'Jack me! You've only gone and found the tunnel. Yay!'

'Doesn't look right, looks damaged, Bit.'

'Let's take a look.'

The closer we get the worse it appears. The horseshoe edge is ragged and drooping. The tunnel's blocked. 'Hit by something?' I query.

'Bomb?' he ventures.

'Could be, or explosive. Rat I knew found a cache of dynamite. Probably plenty around to be found.'

'So, Rats or troopers did the damage.'

'Either or both, but look up there, Kai. Tunnel's not completely blocked. I can see a way in.'

'Mighty small way! How wide you think?'

'Six feet, easy. Room enough, by miles.'

'Yeah, but look up *there*.'

Above the hole hangs an obese mass of earth, kept from falling by a jutting finger of stone.

'Could drop any second,' he says.

'You think? I'm taking a gander inside that hole.'

'Hell's teeth, you can't. What would Striker say?'

'Wrong thing to say, Kai. Should have kept your hell-mouth shut.'

He's spluttering a laugh as I start climbing. The bricks sticking out of the blockage make it easier than I thought.

'I can see inside. I'm going in.'

His shouts are lost as soon as I get inside the hole. Sitting on the lip I scrabble for my candle, and spark a light. I still can't see beyond my boots, but the sound of the sparking gives a hollow echo, like I'm on the edge of a great empty space. Satisfied I've done all I can I wriggle back outside. Further exploration would need ropes, ladders, better lighting and time.

So, what did you see?' he says, craning up.

'A big hole, Kai, and I didn't exactly see it, I heard it. It's vast.'

'How far did it stretch?'

'Couldn't tell without climbing down. Only had a candle didn't I? Could be a clear run to the other side, could be a cave-in ten yards further on. I don't know, right?'

'So, what d'you think?'

'Same as you, I 'spect. Too risky.'

'Yeah.'

'Hold on. Hear that, Kai?'

'What?'

'Shh. Listen.'

We hold still, me staring at the track, him at the sky. But it's gone quiet, whatever I heard before isn't there now. All I hear are the faint sounds of owl hoots. All I see is a small creature running through the grass. All I smell is the mouldy air of the tunnel.

But then the quiet is shattered, the heavens rumbling like the old gods are marching back.

'Zat Thunder?' Kai shouts.

'Frink, No! That ain't thunder, Kai. It's weapon fire.'

We race back to the earth berm and stand straining ears and eyes.

'Up there.' I point at the moon-silvered aircraft spitting gobs of electric-blue phlegm at the ground, before soaring back to the clouds.

'There's another,' Kai yells, pointing a second flier shooting cherry-coloured bolts.

I'm screaming curses on every woman who gave birth to a black-souled trooper. 'They got us, Kai. Found the tribe! We gotta get back.'

28

How we run! A rain-cloud bursts over us, real thunder rumbles, smoother than trooper fire, but we don't stop. I stumble, Kai hauls me up, then he falls and I help him. All the time I'm screaming curses and praying for Striker and my Brown.

There's the berm ahead. Got to run faster, but Kai grabs my arm—figures on the track. First thought, troopers! Then recognition hits, it's Asa and Fee. We meet, the four of us, drowners going down for the third time.

'Fly-bys,' Fee gasps. 'Jehu got one. One escaped.' She stops for breath, and Asa carries on.

'Striker said to find you. Trusted you to find ... way. Rest ... following.'

'No choice, Bit,' Fee says, breath gained. 'Tunnel or troopers.'

My turn. 'We heard firing? Who's hurt?'

'Later,' Asa answered as several more figures slide down the berm. I recognise Striker and Jehu toting Mai's stretcher. Big K'tau's with them, Kevan draped across his shoulder.

'The tunnel?' yells Striker.

'Not sure,' I shout back, shaking my head.

He staggers up to me. 'What d'you mean? You think there's a chance?'

'Slim chance.'

'Slim's better than what's behind us.' He turns and shouts

'Come on, safety ahead.'

Beron takes Kevan from K'tau and I take Brown and then I head in the direction of a tunnel that might or might not offer safety. Kai turns with me, doubt and fear writ large upon his face.

The earth berm is a major hold-up. By the time everyone's over, trooper craft have zeroed in, firing blue and red. As well as the big stuff, wasp-like fly-bys zoom in, stinging and slashing.

'Not far,' I pant, but no one's listening.

Tunnel's ahead, screams and firing behind. I'm up the blockage and in the hole, no time to guess or gauge, just let go and drop, praying for a soft landing. Luckily that's what I get. There's no big drop. 'Slide the stretcher,' I scream. 'Slide it, damn you, slide.'

And through the hole slides the muddied stretcher and I guide it away as other white eyed, mud daubed figures follow in swift progression. I seize the chance of a lull to scramble back outside.

More of the tribe appear, attempting the slope, desperation driving them hard. 'Mind the sides,' I warn.

Weapon fire ceases and the aircraft climb into banking turns. They'll be back guns blazing, before very long. I stare up, the overhang's still hanging solid, but the sides of the entry hole are crumbling. How long? Frinking nard, how long?

'Hurry,' I'm shouting, so loud, my lungs are gonna pop. Another few slide in, more are climbing up. The planes turn. They're coming back. One more in, another two and I'm down slope shouting and pushing them on. The guns are firing, someone's hit, tumbling down in a flurry of arms and legs.

Can't see anyone climbing, there're no more runners, just plane noise, blue zizzing phlegm and blood-red bolts.

I'm on the lip and there's no one climbing, just a loose-limbed body rolling down and down. A bolt hits the slope, impelling me inside and dislodging the tenacious overhang. With a slurping, rolling roar the hole closes and darkness falls.

I slide into the dark, expecting the earth to crush me and all who entered because of me. What have I done?

Then a voice breaks the dread silence, 'Well that's it folks, they ain't getting us today.'

'That's Kai,' I say, my voice sounding loud in the silence. 'Know that chirp anywhere!' A wave of laughter smashes the silence as folk realise they're still alive. And for one brief moment I forget the bodies lying on the track.

Torchlight flickers on, then off as Eily calls, 'One at a time. Save your batteries.' Next sec I hear Striker's voice, and the hard knot inside my belly loosens. 'Roll call, guys. Sing out your names.' I listen and count. Thirty two. Twelve gone. How many injured? That was the next count ordered. And we're fortunate, ten hurt but only Mai and Lialle need be carried. Kevan's on his feet again.

Eily calls out and her voice is strong and confident. 'On second thoughts I believe we should light a few more torches, according to the map this tunnel's not overlong and the air smells fresh enough. May as well put the few we have to best use.'

I breathe in deep, and she's right, the dust is settling and the air's clean. So no blockage, we've a way out. I get up. I've twinges, scrapes and grazes but I feel frinking great. Now to find Striker.

Later, after a much needed rest I'm still smiling, as I walk with Striker who's leading us down the tunnel, holding one of the precious torches. I got Brown wound about my neck like a winter muffler, and I call warnings of obstructions to Kai who passes them down the line. First off it's brick, tiles, concrete lumps and fallen earth. It's easier walking close to the walls avoiding the train rails, but as the walls bow outward and the bricks start to crumble I'm back to track walking.

Leaders and warners change and change about, the pace slows as folk stumble and fall. And grumble.

'At least we're walking dry,' I say to Nab, loud, to silence the moaner right behind me.

'The tunnel slopes,' Nab says, then turns to the moaner, 'And the roof fall stopped the troopers following. Be glad of that, you miserable grouse.'

'Shut your mouth you stinking Rat,' the moaner mumbles. 'It's you lot got the Party after us.'

Nab stops sudden like, and the grumbler walks into her, 'Say what, Quilla? You blaming me in particular, or Rats in general?'

'If the glove fits wear it.'

'Shut it, Foxy.'

A wild yell from Kai, halts the incipient fight, 'Tunnel end in sight,' he shouts.

'Smell that, Nab?' I say. 'Fresh air, greenery. Last lap.' I hustle her to the front of the line to see just what Kai has found.

Instead of the damaged exit I expect, there's an open half circle, shielded with hanging greenery and growing shrubs. Daylight rays through the mass of ferns and tangled brambles, the rails hidden beneath matted ivy and bindweed.

'Quiet,' whispers a voice into the dead silence. First I can't hear anything but the blood rushing through my veins and the pounding of my heart, then as I rein in my excitement I hear water dripping and the shush of wind on leaves.

Eily pushes out through the cascade of brambles. That frees me, and everyone else, to leave the dark and walk towards the light.

The brambles pull and bite, but no one stops or cares. It's early morning by the light and it's raining.

'It's a jungle,' Kai crows. 'We'll be hidden from spy craft.'

That starts a babble and I pick up the odd sentence.

'Any signs of troopers?'

'All quiet, no planes, no fly-bys, nothing.'

'That's good, but …?' a voice stutters from close by.

'How come the tunnel wasn't blasted flat?' questions another worrier, standing by my right shoulder.

'My thoughts exactly,' I say into the silence that follows.

'Could be the troopers thought the landslide did for us? Kai ventures.

'Could be those fly-bys were auto-drones,' I say, loud and clear. 'Dumb machines didn't think it through.'

'Reckon you've nailed it, Bit. I'll go with that.'

A chorus of agreement lightens the mood.

'So what now?' asks a perked-up Kai.

'How about we set up camp just inside the tunnel,' I say, trying for upbeat. 'We'll send out scouts, yeah? And rustle up a meal?'

Doesn't take much encouragement to get a fire going. 'Don't worry 'bout the smoke,' says Fee. 'The foliage will break it up.'

The fire made from dry sleepers torn from the track burns hot, and almost smokeless. It soothes the hurting and eases dark thoughts. Manas surprises us with a flask of firewater brought from the ludus. It's a mere mouthful, but sufficient to toast Spartax.

Before we sleep Striker and I talk. 'Think they *will* come after us?' I ask.

'Like Kai said, they might think we're dead, suffocated under the dirt fall. And like *you* said, if the fly-bys *were* auto-drones …'

'But what do we do next? What if …?'

'Leave the what-ifs till tomorrow. Right now we need sleep.'

'And when we wake?'

'We forge on.'

29

Striker calls a Meet the very next morning. It doesn't happen. More'n half the teamers are off hunting. They come back fired up with sightings of deer herds, forest boar, flocks of game birds and a fish-packed river.

The Meet *does* take place—two days down the line, when a pelting rainstorm deters the hunters. As the teamers gather I sense that Striker won't manage to swing a move from this campsite.

Jehu calls Striker to speak and he gives all the reasons to move on: we're too near the last trooper sighting; the troopers have fly-bys and manned aircraft and distance means nothing to them; finally he reminds them that Templeton is expanding his territory and this place is ripe for exploitation.

Foxy Quilla gets next talk space and speaks all quiet and reasonable, 'It's clear the troopers think we're goners. Why not delay the move, get some R&R, send out scouts and hunt up travel food?'

Quilla takes the day—we're staying.

Striker still believes it's safer to move on. Jehu, Eily, the Clan and one or two others agree, but Striker vetoes going it alone.

'It's not just the Clan any more, we're a tribe now. Thirty have more chance than ten. But I'm not convinced this place is the Eden Quilla thinks.'

'What do we do?'

'We'll volunteer as scouts and be very, very wary.'

Two mornings later I wake early, to a drizzly threatening dawn. I wake kinda trepidatious, my mind on Mai, and go check on her.

I get to Eily, read her face and don't need to ask.

We bury Mai in Wilderness soil, though she wanted to be burned. But rain-soaked wood won't burn, and there's the problem of fly-bys so we bury her in the place she yearned to be—the wild, free land.

Kevan, mended but frail, gives the eulogy, Striker says the Words over her grave and Jehu gives the haunting cry that tells of the death of a valiant Rat. We eat her funeral feast sitting in the tunnel listening to the rain fall and the wind keen, and mourn our loss.

Next morning I wake restless and wake Striker. We're the only souls up and about and I tell him I'm going into the tunnel, to check on the blockage, see if there's any slippage or signs the troopers have sent boring machines.

'Think that's likely?' He says.

'No, but I'm not sure we're ultra-safe squatting here.'

'So, if the tunnel's still blocked?'

'Then I want to check out the entrance, suss the track. We need up to date info 'stead of false hope.'

'When do we go?'

'Go where?' says Kai, making me start, he's crept up so quiet.

'Shh! We're going to do some checking.'

'Count me in. I want to *do* something.'

'Count us all in,' says Manas. And there's the rest of the Clan plus Asa, Fee's glue-boy as Kai calls him since he and Fee have pair-bonded and stick close together.

Creeping through the tunnel past sleepers sharpens the edge dulled by days of drifting. Takes time but when we reach the earth slide blocking the tunnel nothing's changed. Kai checks carefully by the light of what has to be one of the sole remaining battery torches. Trust Kai to pick up a valuable trifle; boasts he was a nimble thief before he was nabbed.

We can't see anything and can't hear anything, but that don't mean there isn't anything waiting outside.

We slide back past twitching sleepers, head past the hanging greenery and start the climb to the top of the hill above the tunnel.

Sun's high, has to be well past noon, time we reach the summit. We take a breather sitting under trees eating cold meat from Mai's funeral feast and talking about her.

'She was getting better,' Manas says, soft voiced. 'Talking strong, sitting up, even took a couple of steps. Then … then she …'

'She always wanted to be burned, you know,' Kai said. 'She said going up in flames was better than melting into soil.'

'Yeah, but even Quilla wouldn't risk smoke signals. Mai would understand.'

Brown bustles back with a fat mouse in her mouth and shares it with Silk. The crunching captures eyes *and* attention. Meal over, ferrets pocketed we set out to cross the hill to glim the results of the trooper action.

'No need to rush,' says Striker. 'We won't be missed.'

It's much harder to trek over than under and we don't rush. We sight the glen and rail track as dark falls.

'No bodies,' I say to Kai. 'Animals ate 'em?'

'Could be trooper-took,' he replies.

'Strafe marks aplenty. No trucks or diggers, looks like they *were* sold on us being killed.'

'Reporting certain success, no doubt. With bodies to prove it. Any use climbing down, Striker?'

'None whatsoever.'

'Right,' I say. 'How about rustling up a rabbit or somesuch? I used to roast a mean rabbit dinner for me and my dad.'

We walk back the way we came and I explain about fire

shelters and dissipating the smoke and the correct way to skin a coney, to non-Rats, Asa, Fee and Kai.

Then Striker says I could give a class in snare setting, to while away some time. 'And just for interest, there's a prize for the fattest rabbit snared.'

Nothing like a bit of healthy competition to raise the spirits, but it's half way through the night before we sit and eat. And who wins the prize of a fold away dagger? Kai, natch.

After a few hours' sleep we head back to the tunnel camp, relaxed and smiling.

The smell alerts us, the acrid stink of burning bedding … and worse. Burning flesh smells like roast boar, but with a far sweeter edge. Smiles wiped we move with caution to the tunnel lip, lie down and look over the edge.

It's bad. The hanging greenery curtaining the tunnel is strewn and trampled on the ground. Blackened sleep sacks lay in smouldering piles with the racks of curing skins tossed, broken and mashed into the stinking mess.

It's the fallen trees that puzzle me, a second look shifts perspective, it's not tree trunks, but bodies, not branches but limbs. Nothing stirs, 'cept flapping crows, spiraling smoke and the snap of half-burnt twigs.

Slowly, with no need of haste, we descend and gather in the dell. 'Search and tally,' Striker whispers, and glad to be told, we obey.

All in all eleven of the bodies are teamers, Quilla among them—two strangers close beside her, one stuck with Quilla's favourite knife. Eight more unknowns lie dotted among our dead.

'Surprise attack and they're not troopers, Striker, these bodies look to be Rats.'

'That's my thought, Bit. What say you Nab? Manas?'

Nab answers first, 'Rats, certainly. Unknown tribe.'

'Can't be,' Manas says, frowning. 'Rat's don't leave their dead.'

And with that came a high whistling hum and Manas drops

arrow shot and a screaming dervish slams me down 'fore I can shout warning. Last thing I see, Manas's eyes, fixed and empty, then … I'm gone.

I wake, head down over a bony shoulder, nose pressed into badly cured leather, jogged and swayed as my captor lopes across bumpy ground. 'Brown,' I groan and something squirms in not one but two pockets. The pain in my head outs me before I can think of what and why.

Flung down and conscious again, in the midst of bodies in a similar pose, I see Striker's face and breathe again. It's night, and there's a fire burning and I smell roasting meat, animal not the sweet stink of man-flesh. Trees circle a small clearing, stars peep through over-arching branches.

'Awake are you?' A skin-clad stinker pokes at Nab, she snaps at the finger, earning a whacking cuff for her effort.

I try a Whip Tail call, I want this stranger Rat to know we too are clansmen, but someone behind me takes offence and knocks me out.

More jogging, but the guy who totes me smells different, I rouse, but remain limp and mute. Something wriggles, again in two pockets and I finally figure I'm host to Brown *and* Silk. Who else would the kit turn to if not her dam?

The jogging stops, challenge spoken and returned, and after more and smoother footwork I'm slung down into somewhere dark, onto something hard. Further thumps tell me others have been dumped with me. A door scrapes closed, a sliding wood on wood and I'd guess we're penned in some cell … somewhere.

'It's me, Bit,' I venture. 'You there Striker?'

'Yeah,' he says hoarsely.

'Who else?'

A roll call tells me that we total six. Manas is no longer with us, but Asa is.

'Manas was right, Rats do come back for their dead.'

'Picked up some live ones same time, didn't they?'

'Bit?' It's Kai. 'What happened to Silk?'

'She's safe in my pocket. Reckon she followed Brown's scent after … She needs looking after. You up to it Kai?'

'Bet your life I am. Can't get to you, I'm tied.'

'So am I. Whistle and she'll come.' At Kai's whistle the scrabbling started again, but stopped as Silk left me and jumped to Kai. I heard him crooning to her and Silk creeling back.

'She's licking my face,' he said.

'Licking blood, no doubt. You been cut?'

'Arrow grazed.'

'Shh. Visitors,' a voice hisses.

The door grinds open showing a figure lit by a pair of burning brands. Figure's wearing trooper boots, cloth trews and a leather jerkin. As well as the two brand bearers there's a fem dressed similar. She doesn't blink, her gaze steady as the arrow in her drawn bow. All four of them bear facial scars and tattooed arms.

The guy steps forward, looks from face to face and stops at me. 'Bitch Singer of the Whip Tails?' he says and I look up at his fish-belly face, mouth cracked and dry, my throat hurting sore. Can't answer the worm even if I wanted to.

The silence stretches till a fifth figure makes an entrance and my heart lurches, slows, then races. His hair's completely white and scraped into a plaited tail, face weathered near black and seamed with fresh scars, some the precise marking of chiefdom. But his lone eye is still as keen as ever. One Eye lived!

He steps up to my questioner, 'Get them out; it's her.' Then walks back out before I can moan or mew.

'Up,' yells fish-belly and takes out his knife. 'You'll have to walk, I'm not carrying you.' And he cuts the thongs that bind my wrists and ankles, doing the same to the others. But he speaks right into my face. 'Don't be stupid, now, that venner won't be the only eye watching you. Move wrong, even think about moving wrong and you're crow bait. Understand?'

I stare back, mouth tight and he shouts again, 'Understand?'

Answer him? He'll wait forever to get an answer from me. He steps forwards, knife raised, and it's the steady eyed fem who calls him off. 'You want to cross the one-eyed venner?' At that his arm drops and he turns for the door, muttering curses.

Outside I see our cell is just one of a line of grass roofed, mould marked stone cottages. We're pushed and prodded along a crumbling roadway overshadowed by ancient wide branched oaks. One Eye's not in sight, gone like a blown out match.

Up ahead a stone walled church stands silver grey in the moonshine. On the crooked steeple dangles a twisted weathervane cockerel.

The path to the church door winds through a clutch of leaning grave markers. When we reach the grey oak door One Eye's holding it open, his face blank as a wiped slate.

Inside the lobby the stink of must and fungus makes me shiver. Another oak door leads into the church proper, a pewless space lighted with wicked fat-blocks smelling so foul my eyes start stinging. One Eye leads down the white walled room between rows of silent, watchful tribesmen sitting cross legged on the flagstones. A strong draught blows in through glass free pointed windows.

Instead of an altar, there's a carved, high-backed chair. Seated on that throne is a man with tight curled hair and a beard of extravagant wildness. Behind the chair huddles a clot of disheveled figures—the remnant of the teamers.

One Eye bows to the throne sitter, before moving to one side. The chief waves our guards away and examines our faces. He's frowning. The last face he stares at is One Eye's.

'Tomos of the Reapers,' One Eye says, real serious. 'I, One Eye of the Quester Clan ask leave to speak.'

Questers? The word jabs me like a spear, bringing memories of the night Throat Tearer won hearts enough to take a new clan to the wilderness. So, One Eye found them after Talon's betrayal.

The chief nods and One Eye draws breath and speaks all formal like a true venner.

'I speak for your captives, to ask … no, beg their freedom. I have spoken at length with them and learned they are a tribe newly escaped from Templeton's compounds. Pursued by troopers and under heavy fire, the survivors hid in a disused railway tunnel. Further firing destroyed their way in, curtailing pursuit.

'Chief of the Reapers, I truly believe these prisoners present no threat to the tribe, are no allies of Templeton, and are as mice to his tomcat.' He pauses as Rat laughter spreads through the listening gather. All quiets as Tomos rises from his chair, his gaze sweeping over the gathered tribesmen.

'I hear One Eye of the Questers. One Eye the venner, the teacher, who says these folk are a tribe and deserving respect by virtue of Rat lore. But *I* say they are cits, NOP incomers, and as such, merit culling.'

The Rat congregation growls, whether for us or against us, there's no telling.

One Eye speaks, voice pitched deliberately low. He captures the ears of the gather and the growls die.

'Tomos, as a Rat leader you are bound by Rat law. A Rat has right of speech before condemnation and as a one-time leader and now venner of the Questers, I invoke the right to speak on behalf of captured kin.'

He looks at the seated Rats and then at the Chief Tomos, none demurs, and he speaks again

'Stand, Striker and Bitch Singer, once pack members of the Whip Tail tribe. Stand and speak for your lives and the lives of your new clan.'

We stand to the banging thump of fists on palms—the Rat host showing eagerness to hear more. With none to gainsay, we begin, taking turns to spin our tale using a blend of word and signage. All Rats love a tale and I take care to make eye contact with as many listeners as possible. As the story of treachery, torture and the creation of a new tribe forced to fight in the arena, unfurls, even Tomos sits forward on his carved chair intent on every word, his eyes following every hand sign.

I finish with our flight to the Wilderness, mourning clan members lost to trooper fire and also to the knives and arrows of the Reaper tribe.

Striker calls the prisoners to sing out their names. Six names sound out, Eily and Jehu are not among them. I sign to Tomos. 'Leader of Reapers, I cry peace. We of the Teamer Clan would swear oath to you and join your fight against the troopers of the New Order Party. What say you, mighty chief?' I stop signing to the chief, and sign to the congregation instead. 'What say you, o mighty tribe of Reapers?'

Silence greets me, a deep cold silence that's broken by an ear-battering roar, like every Rat is shouting YES. And then the hooting begins, a pulsating throb that matches my beating pulse. One Eye's mouth droops to a one sided grin. They're for us!

Tomos raises his arms and the hoots subside. 'The tribe has spoken. Welcome Teamer Clan and join your brethren in the Wilderness.'

No mention's made of the ambush. The dead of both tribes are honourably burned, including Mai's resurrected body. After, there's a feast like no feast I've ever dreamed of. We stay with the Reapers for what I guess is a kinda probationary period, under Tomos' watchful eye. He talks to each of us in turn, gets acquainted with the ferrets and gradually his attitude softens. A month on, we leave with One Eye in search of the Questers.

30

There's twelve of us walking with One Eye. Striker and me, Fee, Asa, Nab and Kai, plus Kavan, K'tau, Weasel, Tink, Hulda and Sun—we're the Teamers, a new clan. I suppose it's fourteen if you count Silk and Brown. There's been no sign of Robber.

We set out early morning, after a breakfast of bread and cheese. The walk started quiet, it still is.

'So, Bit. Want me to tell you my story?' says One Eye.

I shrug a yes, and Kai and Striker move in close.

'It was pure luck that kept me safe after Talon juded us. Soon as I saw you and Striker netted, I ducked behind a pile of rubble. Came a fire blast and I woke up covered in the stuff. Time I clawed free, the sky was silent the troopers gone. Had no choice but head for what was left, the venners and the young of both tribes. I had to convince them to follow me into the Wilderness in search of Throat Tearer's Questers.'

He quiets for some few moments, 'Took a power of persuasion to get those venners to risk the young in the Wilderness, but the Whip Tail young were all for it and convinced the Crow kits to join forces. With them on my side the venners had no choice; seek the Wilderness or lose the ratlings.'

'How long did it take to find the Questers?'

'Don't matter how long, we found them. There were enough markers left for Rat eyes to see, in spite of plant growth and weather damage. And, hell weren't they pleased to see new life brought to the tribe.'

'Throat Tearer still alive?'

'Sure was. But a year or so later he died in a winter flood. They elected me leader and I served till I'd trained up a fine replacement in Blade. Now I'm venner advisor to him as well as traveling to other Wilderness settlements making sure the young stay on the right track and the lore is bedded deep within the clan mind.'

The silence is broken by questions about life in the outback and One Eye's all too pleased to tell us what we need. By the time we reach Quester settlement I'm surprised to see how permanent it looks and say so. Striker gives me his thoughts. 'No troopers, Bit. No need to be always on the move.'

'I noticed the crop fields,' I say.

'And animal herds,' puts in Kai. 'Look, cows and goats.'

'We keep fowl as well,' adds One Eye.

Blade and the Questers take us willingly, glad to see the tribe grow in size and strength.

In this wild, free land time flows easy; treacle from a warmed spoon. Cocooned in peace we Teamers blend with Questers, two tribes united in brotherhood. Cocooned, Striker and I bond tighter, our love softening the ache of childlessness. But the hatred we feel towards those that caused it lingers like the taint of a half-buried corpse.

A few weeks on Striker wakes me from a restless, dream-ridden sleep.

'More bad dreams?'

'Get 'em most every night, though some are worse than others. Can't fight them, can't stop them no matter what I do. I can work my guts out, tire myself to exhaustion and still they come. I'm either back in the CRC—Dumb Dor again, or worse, tortured by Templetons med-techs.'

'Think I don't get flashbacks, Bit? Well, think again. And you know something, Bit? All these evil dreams stem from hatred. All the hate we feel for Templeton, his murderous troopers, his sadistic techs, festers inside us like … like a septic boil, or a volcano spilling molten lava.' He sits up, draws a giant breath and then speaks on. 'I've seen how hatred withers lives, eats away at love, so I want you and me to swear that we won't let Templeton ruin this new life. Bit, we can't allow that monster to destroy *us*.'

'Yeah, but it's not like he's here so why aren't we free of him? We left him far behind, didn't we?'

'Him we escaped, but what he did still haunts us. You curse him on wakeful nights, you kill rocks 'stead of him, you dig the fields with fury, like you're digging his grave. You've allowed him to possess you.'

I open my mouth and he puts a gentle finger to my lips, whispering, 'I know, I know, my love, it's not just you. I feel the same. Believe me, that bastard lives in my head, too.'

Silent now, he wipes my eyes and draws me close, for comfort and the spark of loving.

Afterwards we talk of plans and new ventures. 'But to move on, Bit, we must free our minds of dreck. We have to rid *him* from our thoughts—we need to *exorcise* Templeton.'

'What, you think I haven't tried pushing him out?'

'Yeah, but by yourself. You been working alone. It might be better if we worked together.'

'You say that, but we'd tread the same old track. What we need is advice from someone we trust. Face it Striker, we need outside help. And I know just the guy.'

'You mean …'

'Yeah, One Eye. That frinking bastard Templeton is not gonna beat us, we're Rats, remember?'

'If anyone knows about exorcism it's sure to be One Eye.'

'Then let's go ask him.'

'Now? It's the middle of the night.'

'All right. Early morning, yeah?'

'First thing, Bit, first thing. Now settle close.'

One Eye organises a ceremony for the twelve former Teamers, but soon as the word gets out, the whole tribe of Questers want in.

A week later on a fine bright afternoon, in a fallow field wide enough to hold every single Quester, One Eye calls the gathered clan to order in a loud strong voice.

We're all here, young and old, standing intermingled, standing united.

He begins by getting us singing a hymn taught to young ratlings, *All Things Bright and Beautiful*, a song of praise to God for creating the flowers and animals of the wilderness, the ever changing seasons and the precious land that fosters us all. And listening to the singing, I hear echoes of other songs, other times: of being forced into the church choir by my 'wicked' father and made to learn the hymns which brought comfort to my dad as he lay dying. Of being taught the tribal chants which celebrated births but also paid tribute to the dead. Of being captive in the CRC, finding solace in the song of a ferret's heartbeat, and then finding new life with the teamers. Ups and downs. A turning wheel: I find comfort, and an *easing* in that thought.

Then One Eye relates our blessings: our community of loving friends, our escape from tyranny and our priceless freedom, pausing at every phrase to allow the clan's intoned Amens, and Glory-Bes to ring out loud and clear.

He speaks of past times, of sorrows endured and battles fought, and then calls clansmen to stand and recite the names of those lost and gone before. Striker stands and includes Spartax in his list of lost ones.

When the last name is spoken One Eye tells us that we must look to the future. 'Now join together,' he says, 'and sing uplifting hymns and joyful songs in praise of freedom gained.'

After we've sung our hearts out. One Eye speaks again.

'Brothers and sisters, we Rats carve no names on standing stones, we raise no memorial plaques. Rats celebrate the names of the lost in each Rat heart and each Rat memory. As long as one Rat lives, those names, those Rats will be alive.'

A thoughtful silence endures for some minutes, then ceremony complete we feast on spit-roast hog, mud-baked trout then tackle honey-daubed fruit pies while supping bitter home-brewed ale. Blade, our leader, bids One Eye mark the date in the annals as a festival to be celebrated yearly.

Our first-year harvest is a good one, so good a new barn is built to hold the produce. Blade sends messages to the nearby tribes, inviting them to share the bounty and we meet with Pied Birds, Tree Creepers and the Two Headed Crows.

Kai pays particular attention to a certain sweet-faced Pied Bird fem, name of Magan.

As the year turns we get used to hunting game not men, visiting clans not toxic waste sites, and digging veg plots not graves. And there's the children that need teaching. Not mine or Striker's, but those born to the un-neutered. We school the older ones in the fighting skills we learned in the ludus. For me, it helps root out the seeds of self-pity that remain. Kinda like ridding the veg plot of weeds, you gotta keep at it lest you be overrun. We have chosen to look forward. We're together and that's what counts.

Since the Harvest Meet, Kai's been chasing Magan, but she's proved to be a darn good runner, with suitors galore. So I make it my business to waltz over to the Pied Birds territory and offer training sessions to their younglings. After the sessions I schmooze with the fems and find out that Magan's looking for a stayer, a mate with determination and drive. I give this useful info to Kai, and tell him he has to up his game.

'How?'

'Easy, try talking to her. Visit the Pied Birds camp, go hunt with them, invite them to hunt in our territory, get friendly,

Kai. Don't make it too obvious you're after her, be casual, but determined.'

'Easy you say? Casual, but determined? That sounds pretty damn complicated to me, Bit.'

'Just get to know her, Kai. Find out what she wants, what she's looking for.'

'OK. I'll have a go.'

Then he sorta disappears and I don't catch sight of him for days on end. When I do collar him he tells me he's out at first light hunting conies, and building up a fine stock of skins.

'But I'm not neglecting my duties, Bit. I'm working on beautifying my dwell *and* working the land.'

'What's got into you? Why you doing all this?'

'Cos I did what you said. I made friends with some Pied Birds, and one of 'em's Magan's brother.'

'Ah, so what did he tell you?'

'That she needs a winter coat.'

'And *that's* why you're gathering coney skins.'

'Hunting, curing and stitching them into a toasty warm coat fit for the Snow Queen, herself.'

'When will you finish it?'

'I'm aiming for the end of September—Michaelmas. Say Bit …'

'You want help with the coat?'

'Not the coat, but I could do with a hand tarting up my dwell. See, if she says yes …'

'You want a spruced up dwell to present to her then and there?'

'Right.'

'Fine, me and Striker will make sure it's duded out well before Michaelmas.'

Time comes and after the Festival table's cleared Kai presents his lady love with a neat-sewn hooded coat made from the finest coney hides.

Magan moves into his well fitted, spruced up dwell that same night.

Another year passes slow and steady like the last, the peace interrupted only when Kai and Magan's giant boar goes on the rampage, giving the whole tribe a laugh as he tries to lasso the beast. Magan brought the sows with her when she settled with Kai: the young boar he trapped himself.

This winter shows signs of being long and hard. First snowfall came early, a bare month after the third anniversary of the exorcism. But the barns are full of grain and roots and we have a plentiful supply of salted, smoked and dried meat. Last summer was a good one and Kai's pig-herd well populated, so Blade and his Second, Striker, are confident the tribe will survive without undue hardship.

That first fall is slow to melt. Four weeks later the iron-hard ground is still patched with drifts, and the sky's an ominous shade of pewter, foretelling further downfalls.

Been out all day, with Striker and the ratlings, been playing hide and seek, chase the dog, and collecting hips and haws to add to our winter stock. Striker offered a prize for the biggest collection. It was like being born again, like I was given a second chance. It was *fun*.

If we'd had young of our own, it would have been just like this. But thinking so rakes up old hates, and that does no good to no one.

Tonight everyone's building bonfires, baking tubers and roots like in those far-remembered days when life was carefree. And now the snow's falling. It's so pretty and I realise that despite everything, I've never been happier.

'If Winter's here, then Spring's not far behind.' I chant, and the ratlings follow suit as we all march off to bed.

When I wake up the trees are snow sculptures, the dwells just lumpy shapes and Kai's knocking at our door, shouting 'Get up you pair of lazies, there's work to be done.'

God how I love this land. Roll on Spring.

31

The day the sky clears and I'm out hunting and I glim a strange wing-stiff bird flying through the tree-tops, dislodging powdered snow. The oddness piques: this bird ain't flapping. It glides closer and my heart judders. This *bird's* a fly-by.

I raise my bow and strike it down with a well-trained arrow, then stamp the pseudo life from its man-made body. This *thing* will transmit no further information. I steel myself to pick it up, yelling warning cries as I head for home.

Templeton's found us. Our peace is at an end.

From that day onward fly-by sightings become commonplace. We shoot all we can, and when the sightings taper off the youngers cheer. Us olders grit our teeth, knowing better.

Our peace and all our dreams are smashed when the blitzkrieg is launched. Heralded by a storm of giant fly-bys it escalates to bombing raids and massive trooper incursions. We fight, but there's no end to them. No matter how many we kill, how many fly-bys we down, they keep coming. We ambush, they flame our cover. We stand and fight and they raze the crop fields and stampede the beasts. Further and further back we're pushed, our numbers reduced with each passing day. Survivors of whittled clans join ours, but still our numbers dwindle.

We get news of other clans, none of it good, but all are determined to fight to the bitter end.

First it's just us Rats in their sights, but as time goes on and we keep fighting, Templeton's forces attack the very fabric of the Wilderness. Aircraft spray yellow powder from the clouds, coating grass and leaves, so that when rain falls the leaves perish and the grass shrivels into dust.

At the last, Striker leads a clan made up of Questers, Tree Creepers and Pied Birds. We run and fight, dropping in ones and twos till we number just thirteen souls. We've all lost loved ones, friends, not-friends and now, I'm down to the five I cherish most; Striker, Kai and One-Eye, Brown and Silk. My real and greatly treasured family.

We're on the run, harried by troopers 'chuted from giant air-carriers. We head for the hills, not stopping to rest, despite the absence of fly-bys. Out of sight doesn't mean out of mind—this new generation runs silent. All of us are worn to the bone. I can't remember when I last slept soft or ate a decent meal. I've seen game aplenty, but we can't afford the time to hunt.

Sky sounds! Strafe craft. Don't know how, but they spot us despite the tree cover. Blue spears drill down from the heavens, burning through leaf branch and flesh. Run, we gotta run. Nothing else we can do.

What's that? Fly-bys! Zipping in and out, targeting us Rats like game birds.

I get behind a tree take aim and shoot one down, a second fires an actinic lance, it hits my shoulder and I drop my trooper-got gun. I follow it, rolling downslope to deeper cover. Fly-by fires again, I feel the hit, but not the pain. I roll and keep rolling, landing in a gully. No firing, nothing in sight. Has it gone? Could be it's chasing fresh prey. I check for wounds. Shoulder's bad, arm's useless. Where's the second hit?

I soon find out. It took my Brown-girl.

The pain of losing her is worse than the shoulder burn, worse than when my dad died. She's gone. Oh dear God, she's gone.

I've lost my dearest little love.

Rage drowns sorrow, hate rises like magma in a vent, the pressure explodes and I rise and run, pounding and pushing and damning Templeton and his cohorts to eternal, scalding hell.

I sprawl over a bent-knee oak root, my tears flowing like a monsoon after drought. As the last hiccup dies I scrape through leaf litter to the cushion moss and cut a square with a knife thick with trooper blood. I lay her down curled like she's sleeping, nose to stubby tail, cover her with a blanket of moss and heap the leaves back over. I pat the mound and crawl away.

I hide in a brambles till it's quiet then start the hunt for Striker and the rest. I don't wait long enough; a trooper finds me first. He hits and kicks, but my grief at losing little love, my Brown-girl, numbs the physical pain, lost as I am in misery.

I come round, it's dark but I know from the smell I'm in a holding tank. Remembering Brown, I groan, and a voice says. 'Bit? that you?'

'Kai?'

'Yeah.'

'Striker?'

'Him and One Eye in another tank.'

'Silk?'

'Alive. I freed her soon as the troopers got me. She'll be fine in the wild.' His voice catches, he clears his throat and asks after Brown.

I can't answer, can't speak, the pain too great.

'It's all right, Bit. You don't need say.' He pauses, swallows then says, 'It's just the four of us, Bit. They're taking us straight to the labs.'

God, oh God, oh God. Will I ever get to see Striker again?

Templeton's won.

He robbed me of everything I hold dear, destroyed my hope of children, condemned me, my lover and my brothers to die in the labs, and he killed my Brown as surely as if he'd fired the bullet that took her life.

Now that he's exterminated the clan I called family, he'll wreak havoc on my beloved Wilderness.

Got no weapons, 'sept my burning hate and strength of mind. So I use that strength to curse the frinking monster till the carrier delivers us to the labs.

32

The labs: where all imagined horrors are made real.

Shut in a cell where the walls hold day forever captive, I'm never cold and never hot. A sonic chamber destroys my waste—without a frinking sound. One time I 'tempted to write my name in faeces on the floor, but the stuff just wouldn't stick. This place is a tomb of silence. First day I shouted till my throat burned dry, just to hear some narding noise. When I put an ear to a wall, there nothing—no crash of doors, no march of feet and no prisoners' cries. It's like time's frozen. Could be I'm the last soul left alive in a robot-run world.

I can't even see myself—the walls suck away my reflection. I'm a nobody, a nothing, a non-person.

Can't even alter stretches I wear. Like the sleep mat they don't rip or tear. 'Sides, if I take them off, I'm seen by invisible eyes and don't get fed till I put them back on. I tried marking the walls, kicking and scratching till my nails were ripped and ragged, yet as I look around there's no dents or scratches in this perfect place. It's like I don't exist, like I've never been.

There's a hidden place within one wall that delivers the food. Soon as the hatch opens I snatch the offering, never knowing when the next will come. Times it opens twice in fast succession, times I'm parched and fainting before food comes again.

I'm hungry now. Can't remember when it opened last. So I

watch that wall, and watch, and watch.

Soundless, the hatch springs open. I grab the tray, eating quick before it turns soft and melts. First time it happened I near died of thirst. Trays have paired depressions, one for water, one for gloop. Got to scoop the gloop first, using fingers 'cos they don't send spoons. No matter how thirsty I am the gloop gets eaten first. Tip the tray to drink the water and the gloop slides off, and slides into the crapper. Reckon the floor's made tilted. The taste? Hell it's just gloop, no flavour, no lumps, just grey goo that fills and never satisfies.

Time is skewed, can't tell how fast or slow it goes. Got no hair, they depilled it with a spray, but my skin's itching with new-grown stubble. The bruising on my body is faded yellow. How long do bruises take to fade? How long does depilled hair take to grow?

First thing they did when they got me to the labs was separate me from Kai. Later they slapped a med-patch on my shoulder, and hosed me with chem-scrub then cold-sprayed me to wash it off. Dry, they gave me greys to wear and stuck me in this box.

Musta put a load of calmer in that last batch of gloop. Been sleeping a lot lately, dreaming of the Wilderness where drinking-water *tastes*, where food is chewy and meat fills and strengthens. I dream of slitting troopers' throats, waking in this no-place clutching an invisible knife, wishing it real so I could cut my own damn throat.

Bin too calm, too passive. Time to wake up. Fight Bit fight, they want you sleepy. Remember the ludus, how the warm-ups energised?

I start the moves and promise myself a workout each time I wake, pretending that I'm training for the arena. I got no knife, but my body's a weapon I can hone. One time someone's gonna feel its edge.

Weeks, years or maybe only days pass, but I master the warm-ups, and body flowing smooth again, I begin the dance of death that Jehu taught, way back in Spartax's Hold. I aim each stab and thrust at an invisible med-tech. Stiffened fingers gouge an eye, a palm crunches a windpipe, an elbow smashes a tattooed face. Again and again I move through the katas, growing in strength and determination. Hate is an energizing fuel. They come for me, I'll be ready.

I'm working through a kata, toning the kill-muscles, when a noise shocks me from my trance. I stare at the wall as a door opens, revealing two bull troopers holding hi-vee rifles at the ready. The eye-cams on their tight white head protectors follow my every move. Troopers, yeah, but not garbed in city black or wilderness camouflage. These wear whites with the NOP sigil, a red squiggle, marked on breast and sleeve. The taller one, bearing two stripes on his shoulder, barks a command in a tight sharp voice while his dough-faced oppo grips his rifle tighter. Reckon he's met Rats before.

'You. Don't move, stand quiet. Move when told and not before. To the corridor, left and go with red. Move!'

What he says makes no sense, so I stay still. He frowns and sighs and shouts again, 'The red track on the floor, you stupid Rat bitch. It's your lucky day. You're next in line to make nice with the med-techs.' And he smiles. 'See that Jensen? I'd hazard a guess this Rat's met techs before.'

I've let them see my fear. Been alone too long, me. Blank the face, Bit, you're back in the shark tank.

As I step out of the box, I falter and dough-face prods me with the rifle. From silence, I'm in noise, from soft light I'm in glare, from nothing I'm in everything. The glare is eye-watering and there's a mass of snaking lines set into the floor; coloured, confusing lines. My stomach roils, I retch. Dough-face lifts his rifle.

'Stand down, trooper,' Two Bars orders. 'Hit her and she'll puke. And guess who gets to clean it up?'

He allows me some seconds and then orders me on. Okay so I have to go with red. There's a red line in the floor, just one among so many. Eyes down I follow it and gradually my guts settle and I can look around.

This place is hi-tech heaven. I'm walking through a curvy, glistening whiter than white tube. It's lit brighter than the brightest day, unlike the muted bloom of my cell box. The air is strangely perfumed, but if they're aiming for forest scents they've missed by a long mile. We walk and walk, following red. A blue line branches into another tube, then a yellow snakes away. We keep to red, not stopping till the walkway ends and we're faced with a massive open sided loop. This loop, like a giant wheel, is turning. It's not a round wheel, more of a long oval and there's a gap between it and the corridor.

'Get on,' Two Bars says. I don't understand. Then I see people standing on shelves inside the wheel. It's a hellish version of Spartax's lift. Two troopers pass downwards, they glance at me and look away. A few yards to my left the loop's rising upwards. Two shelves packed with gaunt-faced dweebs dressed like me in grey coveralls and accompanied by thug-faced troopers, float past and up. Prisoners. I scan but don't recognise.

A hand shoves me and I step forward onto a slow-moving shelf. Down and down we go, passing level after level. How big *is* this place? Pushed off, I end up next to a wall sign, LAB ONE. Two Bars presses the sign, a door slides open and dough-face shoves me into a room that stinks of sweat and fear.

Takes the two of 'em to strap me on a cold hard table, a table fitted with hollows for heels, buttocks and head. Can't see any black columns, no snaking cables, but this glossy white room's a torture chamber, sure enough.

A door swishes, the troopers come to attention, boots like gunshots. After a cold voice bids them leave, they march out. A door swishes shut, and I'm alone, 'cept for the sound of soft footsteps slip-sliding across the smooth floor, and the cloying smell that reminds me of what they sprayed on the bagged bodies before before they slung them in the burial pits.

The footsteps stop at my table, and I see two figures clad in scarlet stretches, faces marked with the snake and staff tattoo.

Unlike the grey-techs I met before these are hairless; lacking even lashes and brows. One is wrinkled old, the other smooth-faced young. Both wear an identical expression of scientific detachment. An expression I remember from years back, on schoolteachers dissecting frogs and rats.

I can't hold back the screams that fall unheeded into the black hole of their concentration. The young one reaches under the table and fixes a strip of strong tape across my mouth, his expression unchanged as he looks at me, the specimen, the guinea pig ... the lab-rat.

A nod from the old one sets the other spraying an acrid mist from a tube, and my prison greys are turned to dust. A second tube sucks the dust away. Next he clips wires to my skin.

I wait for the pain I know will follow, but nothing happens, 'cept they talk in dry, whispery voices. I hear *pain threshold* and *tolerance*, but the rest is indecipherable tech-speak.

Then something does happen, the table begins to vibrate. Spindly machines grow from the edges and the young tech pulls a stretchy cap over my skull. The cap sucks tight, dragging the skin of my face to my cheekbones. I feel the prick of needles on my scalp, suck in a deep breath and wait. I count to ten, nothing happens, and I relax ... into an eruption, a fountain of volcanic pain. Lights flash inside my head, sounds rage like whirling storm winds. I can't open my mouth, the gag has stiffened hard as plaster. I suffer this trapped agony, whimpering like a tortured dog, until the young red-tech speaks, using plain words that I can understand.

'Readings have stabilized, Master Verrier. Physically the subject is able to undergo the experimental process. Are we to begin?'

The elder nods, then wheezes gruffly. 'This brain is producing the required T waves, Mardell?'

'Yes Master Verrier, a very vibrant signal indeed,' replies Mardell.

'Proceed.'

33

'Preliminary phase or alpha, Master Verrier?' the young one asks.

'Subject appears strong. Go straight to alpha, it obtained the most vibrant response on the last subject. We will start on the basic level.'

I brace, expecting pain. It doesn't come. Verrier looks at Mardell, 'Ah, no distress. Notch up, Mardell.'

There's a click followed by a rising hum—and the onset of pain. Verrier hisses satisfaction. Another click increases the pain/hum. I whimper, then stop, unable to breathe, let alone scream.

'Remove the gag, Mardell. I need a record of any vocalization.'

The young tech rips off the gag but I'm silent as the darkness takes me.

I come around, pain-free and elsewhere: not in my cell and not in the lab. For one thing it's dark; the first true dark I've experienced since I was taken from the wilderness. For another I can smell real honest scents, not the artificial musk the red-techs favour or the faux stink of the corridor. What I smell is real: blossom, leaves and fruit.

I can't move, my limbs are strangely heavy. Straining tires me all too fast. Why am I suddenly so weak? What's in my right hand? I will my hand to move, to close about the thing—an oblong with a thin cable growing from one end and a raised circular button that moves at my touch. Nothing happens and I press again. A door opens in the wall opposite and light streams in, allowing me to see where I am. I'm in a bed with a metal frame. I turn my head, slowly because it takes much effort, and see a metal locker next to the bed and an armchair next to that. Footsteps alert me and I look towards the doorway and see a woman with blonde hair plaited round her head like a crown. She's wearing a loose white coat. She clicks a switch on the wall beside the door and in the pale new light that's born, she walks toward me. She smiles and her lively blue eyes crinkle and she hasn't a single tattoo imprinted on her face.

With a huge effort of will I raise my hand to hers, we touch and the buzzing agony bursts anew. Blackness swoops and carries me away.

I wake back in the torture room, the reek of false scent in my nose in vile contrast to that other place where the smells were as real as the scents of the Wilderness. At first, dizzy and nauseous, I hear only babble, but as the dizziness clears I make out tones, then words, but stay unmoving, unresponsive … listening.

'Something occurred, Master. I observed a spike.'

'As did I, Mardell. A spike I observed before Subject 300 expired.'

'This subject has been affected, Master. Shall I return it to its cell?'

'No. We need more data.'

'But …'

'You question me?'

'Never, Master. I merely wish to inform you of the subject's weakened status.'

'Duly noted. Now re-calibrate the instruments.'

'Re-calibrate?'

'Set all dials one quarter higher.'

'Yes, Master.'

'And update the comp-record of subject …?'

'306, Master. This is Subject is recorded as 306.'

I wait, holding still as the machine powers up. No matter what pain comes I will not acknowledge the hurt. The pain mounts and I submit, riding the pain, allowing it entry. We co-exist, the pain and I. Resistance dams the pain and allows the agony build. This time I will let the river run.

'Increase the delta wave,' Verrier orders.

The pain-river spates.

'Again,' he says, and the bore runs strong, carrying me away on a giant rolling wave …

… back to that *other* place, and the metal framed bed. This time it's day, not night and I can see much more. The locker next to the bed is painted metal, the vase upon it is full of real flowers—heady freesias, same as Dad used to buy for Mother. The easy chair next to the bed is upholstered in shiny blue. I widen my view and find a window, wide and oblong, the slatted blinds preventing me from seeing what's outside. I stare at those blinds, willing them to open until I hear a door opening. I expect the white coated fem, but it's a man; old, but not ancient like Verrier. He's sad-faced, grey haired and wearing the kind of clothes folk used to wear a long time past; wool trousers, a check jacket, shirt and tie.

This man walks to the bed, drags the chair closer and sits holding my hand. He talks, speaking like he's weary, but he's not looking at me, he's staring into the middle distance, like he's speaking into a void. First off, all he says is scribble, but the longer he speaks the more words I recognise. It's his accent that's mucking me up, and the way he uses old fashioned words in roundabout ways. But the longer he talks the more I understand.

Suddenly, like a switch clicking on, it all comes clear. He's telling me about some kid called Dor, or Dor-ee, and how she was a faddy eater. How one time she wouldn't eat anything white, not even ice-cream. He looks so sad that I squeeze his hand and he cuts the story short, staring at me like I've grown a second head. Then he shouts, 'Nurse!' and smiles like he's caught a prime boar with enough meat to feed a small tribe for a month. When I smile back he starts to cry. The door opens and a girl in a blue dress and white apron trots in. I smile at her anxious face and then she, the room and the crying man fade and shrink and I'm back in the lab staring at Verrier and his lupine grin.

'Quite a result,' he says. 'We must try again.'

'Now, Master?'

'Yes now. Speed is of the essence in this investigation.'

'Master, is it wise to subject this specimen to further experimentation? Perhaps one of the others?'

'Wise, Mardell? A *second* questioning? You hover on the very brink of insubordination. If there was time for delay I would not hesitate to replace you.'

'It's just that she … it … is failing fast. '

'What of it? The results are encouraging. Never have I seen such readings. No, we will pursue this line of enquiry with this very specimen. By all means give the data to the lesser technologists to see if they can duplicate the results with their own experimental animals, but it might be that this specimen is the key to the long-sought conundrum.'

'Do I inform the General?'

'You take much upon yourself, Mardell. It will be my express duty to inform our Leader when there is *conclusive* evidence. Until then you will contact no one, do you understand?'

'I hear you, Master Verrier.'

'Set the retro-chron to one thousand microns.'

Mardell's gasp prepares me and as the frequency escalates the pain roils over and through me, and I'm translated, transposed to that alter-world buried in the past, and find the slatted blinds raised and the oblong window uncovered. At last, I can see outdoors. At first it's enough to see the blue sky and watch the wind push clouds about but then I feel the need for more. It seems to me that this visit I feel stronger. Time to sit up. It takes much effort, but I do it, and resting on the pillow I see trees and grass for the first time since they dragged me from the Wilderness. When I can bear to look away, I study the room.

The floor, tiled in alternate red and cream squares, is clean and undamaged. Purple and pink phlox flowers fill the glass vase on the locker, and the smell is as I remember, real and sweet. A magpie flies past the window, followed by a second. I remember the rhyme my grandmother taught me, way back before the Crash. One for sorrow, two for joy, three for a girl and four for a boy, five for silver, six for gold and seven for a secret never told. I've see two. Good, I'm well overdue a jolt of joy.

The outside is strange, because all buildings I glim are undamaged, and they're not the grey prefabrications erected by the NOP. They're old style buildings built way back, with unbroken windows, weed-free roofs and solid crack-free walls. No ruins? *When* am I? How far back?

The door opens admitting a fem in whites, she of the plaited hair. She takes my wrist and I feel my pulse beat against her fingers. She shines a penlight in my eyes and she's talking all the while, slowly so I can understand the words.

'It's nice to see you awake again, and sitting up. A definite improvement. Physio for you tomorrow. You'll be up and about before you know it.'

She smiles at me and pats my cheek, 'Your father is so pleased at how you're doing, Dorrie. He'll be thrilled to know you're sitting up.'

She's waiting, expecting a smile, a word, but I can't think, can't do anything. She called me Dorrie. I was dumb Dor in the CRC. She calling me by my slave name? Those bloody red-techs. Twisting my mind, that's what they're doing. 'Why?' I scream, startling this dream fem like she was real. Her outline wavers and I'm sucked away, back … or forward? Into reality or nightmare?

Can't see anything, but I can hear voices and can smell the red-techs' tainted odour. One voice belongs to Verrier. 'Mardell,' he cries in a hoarse excited voice, 'look at this reading. No, here on the secondary retro-chron. I've seen this pattern before. It was recorded immediately before 298 burnt out.'

'I see it, Master.'

'Look closer. Note that it occurs immediately after the buildup of T waves as exhibited on the main retro-chron.'

'A malfunction?'

'No, absolutely not. The instrument was checked and after that last usage. There is no doubt in my mind that this is a highly significant development.'

In the pause that follows, I utter a groan, sneaking a peek through half open eyes, before relapsing into passivity. One quick glimpse was enough to show their changed expressions. Subject 306 has become human.

'She blinked, Master. She's conscious.'

Verrier clears his throat, 'Hm … you there. You, ah, experienced something, describe exactly what it was.'

I shut down, shut him out and let go of consciousness. You want me? Come get me, creech!

34

I wake to the almost forgotten smell of almonds and the feeling of warm hands massaging my leg. A white coated girl with skin as brown as Kai's, and with the same tightly curled hair, is the masseuse. I feel a growing warmth as the girl kneads one calf and then the other.

'Now we'll try something different,' she says. 'I'll push your leg while you push back, you need to make your muscles work harder to get stronger.'

She smiles encouragingly, 'That's it Dorrie, work with me, push … and push again. Rest … now again, push. Very good. Now the other leg. Better and better, at this rate we'll have you down in Physio working on the large equipment. You'll be walking before you know it.'

I stop responding, I'm not going to push or do anything if she keeps calling me that hateful name. I won't have her manipulating me like those red-techs.

She stops and looks at me. I stare back, defiant.

'What's the matter? Have I hurt you? Where? Try and tell me.'

My jaw is stiff, my tongue's wooden, I try for words but all that comes out is some kind of moaning drone. The girl presses a red switch on the wall, footsteps sound and two more women bustle in. One in a blue dress, white apron, the other's the fem with the crown of braids.

'Dr Morton. I believe Mrs Hart is trying to speak.'

The plait-haired fem takes my pulse and runs her hands over my body checking for hurt. I'm trying to speak, and the effort sends heart and pulse racing. My head's jerking, my lips are moving, but the med's approaching, something pointed, a needler in her hand.

'I'm going to sedate her. Nurse, hold her arm steady.'

The woman in the blue dress takes firm hold of my arm, but before the needle reaches me I scream, 'NO.' The needle halts and I hold very still. I say the word again, but quieter, 'No,' and the needle pulls away. Relief swamps me and I relax against the pillow. The nurse offers me a spouted cup and I taste clean water. All three watch me, like I'm a performing monkey.

'No sleep,' I whisper, 'and please don't call me that name.'

'Fine, Mrs Hart,' the med says evenly. 'We won't call you anything you don't want us to. Stay calm and there'll be no injections.'

Then she turns to the nurse and asks her to contact my family and tell them that I've started talking.

'What family?' I ask, mystified.

Kai's twin pats my hand, 'Don't worry about that now, it's early days. It'll all come back given time.'

The Med says, 'You need rest. I'll pop in later to see how you're doing.'

All three of them leave the room, and in the quiet comes a voice stealing into my befuddled mind, a voice that taunts and goads 'Shift your useless carcass DumbDor,' it says. 'Want the reclaimers to catch you slacking?'

I want to scream. I draw breath…

…and next blink, I'm back in my cell with my head about to burst and two red-techs watching me like cats with a spider. One bends down and injects a stinging coldness into my neck.

'Subject is failing. She should not have been transported here. Code Master Verrier, inform him we are returning the subject to Obs One. And alert Life Support.'

A blank …

… and I'm in a see-through cylinder, swathed in rustling foil. A face stares at me through the transparency—Verrier. His words come muffled but understandable. 'She's stable. Remove her from the pod and take her to Obs 2.'

Two techs lift me out.

Blank.

I'm on a trolley, attached to a small tick-bleep box, noising like it's in overdrive. Once inside the door marked Obs 2, they stand by me staring at the ticking, bleeping machine.

'Did Verrier trace the time line?'

The other shakes his head. 'Not to the exact source, but he's confident it's the same time-node each visit. He's named it Nidus Prime.'

'When is he sending her out again?'

'Soon as her phase stabilizes. He lost the others by moving too fast. He'll not risk losing this one.'

'She'll die, though, won't she?'

'Eventually. They all do. Brain dead every last one. But he has high hopes of this one lasting longer.'

'Anything transmitted?'

'Blurs, that's all. They are working on the images as we speak.'

'So we get hell from the senior techs till she's fit for another run?'

'I don't think so. Verrier seems to think success is in our grasp. He's trying the same phasing with the other three likely subjects until she's ready. I have to start the procedure with them, while you monitor this one closely.'

I want to stay awake and digest all I've heard but I can't prevent my eyes from closing.

35

Two days later, I'm weak as gnat's piss and they're wheeling me from Obs to the lab. Must be heading for another torture trip. Way I'm feeling this'll be my last. Do I care?

What I want is peace, and off this damnable wheel. Verrier pulls my plug? Fine by me. I begin breathing, regular, slow and deep. Relax … let go. It'll all be over soon.

Verrier pulls the stretch cap over my skull. Verrier with his sly smile and a new light in his dead eyes. Expecting big things, this turd. I want, no, *need* him disappointed. Pity I won't be alive to crow.

Pain attacks and I surrender willingly … and I'm in the other place. I feel a monumental disappointment that I'm still alive. How long will it be till Verrier drags me back?

The sad grey man sits in the easy-clean chair holding my hand. This time I understand every word he says, 'Dorrie girl, you're back again. I'm here, you're old dad's here. They said talk and I've talked myself hoarse and you're awake and the doctor said you spoke. I've prayed so very hard, and now my prayers have been answered.'

He's wrong, this old man, wrong or mad. My dad's dead, rotting under rocks and I'm *not* this Dorrie girl. Got to tell him, Bit, set him straight. Dream or no dream you got to say the truth.

I work my lips. They're looser than before and my throat's

not dry. 'Look,' I manage. 'A mistake.' I stop, it's come out wrong. Right words wrong voice—too light, higher in pitch. I cough and swallow to clear my throat. 'I'm not your Dorrie and my dad's long dead.' That's all I can say because those few words have wearied me beyond belief. But he's not listening, it's been a wasted effort. He holds my hand tight as a bandage and he's crying like he's chopped a pile of onions, sobbing *Dorrie* over and over like he's groove-stuck.

He presses the red knob, push, push, push. The doors open and the nurse arrives.

'Nurse,' he says. 'She's talking. Proper talk, not gabble. Tell the doctor my Dorrie's back.'

He's still holding my hand and sobbing when the plait-haired medic arrives.

'She's not making much sense Doctor. She's says her name isn't Dorrie and I'm not her father.' He lets go my hand and stands to face the fem. 'Is it normal,' he lowers his voice, 'or is she brain damaged?'

'Mr Osborne, don't worry.' The med's voice is calm and even. She walks him from the bed talking softly, yet I hear every word. 'Your daughter has been comatose since the accident. It's been six months, Mr Osborne. You must not expect her to snap back to full awareness like a switched on light bulb. Just as it's taken time for her to achieve consciousness, it will take time to recover her sense of self and for the past to surface. But I must inform you that very often some memories are never recovered and in some cases the resurgent personality is significantly changed.'

The man looks at me and back to the fem and all the joy's been wiped from his face.

'Mr Osborne, our medical staff is working on developing her motor skills. It is up to you and your family and friends to help recover her past. Perhaps visitors can bring in items that might jog memories—photos, music, favoured possessions. Most of all talk about her likes and dislikes, her hobbies and holidays. Try and fill in the blank spaces for her. Hopefully the memories will return fully, but there may always be significant gaps.

'I need to examine your daughter now, Mr Osborne.'

She comes to me and shines the little light in my eye, 'I'm going to take your pulse and blood pressure, Mrs Hart.' She's smiling as though she's really pleased with me and I risk a smile back.

'You're coming along splendidly, and as soon as you start eating I'll have the drip removed.'

I look and there's a narrow tube stuck in my arm, it doesn't hurt and as I read the med as honest I don't rip it out.

'I'll leave you with Mr Osborne for now, but nurse will pop in later to try you with something light.'

She and the nurse vanish, leaving behind the man who says he's my father. He's convincing, I'll say that for him. Obviously he believes what he says. He convinced the med, that's for sure. He seems harmless enough. I could take him, if I had to.

Now he's babbling on and I can't think. What happens if I wake up in the lab? Frink, what happens if I don't?

I focus on to my so called father as he tells me he's off to spread the good news. Telling me Gabe'll be in tonight. 'Don't worry, I won't visit, you two will have some catching up to do.'

And he's gone, leaving me wondering just who this Gabe might be. I'm tired, but scared to sleep in case I wake up confronted with red-techs. Another of the blue-dressed nurses comes in, hairbrush in hand. 'I'm Nurse Andrews, you can call me Nell. Nice to see you awake. Fancy your hair tidied?'

I smile and nod, she's cheerful and pleasant and completely tattoo-free. She brushes my hair with firm gentle strokes and 'Want to check the mirror?' she grins, holding up a looking glass. I look, but it's false … wrong. It's not me, it's some fem I've never seen before—round faced, mouse haired with slate blue eyes. It ain't me. My hair's black as coal dust. I got green eyes and a pointed face like a cat's. This woman in the mirror can't be me. I reach for the mirror, so does the mouse haired fem. I move, she moves. It's my arm … she is me. My guts twist, there's bile in my mouth. She … I … grimace and swallow.

'That's not me,' I shout in *her* voice. Takes a needle to shut me down.

36

I'm awake but I don't wanna open my peeps. What if I'm back in the lab? No wait, I smell freesias. No flowers there; I'm safe in the other place. Got to think, get things straight. First I gotta be glad I'm not in Verrier's grip. Anywhere's better than that. Hell, dead's better than that, don't matter a straw where *here* is. Second, if I want to be Bitch Singer of the Whip Tails, I'm damn well *gonna* be. This Dorrie stuff can wash down the crapper for all I care. I'm a Rat so I'll think Rat. I'll work on getting fit, avoid mirrors and leg it soon as poss. There, thinking done. End of.

Nell, the nurse, brings in a tray and tries to feed me. I'm not having that! I grab the spoon and manage to get half the bowl of pap inside me with just minor spillage. That fills me but if I'm getting out I'll need to build strength so I eat till the bowl's clean. I don't quibble over a spout-cup and drink the fruit drink without spilling a drop, then fall asleep before Nell removes the tray.

Awake again, I try to get my legs moving. I fail. Later, after another bowl of sticky sweet stuff, the nurse tells me it's visiting time. Minutes later in comes a big guy who hovers by the open door like he don't know whether to come in or run away.

'Dorrie?' he says and smiles a sickly smile. I look at him, and hell's bones he reminds me of someone. I'm frowning as he lets go of the door and slides to the bedside. Soon as he gets close it clicks. It's the eyes—one blue and one hazel. Frink, this guy's the dead spit of that lying treacherous nard who sold us to the troopers. He's Talon to a T. Jeez, now I got One-Eye whispering in my head, *Never trust a man with different coloured eyes.* Right, like I need telling?

Guy pats my arm, pulls another sick smile and perches on the bedside chair like he's sitting on a snoop mine.

'Um, sorry I wasn't here sooner, they rang, but it's a bad time at work right now. You know how it is. And there's Bronnie, of course. And, well, it's been so long. I mean, six months unconscious? They said ... I wasn't expecting ... they told me ... The words peter out and he sits drooping like a scolded cur. Reckon he'd like me to help him out. Fat chance, frinko!

I wait, he waits, then he tries another thick-lipped smile. Now he's fidgeting. Hell if I want info I'd better prime the pump. So I fake a sickly smile and it does the trick. He relaxes, slides further into the chair clutching the enormous bunch of tired no-scent blooms.

'They said you were on the mend. I'll bring Bron as soon as they say it's okay. Oh, and Babs says hi.'

The silence stretches so I throw him a bone. 'You're Gabe? Sorry, but I'm still fuzzy. Can't remember much at all. Meds say I'll need a lot of help to get things back. Might never get some stuff back. I can talk all right, can't move much and I remember very little.' I wonder how he's going to take this and I watch him close. He sighs. Frink's relieved!

'I'll help, Dor. Everyone will help. You'll be back on top form in no time.'

I'm watching him same as I'd watch a trooper snitch, marking every sideways glance, every greasy squirm. This guy is not relishing my recovery one smidge.

He stands, sticks the flowers on the bed and takes an envelope from his jacket pocket. 'Here,' he says, then nods, pats my hand and shuffles out without a backward glance.

I rip open the envelope, something I haven't done and haven't thought of doing for more years than I care to remember. It's a greeting card with Get Well Soon printed on over a field of unlikely flowers. Inside there's a hand written message, To my dearest wife, from Gabriel xx

So that's who he is. The guy who greeted me like I was a friend of his grandmother's is Dorrie's legal mate. Wasn't he supposed to love her? When the troopers tore me from Striker it was like my guts were slashed. It still hurts when I think of him and I still can't bear to think of Brown. And he, that frinking Gabe, just pats her hand, the wife who was dead made alive again.

The flowers he brought fall to the checkered floor and I burrow into the pillow crying for my lost ones.

37

Been crying a lot lately. Don't want to, can't seem to help it. Nurse Nell says it's natural, part of the process. She doesn't know I'm crying for a lost world—and a father who called me his dear Cass.

I've heard patients talk of coma dreams, of waking up convinced of things that relations say never happened. What if that's true of my memories? What if they're fantasies? What if I'm the one that's got things screwed. Perhaps I *am* this Dorrie, perhaps Verrier and the labs are coma dreams? Yeah, but what about Spartax? And what about the rest of my life, the Crash, the Rats, Striker and my Brown girl? All of it so very real.

The medics tell me feeling depressed is normal. They say I'll get over it. I think they're talking shit.

Today a cheerful med informed me that I was to start physiotherapy down in rehab. Gonna do something called occupational therapy, stuff like painting—creative work to get my hands and mind limber. Perhaps, with a limber mind I'll be able to separate truth from make-believe.

Dorrie's dad pops in most mornings, says he'll leave the evenings for Gabe. I don't say I've only seen him the once. Wouldn't want Gabe getting the idea I want more of him. Today her father noticed I was having a hard time calling him Dad.

'I don't mind what you call me,' he says. 'Call me Henry if it's easier.'

'I'd like that, and for some reason I don't see myself as Dorrie any more. It's like I'm a new person and need a new name.'

'O …kay. You want a film star name?'

'No. I thought, Bit.'

'Bit? Like your Gran?'

I must have shown my puzzlement, so he explained. 'My mother was a tiny woman. Five foot and one half inch tall she was, and never let anyone forget that last half inch. My dad was a brawny six footer. Your gran's born name was Elizabeth but Dad called her his Little Bit. So all the family called her Bit or Bitty. It's good Dor … Bit, things are coming back. Told you they would. Everything is in there, we just have to winkle it out. Right then, love, Bit it is.'

He was so happy he near skipped from the room, leaving me feeling bad for spieling the lie. This visit I found out who Bronnie is—Gabe and Dorrie's three year old daughter. And she's coming to visit this afternoon.

So, I sit in the shiny blue chair that the nurses sponge clean every morning, staring at the door, feeling nervous. It was hard enough lying to the old guy, how can I deceive a child? She'll trip in expecting her mother and she'll get … me. She's bound to know I'm fake. Young creatures have a nose for the truth. She'll yell, and then what?

Wish my legs are strong enough to run me away, but even a week of therapy can't work miracles. Sharon, the curly haired Kai look-alike who finds it easier than the plait-haired med to call me Bit, says I'm the most determined patient she's ever had. Wonder what she'll say when I up sticks and walk away?

Frinking hell, they're here. Gabe's carrying the child, her head's tucked into his neck. Smile Bit, she'll want to see a smile. She's a little thing with hair the same light chocolate as Brown's. And when she lifts her head from her father's shoulder her eyes are as bright and dark as a ferret's, and for a moment grief strikes me afresh.

Gabe puts her down. She doesn't make a move towards me, just lets go his hand and keeps her eyes to the floor. I've never had much to do with little children, the venners were in charge of the kits. In the Wilderness I taught fighting and tracking to the older ratlings, didn't deal with tinies one-on-one. Caring for Brown taught me a trick or two, disinterest and distraction being chief among them.

I look away, making no overt moves and in a little while I reach into my dressing gown pocket and take out the small woodcarving I've been working on in therapy. A figure that I fondly imagine to be a likeness of Brown. I place it carefully on the wooden arm of the chair and smooth it with a finger. I catch a movement as the child takes a half step closer. I risk a look and she's staring at it. I tempt her with a fleeting smile and push the model towards her. She takes a step closer, I hold my breath … and frinko ruins the moment by snatching her up and dumping her on my lap. Course, she starts skritching, don't she? Before I lift a hand or say a word, her stupid father grabs her back.

'It's too soon,' he bleats. 'I said it was too soon. I shouldn't have brought her. Can't you see how upset she is? I'm taking her home.' And they're out through the door like a pair of scared stoats, leaving me cursing all gotch-eyed frinks.

I stow the carving in my pocket, ready for next time.

They moved me yesterday, to a six-bedder. Dunno how long I been in this world, but I'll do all I can to stay away from Verrier's torture labs. I'm weary, sick and worn to the bone, waking each morning terrified I'm back there. The best sound ever is the squeaky rattle of the early morning tea trolley and the sleepy groans of waking patients. All this tells me I'm safe. I've come to love that old trolley and the snoring oldster in the next bed. Can't get enough of the smell of flowers, piss and vomit that tells me I'm still *here*.

I know Striker and Brown are gone, even if Verrier drags me

back to that other place they won't be there. I've faced it—they're dead, like One-Eye and Kai. Okay, so I got vengeance in my heart, but how the hell do I strike back? Verrier's *there,* I'm *here.* How come anger bites deeper than sorrow?

I've decided that from now on I'm putting a rush on getting fit. No more time wasting. First task is to get all the info I can on this new world, ready for the breakout. Gotta lock away the memories; lock 'em in a box and hide the box deep down. Someday I'll open it and mourn for what I've lost. But from now on this Rat's only mission is escape.

I don't see much of Gabe—just as well. Guy reminds me more and more of Talon—same whine, same smile and same damnable eyes. The less I see of him the better. The oldster in the next bed thinks he's great and tells me I'm lucky to have such a 'lovely fella'. Even Nurse Nell blushes when he looks at her. I can't figure it out. Put it like this, if he was Rat I'd vote for culling.

I go to rehab regular, sometimes with therapist Sharon, sometimes wheeling myself. They tell me it won't be long before I'm fit to leave. Yeah, but I'll need money to run, and some idea where to run to. Could be I'll have to squat in Gabe's till I find out how this world spins. Once I cut loose I'll be on my own in no man's land. But I'll survive. Hell I'm Rat, ain't I?

I'm getting a haircut today, getting back to ragged short. I may be stuck with nondescript brown but the style'll be mine. The body's taller than I'm used to, but that's fine. It's the previous owner's flab that gets my goat. Just have to keep clear of mirrors till I work it off.

As well as Sharon's exercises I'm doing first level martial katas I learned in the ludus. I got all the moves in my head, and I'm aiming for arena standard. Never know when a killing blow will come in useful in a strange neighbourhood. My biggest worry is that folk will notice I'm a lefty now, but so far no-one's made mention.

Henry tells me tales of Dorrie's childhood and her growing up that I squirrel away against time of need. Not that I expect to be around for long. Lucky I'm supposed to have gaps in my memory, so if I do get mixed up folk are keen to help. But it makes me feel guilty, hearing him talk, because he loved his Dorrie, still does, but she's not here, it's just me, pretending.

I like Henry, he's a good sort, bringing Bronwen to see me when he collects her from nursery school. First time he brought her I gave her the wooden ferret. Didn't actually hand it to her, just perched it on the chair arm like before, and started talking to Henry. She was interested, edging forward for a better look, but still holding Henry's hand, so I pushed the ferret towards her. 'Take it,' I said. 'I made it for you.'

She looked at Henry, who nodded, and then she took the ferret gently, climbed onto his lap and sat stroking the wooden beast it until it was time to go. As they left, she turned and smiled at me. I smiled back though I felt like crying for this motherless kit.

I don't know if Henry tells Gabe what we talk about or how me and Bron are getting on. I don't ask. But she's definitely getting used to me, and I know she loves the carved ferret, it's always with her. Henry says she even takes it to bed. Bron's much calmer with Henry, Gabe sets her on edge. She hasn't spoken to me yet. She's always quiet and watchful when she visits, only sound I've heard her make was that scritch when Gabe dumped her on my lap.

I found out who Babs is—Gabe's mother who helps with Bronwen. Haven't met her yet and I get the impression from Henry that I shouldn't be too upset 'bout that, though he's quick to point out that she's very good with Bronwen.

I think of the child, nights when it's hard to sleep. She puts me in mind of a small frightened animal. Henry told me she hasn't spoken since Dorrie's accident and that's why she goes to special nursery class every day. The one that Gabe won't talk about. She can't or won't speak, she's as mute as I was in the CRC. Maybe that's why I'm drawn to her. But I *chose* to be mute as a way of fighting back, and though the medics say Bronwen's suffering some kind of shock, I wonder if there's deeper reason why such a bright-seeming child refuses to speak?

Got to admit that since I gave her the little carving she's been easier with me. Soon as she and Henry walk in she's on my lap and I'm telling her the old stories my mother told to me. I carved another toy for her, finished it at this morning's OT session by sanding it smooth as silk. It's a figure, a Rat, as much like Striker as I can get. He's got spiked hair and Wilderness clothes—the whole deal, patched leathers, thick-soled trooper boots, and knives, lots of knives. It's so real it hurts. No one in the therapy class knows what to make of it. I told them it was out of a book.

I put it on the chair arm, like before. I made it bigger than the ferret because I wanted more detail. Can't wait to see what she thinks of it.

They're here, and as Bron walks in her eyes go straight to the carving. As Henry fetches a stacking chair, she skips to the bed and stands there, fingers twitching like she's itching to grab it.

'Go ahead,' I say, quiet like. 'It's yours.'

She looks at me and smiles as she takes gentle hold of the manikin. She studies it, turning it end on end, feeling it carefully with her fingers, then she points and looks at me.

'Knives, in case he has to fight,' I say. 'She points again. 'He glues his hair into spikes. Why? Because he wants to. And those are trooper boots, strong made for walking on rough ground.'

Now she staring at me so hard and I know exactly what she wants, but can I say it out loud? 'His name?' I pause, fighting tears, then swallow and say for the first time in this world, 'Striker. His name's Striker.' She grins at me and hops to Henry to show the treasure. He looks at me, his pleasure plain.

'It's lovely. Bronwen loves it, don't you, sunshine?'

She nods and skips back to me, sits on the floor by my chair and I watch with tears in my eyes, thinking of long-past times, till Henry breaks my train of thought.

'That crash must have shaken some new talent into you, Bit. You've never done anything like this before.'

'Perhaps I never tried, Henry. Never gave it a go. Now I'm back, I'm trying everything. Life's too short to hold back; no more holding back for me.'

'That's my girl. Go for it. Life *is* too short. Have they talked to you about coming home?'

'I'm waiting on the chief med. If he says I'm fit then I'm off.'

'Why don't you come to mine for a few days till you get used to things? I've got the room.'

'Thanks, but Gabe says he'll take time off work to settle me in and I want to get used to being home again. You'll visit, won't you? Please. I think Bron'll find it strange having me home.'

'Be in every day, if it's OK by Gabe. And don't you start worrying over Bron. I think you and her will settle fine.'

Don't know what to think of that, since I'm set on skipping out. I've got to get free, haven't I?

Next thing Bron's on my lap and I'm telling her stories of Striker and the pack. When it's time for her to go, she actually kisses me goodbye.

But it's not me she's kissing, is it? It's her mother. It's Dorrie.

38

I'm going home. Chief med told me a coupla minutes ago. I phoned Henry and he's phoning Gabe to say he'll pick me up and stay with me till he gets home from work. Nurse Nell helped me pack my case and I've said my goodbyes, now I'm waiting. They'll want me back for check-ups, but from now on I'm on my own.

Two weeks on and I'm still living with Gabe. Getting free ain't as easy as I thought. True there are big townships and real living cities to get lost in, but there's no Wilderness and no Rats. And you need stuff: documents, idents, tickets, passes. Wads of paper, yeah, but way up top of the list is *money*. And they got a police force here.

A Rat hunts, scavenges, steals; in a CRC they feed you; in the gamers compound you eat like kings. Here? Here you buy. No money; no food. Steal and they lock you away. So I need money and that's a tad difficult with a husband like Gabe, seeing how the guy's a stone-creeping slime-worm. Since I came home he's not given me a penny piece of my own. He's Chief Rat, in charge of money, food, every frinking thing. Turns out I'm not married to the man but to the house. I'm the housewife, he tells me. Oh joy! I get to cook, clean, wash clothes, and soon as I'm real fit I get to shop for his listings, paying with the coins he hands me, taking care to give full account of the coin spent.

Gave me a tour soon as he stepped inside the door, late in from work. And it's *here's the washing machine, dear, and there's the cooker, and look, wifey dearest, here's the do-anything iron.* Only the frinking thing doesn't do it all by its little self, it somehow needs a woman to push it along. It's to make life easier, he says. But there must be something wrong with my poor injured brain, as somehow no matter how hard I try, the washer won't work, the oven spoils the food and that ditzy little iron? Seems that if it's dropped repeatedly on the floor it doesn't work at all. Funny that.

He's paying a woman to service the house, till I 'get back to normal.' Hope he's got long pockets!

Babs visits, often. Dear, interfering, Gabe-is-God Babs. Only good thing about her is that house cleaning is the reason for her existence and ironing is her passion. With our new better-than-anyone-else's iron, she's a she-cat on heat.

She's here today, standing at the ironing board carping like always.

'In my day you ironed everything, from sheets to dusters and you washed clothes by hand. You youngsters don't know you're born. And some,' she grates, pinning me with one of her acid looks, 'some don't know a good man when they've got one.'

I stare back, my CRC face on, while she rolls it all out. 'You don't know how my boy suffered when you were in that hospital.' Not half as much as his wife, I say to myself as she folds the shirt like she's packaging it for sale. 'What he deserves is a helpmeet, a wife who'll minister to his needs.' I look away holding down the urge to tell this woman just exactly what 'her boy' deserves.

It's time for Bronnie to come home and that's another worry, because since I've taken residence she's decided I'm the best thing since chocolate pudding. She clings to me, bedtimes, desperate for me to stay with her. Being honest she's the main reason I'm still here. It's not the money, hell, I'm as good a thief as the next.

It's her—she's my new Brown. And there's something else. Got to admit that if I move on I'll miss Henry. I know it's wrong but I envy Dorrie growing up with a dad like him.

I'm up before the birds most mornings, working out. I'm improving, not arena ready but well on the way. Each evening before Gabe gets home stressed and snippy, I practice outdoors while Bron watches. Babs obviously thinks I'm screwy and she did try keeping Bron from watching. Only tried the once, though. Bron's scritching fit sent her running like the kid had caught my madness.

I've also gone through Gabe's store of newspapers and magazines. First thing I discovered was the date. Back … there, I'd no need of dates, but I remember when I was born, Feb 13 2021. Never forget that do you? And the dates on Gabe's papers say May 1962. I also found out something real troubling. Before the Crash I went to school, learned history, learned my kings and queens. I remember the celebrations when William V was crowned. But here there's no King Billy, no Prince George, no princesses. *Here* there's a Protector. This ain't Templeton's New Britain, *this* is the Republican Protectorate of Great Britain and United Ireland, under the guardianship of Protector Elisha Cromwell, a thin, beak nosed man with cold, dead eyes.

This ain't my world or my timeline, but as long as I'm out of Verrier's clutches who cares?

Another thing I learned was Bronwen was in the car when her mother crashed, and her mother was driving too fast.

'Coo-ee, it's us.' Henry peeps around the back door and shrugs towards Babs, and then Bron barges in to hug me. She obviously had a good time at nursery.

'Say Bit. Want to walk with us tomorrow? It's not far.' Bron starts jumping on the spot and smiling wide. 'Bron wants you to come, don't you Bronnie?'

'All right, I'll come. Long as you promise not to walk too fast.'

'Go on with you, you're fitter than I've ever seen you.' He's smiling, ignoring Babs who mutters about asking Gabe first.

'Has that husband of yours said anything about getting you some new clothes, now you're trimming up?'

'Clothes cost, you know,' Babs says loud, so we can't talk over her. 'Why don't you just take them in? You used to be handy with the sewing machine. I'm sure Gabe would like that.'

'Why don't I walk the street naked? That'll save a few pennies,' I retort, sick of biting my tongue.

'Well, really! And in front of the child. I'll not stay listening to such … such …' Word-stricken she grabs her cardigan and bustles out the back door, leaving the iron on and Henry and Bronwen giggling like loons. I'm glad Gabe's away on a course. There'll be no snitching till he's back.

Today I'm waiting for Henry. Bron's skipping with excitement and I'm ready dressed and looking forward to the outing. Soon as he knocks, we'll be off.

8.45 prompt, he arrives. Soon as he sees me he grins.

'You look all bright eyed and bushy tailed, Bit. And you look just like a fashion model.'

'Aw, thanks Henry, been ferreting in the wardrobe. So I'm presentable?'

'Fit to meet the Protector.'

Last night I'd gone hunting wearables and found this dark brown skirt. It's far too big, but belted tight and topped with a floaty blouse I look presentable, if not the fashion model Henry makes out. I'm wearing a pair of lace-ups that fit, if not perfectly, then a damn sight better than some I wore in my other life.

We walk down the street with Bron hanging between us, alternately skipping and being lifted over pavement cracks. She's got the wooden Striker and the ferret in the see-through bag she takes to school. I scry the houses, still shocked to see them undamaged, lived in and with neat gardens, not overgrown jungles. Henry nods to passersby who smile back; everything is so altered. As we get closer to the school I walk unafraid among fems with children, and keep from staring at a bus stop with folk waiting to ride to the shops or work. It's hard not to stare, it doesn't feel normal, it feels like I'm in the dreamland of Happyville, where folk don't starve, and children play without fear of troopers and sky-attacks.

Time I reach the school I'm wrung out. I want to run and hide, it's all too much to take. But at the classroom door Bronnie holds my hand and drags me inside. She hangs her bag on a peg with a butterfly stenciled above it, then hops off to play in the sand, leaving me. God, what do I do now? Next thing, a fem walks over, holding out her hand. I feel like running, but I don't give in.

'Mrs Hart, I presume?' The fem says. 'So good to meet you. I'm Kitty Brandon, Bronwen's teacher, and I'm pleased to see you looking so well. I hear you are making a splendid recovery.'

I got to speak?

'Y … yes,' I stutter. 'Thank you, I'm fine, now.'

She waits, like she's expecting more, so I carry on. 'Ah, and how's Bron doing?'

'Well, Mrs Hart, I expect Mr Hart has told you how worried we've been about her. I've been working closely with Mary Clarke, the peripatetic speech therapist, and though progress is slow we've all remarked how much happier she's been since your return home.'

'Miss Brandon?'

'Mrs, actually.'

'Right.' I take a breath and the words come. 'Mrs Brandon, is there anything I should be doing to help things along?'

'Just the usual, you know talk to her, tell stories, sing and recite rhymes. Encourage her to join in. I think that now you're home again she'll want to use words again.'

My heart drops. 'You think it's important for me to be with her?'

'Mrs Hart, I believe it's vital.'

Bron's happily playing so I walk back with Henry. Somehow

I don't feel like making conversation.

'Want to pick her up with me at lunchtime?'

'Fine,' I say, but it isn't. Seems like I'm more important to Bron than I thought.

Later when we pick her up, we walk to Henry's house, it's in the opposite direction from Gabe's and after a glass of squash I say I'll walk home with Bron.

'On your own?'

'No, there's the two of us.'

'Can you remember ...?'

I reel off the memorised rights and lefts, which surprises him. But he doesn't know how Rats are trained. Of course we get back okay, to find a freaked out Babs has informed the police we're missing. When all that's settled I get a feeling that dear Gabe is not gonna be best pleased.

He'll be late home again, so I take Bron up to bed, putting the school bag on the table by the door. I kiss her good night and she pulls my sleeve, I offer her a drink and she shakes her head. A biscuit? No. What then? She frowns, I shrug, she pouts and I lift my hands. What? She frowns harder then signs angrily, '*Animal, want.*' I'm staring in amazement and she signs again, slower. Clawed hands, animal. Hand brushing chest, want. Shocked, I retrieve Brown and Striker from the satchel, and with her ferret in hand and Striker under the pillow she snuggles down and closes her eyes.

I walk downstairs wondering how come she signs. Then I get it. Bron's a watcher, been watching me since I walked into the house. Sometimes when I talk I sign. An old habit, hard to break. And when I tell stories of Brown and Striker I sign like a Rat telling a campfire tale. She's picked it up. She might not vocalise, but the child's as bright as a new-minted coin.

I sit on the settee to think, to decide. I want, need, *ache* to go live my own life, not Dorrie's. But how can I just up and leave Bron?

I'm drinking a cup of tea when Gabe bursts in like a bull

trooper on a raid. No need to ask who juded me out.

'How dare you worry my mother like that,' he storms. 'Who said you could go swanning off without a by your leave and cause so much trouble?'

He thinks he's ticked off, well I'll show him ticked. I stand and face him, 'So, who boiled your goat?'

But he just rolls on. 'Where did you go?'

'You know very well where I went. I took Bron to school. Why the fuss?'

'I told you to wait until my day off and we'd go together.'

'So?'

'So why did you walk back on your own?'

'I managed fine. Henry showed me the way. Look, I crossed on the crossings, I held Bronwen's hand. We. Were. Fine.'

'But I TOLD you.'

What's with this loon? Look at him, red faced, puffed and pouting like a thwarted kit. Now he's drawing back his hand, he's only going to hit me. Yeah? I fling up my right arm, ward the blow and jab a left-handed finger punch into his unprotected lardy gut. Nice. He goes down and I'm tempted to put the boot in, but it's not necessary. I just walk away, stepping carefully on his outstretched hand. The crack of bones stirs memories.

Leaving him to his pain I join Bronnie and her wooden friends in bed.

39

I get up to fix breakfast half expecting Gabe to be curled up on the carpet, but he's gone and so's his car. Trouble postponed, I drain him from my mind and concentrate on expanding my horizons. Breakfast eaten I turn to the child. 'Right Bron, for starters it's Saturday so you can take me to the shops.'

She's up and at the door before I can say go. I'm about to step outside when a thought strikes. 'Hold on. We can't go, your father hasn't given me a key.'

She's not fazed in the slightest, running to the cupboard under the stairs and taking a key off a hook and giving it to me. I sweep her up in a hug, 'You're a good clever girl. Come on, let's go.' I slam the door, pocket the key and we're off down the street.

Got no money, but I don't hanker to spend, I just want to do a recce and check out the neighbourhood. I used to go to the shops with my mother, way back, once upon a time before the world crashed. When was that? What was I, eight, ten? I try and count the years passed, and fail. How long I was in the labs—months? A year? More? Enough to skew all sense of time, that's for sure.

Bron leads me to the half dozen shops in the road that branches off ours. The first one's a newspaper-cum-tobacconist and Bron makes sure to point out her favourite sweets displayed in the dusty window, partially obscured by cigarette and tobacco come-ons. There's also a cork board fixed to the door with a host of For Sale notes tacked on. Bron eyes the sweets while I read the notes. A pink one stands out, and it reads 'French lessons given. Strict teacher, punishment guaranteed.'

A tiny woman in a wrap-around pinafore, her hair straggling from a wispy bun, opens the door and smiles.

'Mrs Hart, it is you. I recognised the little girl, but I wasn't sure it was you till you were right up close.' Her eyes move from my shorn hair to my tightly belted coat. 'Come you in and say hello to Billy. He's been asking Mr Hart about you regular, he has.' She takes a breath then yells, 'Billy! It's Mrs Hart.'

A voice from inside calls welcome, and Bron takes my hand and drags me into the shop where an equally short but extremely stout man with greased down, iron-grey hair waits to greet us.

'Mrs Hart,' he beams. 'Does my soul good to see you up and about, it does. Here, have these chocolates, you and the little girl. Help put some meat back on your bones.'

The tiny woman, his wife I guess, titters. 'Oh Billy! Don't you listen to him, dear; you're looking lovely. I bet you're taking good care of your mam, aren't you Bronwen?'

Bron smiles broadly and I thank them for the box of chocolates and leave the shop. We walk slowly past a grocer's and get a wave from the ancient behind a counter piled with tins and packets, then pass a window packed with vegetables, and after that a busy and rather smelly butcher shop. Next comes a shop window painted with a sign that says Bank Street Library and Bronwen pulls me into a long narrow room stuffed with tall shelves filled with books.

Bron waves at the smiling woman behind a counter to my left, before leading me to the children's section; a padded bench, tiny chairs and a low red table. She points at me, then points at the bench and I do as I'm told and sit. She fetches a book and waits for me to read the story about a boy and girl and their pet dog. When that's done she hands me a second, same two kids get a new kitten, this time. The tale tells how the cat and dog make friends.

'Right, Bronwen Hart, my turn. You choose a picture book while I go find something for *me* to read.'

I spot a shelf of atlases and travel books. I choose an atlas of the Protectorate and a book about Bridgend, where we live. I need to know everything about the town, and how best to get away from it. The author's name gives me a jolt, it's by a W.H. Temple, my father's name. I sit on a small chair by Bron, till the shakes settle. Then while Bron looks at a book on how to care for pet rabbits I skim through Bridgend and take a quick look at the atlas. I'll come back another day and read some more. Books returned it's time to go. Bron puts her hand in mine, smiling a big open smile and it's like I've been punched in the guts. It's Brown all over again, this child has wriggled into the ferret shaped space I thought forever empty. I've got no choice. I go, she comes with me.

Lost in thought I'm standing looking into the next shop some time before I realise what it is. Name on the window says Peter's Pets and there's a warm pungent smell escaping through the open door. Bron's tugging my hand and pleading silently to go in. We do. Inside she inspects every cage and every tank, staring in turn at mice, rabbits, kittens and gerbils. The huge red-green bird on a perch by the counter catches my eye.

'Interested in the parrot, luv?' says a longhaired kid wearing tight jeans and a grubby body-hugging T-shirt. He looks at me through half-closed lids.

'Just looking,' I say remembering the formula from when my mother and I went shopping all those years ago.

I look for Bron and she's not by the gerbil cage. A spark of fear ignites, but when I see her crouched down by a floor level cage, I go see what's caught her eye.

It's a golden ferret, curled up at the rear of a too-small cage. Nausea stirs at seeing it trapped, remembering how Brown ran free. I chirp and it raises a golden head, watching with shiny dark eyes. The louche counter boy swaggers up.

'So it's ferrets you like, eh darling?'

I get up slowly, stare at him till his shoulders settle, 'How long has it been in that cage?'

He steps back, warned by my tone.

'Look, I just work here. I feed 'em and sell 'em. Any complaints you take to my boss. It's not on my back.'

'It needs exercise. When do you let it out?'

'You joking, dar … Missus. Ferrets bite. Got wicked teeth, yeah? Let it out? 'Struth! You want to exercise it?' he sneers. 'Buy it. It's a steal at three quid.'

Penniless, I turn from the caged animal, take Bronwen's hand and lead the crying tot out of the shop, fighting the desire to steal the ferret and stuff counter boy in a cage.

'We can't buy it,' I say as we plod along. 'I don't have the money.' She tugs my hand to make me look at her, then signs *animal* and *sad*.

She's still crying when we get back to the house. Babs has arrived and is ironing, quacking on and on about nothing till I'm ready to scrag her.

'I'm giving Bron a bath,' I tell her, and as we climb the stairs I hear her muttering about bathing children too much isn't good for them, it washes the oils out of their skin. Yeah, save it for someone who'll listen, Babs. Save it for your precious Gabe.

Bronnie doesn't play with her ducks or the floating turtle, all the time signing *animal* and *sad*. 'I know,' I say, 'and I'm thinking.' But it's not just money we need, I got to think about Gabe. Fat chance he'll allow me something I actually want.

'Say, kid, how about we stroll round to Henry's?'

Course Babs starts wittering when I say where we're going. 'What if Gabe rings? What will I tell him?'

I just look at her the same way I looked at counter boy and, like him, she backs off.

Bron's not crying when we get to her grandfather's, but he sees something's up and tells her to take her squash and biscuits into the garden and talk to Jimmy next-door.

I spill the tale and end up saying how much she cried. 'She

wants that ferret, Henry. But it costs three pounds and that's before the hutch, the run, the food. And ferrets need proper care, you can't just stick it in a cage like a … like a lab rat.'

'Yes, but it'll be you doing most of the looking after, won't it? How do you feel about that?'

'Me? I'd love it.'

'Changed your tune, haven't you? Furry animals used to scare you rigid. Remember Richard's rat nipping you? You wouldn't even pet Aunt Rosie's cat.'

'That was then and this is now. I'd love a pet, problem is I'm pretty sure Gabe won't.'

'That's not a problem. I'll keep it here. There's the shed, it's weatherproof. I can knock up a cage and we can get a book on the right way to look after the creature. See? A spot of woodwork will give me something to do, and caring for an animal will do our Bronnie a power of good.'

For the first time, I hug Henry close and when I let him go he wipes his eyes. 'Come on then,' he says gruffly. 'No time like the present. Bronwen! Want to go shopping for a ferret?'

By tea time we've cleared the shed of junk. Some into the refuse bin, the rest stacked along the garage walls. 'I'll get some shelves for the garage, been meaning to for a while, now I've got cause to.' Henry's happy, I can tell, happier than I've seen him. This project is as good for him as Bronnie. I gave her the sign for ferret and she's using it all the time.

'Okay. Now the shed's clear you have to brush it clean. Bronnie, leave that ferret alone and help your mother while I sort out some timber.

In the end it's getting dark and there's no time to 'knock up' a new hutch, so we leave the ferret in the small cage we bought at the pet shop.

'See Bron,' I say. 'We'll leave the cage door open and the shed door shut. The ferret can wander where it wants. It has fresh bedding, we've fed and watered it and tomorrow we'll help Grandpa design and build the best house ever for … Wow,

Henry! We haven't named it.'

'Naming an animal shouldn't be a rush job, should it Bron? What say we watch and study for a bit? I'm betting if we do that the perfect name is going to pop right up.'

That satisfies her and me. 'Time to go,' I say. Her face drops. 'Okay a few extra minutes. How about you and me go in the shed and play with your new friend?'

Ferret's curled up small, but as we sit quiet on the clean floor by the cage, it looks up from its nest. I hold my breath and offer a sliver of Henry's Sunday joint. Ferret's nose twitches and I hold the offering steady. Bron only gives a small gasp as the meat's investigated and accepted. Bron holds out her piece and that's taken too, then with a pounce the creature's on Bron's lap. As she touches the golden fur, her face lights up and she smiles the biggest smile ever. Hell, it's *worth* the hassle.

We sit till my legs start to go numb, 'Time to go,' I whisper and like an old pro she eases the ferret into its cage and we tiptoe out, two jet eyes watching as we go. Shed locked we say goodnight to a glowing Henry and troop home to face … whatever's waiting.

40

The house is dark when we get back, no Babs, no Gabe. It says a lot that Bron doesn't sign after them. I rustle up beans on toast, and after a quick wash, it's bed for Bronwen. She's asleep before I switch off the light, carved ferret in hand. I tiptoe back to the bed, and take hold of it, meaning to put it on the bedside table, but she grips tighter and opens her eyes. 'No,' she says. Hell flames, Bronnie spoke!

I go downstairs light footed and light hearted: she's turned the corner, she's on the up. I feel good, as good as when I passed Trial and gained my name, and punch the air. Bitch Singer rules!

Instant deflation comes when I catch the sound of a car turning into the drive. Gabe. Headlights flicker across the front window. Yeah, frinko's back.

I'm leaning on the newel post when he comes in. He shuts the front door firmly and looks at me, squint eyed and tight lipped. 'You, *my lady*, have gone too far. They told me to expect personality changes, but that performance? That was insanity.' He holds up a bandaged hand. 'See this? This is what you did, three broken fingers.' He steps towards me. 'I had to go to casualty. I had to *lie*.'

I don't take my eyes off his—he thinks of making a move on me and he'll get worse. He doesn't, instead his tension fades and he smiles. Then that self-satisfied grin turns to a snarl. 'You better stay sane from now on, Dor. And no, I'm not talking drugs or straightjackets, I'm appealing to your motherly instincts. You got a daughter who's depending on you staying sane and acting like you're normal. And I want a proper wife, understand?'

Course I understand. Be a good little wifey and the snake pit's empty. Act independent and Bron's in with the rattlers. At last, the real Gabe, Talon incarnate. *This* was what Dorrie married, poor fem. Little wonder she took Bronnie and ran. Little wonder she drove crazy fast. Bet Gabe rejoiced in Dor's memory loss.

As Striker used to say, 'Strategy, Bit, strategy.' I drop my eyes and bend my head. He likes that and gives a little snigger. But, hell he's never been penned in a CRC. Chief Mont could teach him a thing or three.

I serve the bland casserole Babs left for supper and then wash up. He calls me to the sofa and we watch one awful TV show after another till he says it's time for bed. 'You're in with me tonight.'

I'm lying on Dorrie's bed with Dorrie's man, and when he's done with me, he sleeps and snores, while I think options. For starters I know I could cull him, no trouble. But, and it's a big but, if I do I'll be hunted, and then what happens to Bron? In some ways life was simpler when I was Rat.

Morning, and he's a man in full control of wife and home. 'I'll drop in on mother on the way to work. I'll tell her you're well enough to take the reins, okay?'

I nod, trying for demure and probably failing for lack of practice, but proud-guy keeps on talking. 'I'll give Mrs Brandon notice today. She won't be needed any longer. You'll be cleaning house from now on. And you tell your father you'll take Bronwen back and forth to nursery.' He stops for a few seconds, 'That's all, I think. No, wait, one more thing, here's five pounds, get something really special for dinner tonight. Keep the change, I'll want to check the bill. Right, now come see me off and for God's sake smile will you?'

We see him off and he mouthes kisses. 'See you later,' he calls. Gotch-eyed Frink!

While we wait for Henry, I run the vacuum round, wash the dishes and then go searching. There's a locked drawer in the kitchen cabinet where he keeps stuff. The lock's simple, Kai started me on one twice as hard, back in the ludus.

'Never know when a skill like that'll come in handy, Bit. We'll start simple, two hair grips, a lot of patience and it's a done deal.'

My done deal yields a sheaf of bills and a box with *Cromwell's Fine Dark Chocolate* painted on the lid. Inside I find Dorrie's driving licence and three birth certificates, Gabe's, Bronwen's and hers. There's also an envelope containing her marriage lines, three nice rings and a locket on a heavy gold chain. There's a picture in the locket, a young Henry standing next to a woman who must be Dorrie's mother. I leave everything as I found it and lock the drawer. It's enough to know where these things are. No cheque book though.

When Henry calls I tell him I'm ready to do the daily trip.

'That's good to hear, love. Thought I'd never see the day,' he says, wiping his eyes with the back of his hand.

'Walk with me one more time? Hey, I've got good news. Bron spoke last night.'

'Could this day get any better? What she say?'

'No!'

'That was your first word, you know. The two of you on the mend, marvelous. What did her dad say? Bet he was overjoyed.'

'Yeah,' I say. 'Overjoyed.'

We drop Bron off with a promise to go straight to Henry's for lunch and a long play with the ferret. At Henry's he asks about Babs. 'She still sticking her nose in?'

'Gabe's talking to her today, and the cleaner.'

'Her as well? Think you're up to it?'

'I'm up to anything, me.'

'Shouldn't say it, but since you woke up you've been a different woman. I think you're right, you *are* fit for anything.'

'It's my second chance, Henry. I'm not messing up. How's our creature?'

'Creature's fine. Jimmy next-door lent me a book. Found a plan for a really top class ferret house. Sorted out the planks last night and I've been up since five getting it fixed up. Give me a hand and it'll be done by the time you collect Bron.'

He's right, by the time I leave, the shed's a pleasure palace fit for a top of the heap ferret. We sit in the shed looking at a magnificent construction that fills half of it. There's a place for sleeping, high runs, low runs, climbing posts, look out points, and box tunnels for hiding stuff. There's also a litter box, a food shelf and two water bottles—one for up, one for down, both within easy reach for filling.

'What we going to call the creature, Bit?'

'Got to sex it first.'

'How?'

'Easy,' I say and wave a meat chunk till the ferret shows interest, chirruping like Brown used to. After it finishes the snack it allows me pick it up. 'It's good natured and male.'

'How on earth do you know?'

'I looked at its belly. Males have what looks like a stick-out belly button, but it's not really a belly button. Females are kind of featureless.'

'You *have* been reading.'

I go for Bron and tell her we've a male, a boy ferret and Grandpa and I will choose some names but she'll have to pick the one she likes, because it's her pet.

Soon as we've eaten our cheese sandwiches we go to the shed and give Bron a stuffed mouse with a long tail that she tempts the ferret into chasing. While that's going on Henry and I call out names. She shakes her head after every one.

When the game stops she sits with the ferret on her lap. They're both out of breath. Then she looks at us and her face is working, she's making a giant effort and suddenly out a word comes. 'Quick,' she says and smoothes the golden fur. Then she smiles and repeats the ferret's name, 'Quick'.

'Hello, Quick,' I say. 'Welcome home.'

41

My days and nights are strangely disjointed. Life with Gabe spent CRC fashion, lips shut, head down. Life out of his sight spent either training ludus style or having fun with Bron.

Takes max effort, but the house is clean and the food's edible. It helps that Gabe sleeps heavy, nights. He blames overwork, but I tend to think it's the meds I feed him, the ones 'sposed to help me sleep. But I sleep very well, if only a few short hours each night, seeing how I spend time in re-capturing the killing moves of martial dance. I'm doing well, reckon I could be up to arena standard pretty soon.

Somehow, no one's mentioned Quick to Gabe. Bronwen avoids him whenever possible and when she can't, acts much as I do—dumb. She prattles non-stop to me and Henry, but her teacher hasn't said anything, so I'm guessing she doesn't speak in school.

Quick's real tame, and though he tolerates me and Henry, Bron's his person. I made a leather harness like the NOP teens used, and he's taken to it, or rather taken to the walks in the park near Henry's. Gotta say I enjoy the looks we get from dog walkers as this sinewy creature skitters past tugging a wildly laughing child.

I located the spare chequebook in a locked drawer in Gabe's bedside cabinet and I'm getting passable good at forging his signature. If I was on my own I'd be long gone, but there's Bronwen and now Quick, so escape's been shelved, pro tem. How do you run invisible with a three year old and a fancy ferret in tow?

It's roast beef again tonight, the meat done to a crisp, the vegetables cooked soft and served with thick floury gravy, same as mother makes. Tonight's his early night, so I watch for the car, ready to switch the hot kettle to boil. He insists his tea is brewing as he walks through the door. Creep also wants a smile on my face. Guy wants fantasy, can't take reality.

Today, I can tell from the slam of the front door and the frown dragging at his face muscles that it's been *one of those days.* No false smile, no cold peck on the cheek, just a rush to the drinks cupboard. That bad, eh?

'Do you know who Templeton gave the promotion to?' He takes a long gulp at the whisky tumbler. 'Well, go on, take a stab at it.' I don't, knowing it'd best to keep shtum. 'Lennart. Fish-faced Lennart. And he doesn't put in half the hours I do. But he's a charmer, one of those smooth tongued smilers. Been in the company five minutes. Guess who taught him all he knows about National Ordinance Planning? Me, that's who. And now he's going to be my damn boss?' And Gabe looks at his good wife to play the part.

'There'll be other chances,' the good wife comforts.

'What do you know about it?'

Right, I know how this scene's going to play out

'You haven't worked for years.' He says, his voice rising. Another gulp and he's ranting. 'You don't know what it's like out there. Could be years before something else comes up. It was all the time I lost when you had that crash, and now you're hardly the ideal company wife. It's your fault. You're a liability.'

Now he's in my face spitting whisky drops. 'You and that child of yours. Holding me back, that's what you're doing, the pair of you. I take her anywhere and she starts with the noises and everybody stares.' Glass emptied he gets a refill.

'And I can't entertain like Lennart. *His* wife cooks like a restaurant chef and dresses like a fashion plate. Even his kids are brilliant. Told me they play Chopin and take extra French.' He snorts, 'And I've got *her.*'

He drains the glass and heads for the kitchen. 'Pour me a cup of tea, I'm parched.'

I'm pouring the tea and Bron comes down the garden dragging a tree branch. She's been looking for things to amuse Quick. Gabe spots her and his face sets stony. When she skips in, his face grows dark. She stops, losing her excited colour.

'And there she is. My kid. Looking more like her stupid mother every day and acting just as crazy. My cup runneth over.'

Bron's clutching the branch, eyes fixed on Gabe. He walks over and reaches for her with his good arm, but she pushes back with the branch. His body stiffens, his fist clenches. I'm no fortune teller, but I can see what's gonna happen. I scream a Rat cry, he's distracted and before the fist connects I'm there, slamming his wrist with the blade of my left hand and getting him in the throat with the right. He's down and wheezing. I sweep Bronwen up and hold her tight, both of us shaking like we're fever-hit.

When she's calmer I put her down and check on Gabe. He's breathing, but that throat'll need some attention. Should I put him out of his misery? Hell flames, I'm *wondering*? Times have frinking changed. Was a time, when … I look at big-eyed Bron and leave him gasping, but alive.

He's still twitching after I've gathered some necessities. I frisk him for cash and keys then take Bron and the bags to the car. I've watched Gabe drive, and had a few 'refresher' lessons from Henry and I think I can get by, but it's a hairy ride and I get to Henry's worn pretty thin.

Course I have to answer his questions. 'You drove? Where's Gabe? What's wrong with Bronnie? What's wrong with *you*?'

I stare, clean out of words, but Bronnie rescues me. 'Mammy hit … him. He was going to hurt me.'

'Bit! For Pete's sake tell me.'

The words swoop back, and pour out. Not the whole story, I don't say I'm a squatter in Dorrie's body. Don't want him thinking I'm more'n half way to the fun factory. I just spill Gabe.

'How badly is he hurt?'

'He won't die, if that's what you mean, but his throat's pretty mashed. I hit him hard.'

'Did you call an ambulance?'

'No. I wanted out.'

'We can't leave him like that. What if he chokes to death? You'd be up for manslaughter, if not murder. Look, give me your house key and I'll check on him. I can call a doctor or an ambulance from there.'

He leaves and I make hot milk drinks for me and Bron, who's cuddling Quick. A packet of chocolate digestives later the phone rings. It's Henry. 'House is deserted. I'm coming back. Lock the doors.'

Bron's flagging and after I put Quick back in the shed, and lock the doors, I take her up to the spare bedroom and hold her hand till she sleeps. Striker's under the pillow, Brown's in her hand.

I'm slicing open open a packet of ginger nuts with a carving knife, listening for Henry's key and hear his car. I open the back door, but it's not Henry. It's Gabe and there's a taxicab chugging away.

Gabe's neck is red, there's a purpling line across his larynx and he's puffed with rage. He speaks, in a painful croak.

'Thought so. Get Bron. We're off home.'

'No. *We're* not going anywhere. It's over, Gabe. Take one step closer and I'll poke this carving knife into your worthless heart. D'you understand? I *won't* be hurt and I won't let you hurt Bron.' He's shaky on his pins and paler than a veal calf. 'Look at you, man. Come in and sit down before you drop.'

He has to see from my face that I ain't scared and I mean every word I say. He kinda droops, his puff shrinks and he staggers to a kitchen chair.

His mouth opens but I put the knife down on the table and hold up my empty hand. 'Shut it. Me first. Just listen, will you?' I wait till he's fully focused and then let him have it. 'It's the end, Gabe. It's over. I've changed too much to take it any more. You touch Bronwen or me ever again and I'll kill you without a second thought. And believe me, I know more ways to kill than your average assassin. You want a list?'

He's corpse-pale now, his hand shaking as he touches his neck.

'Think they'll convict me? I've read up on spousal abuse, and I'll make damn sure I'm bruised. Yeah, I'll be the battered wife who killed to save her child. I'll make certain the medics are on my side. And did you know that your daughter speaks fluent now? She'll make an excellent witness. Unlike me she remembers before the crash. And she'll talk Gabe, how she'll talk.'

He tenses, but I don't even try for the knife. 'Think I need that knife to cull a mouse like you? See these fingers?' I hold up my left hand, fingers stiff and stretched. 'I know the sound of fingers pushing through the softness of an eye and the click of a broken neck. I've heard the death rattle of many brave men—killing one soft coward won't mean squat. Convinced?'

He's convinced all right, convinced to a quaking jelly. I smile a fierce Rat smile and watch him wither. 'Better lope off Gabe. Want me to call a cab?'

He shakes his head, and winces. Good, it hurts.

'Hear that, Gabe? It's Henry's car. You'd better slope off, now, before he calls the police.' I laugh with true merriment. 'They get called in, you can kiss all thoughts of promotion a sweet goodbye.'

I put the knife back in the drawer and shut it tight, my back toward him. I leave to greet Henry and when we get back, the kitchen's empty.

I talk Henry calm, half my mind on what I did. I let the creech live! This world sure is changing me. For better or worse?

42

The divorce went through easy as easy, and Gabe's polite as pie. Henry said he's changed his job and is getting friendly with a widow. He's got access to Bron whenever he wants, but it seems he doesn't want it as much as he thought. Can't be much fun taking a child places and not having her talk or look at you. Far as Bron's concerned Gabe doesn't exist.

Out of the settlement I bought a tiny house for me and Bron. It's in the middle of a terrace with the front door opening to the pavement. At the back there's a long ribbon garden that overlooks the allotments where Henry rents a plot. It was thanks to Henry that I got this house, he used to talk to the owner across the fence and soon as he knew the guy wanted to sell he got me a viewing and whiz-bang, I'm a house owner.

Bron loves it here, she talks to all Henry's pals and they load her up with spare fruit and veg and let her walk Quick wherever she wants. I love it here, too. Here, I've a family, a daughter, a father, I got everything 'sept the loves I lost, the loves I dream about.

I keep the house clean because I want to, not because I'm married to it. Henry's painted Bron's room in flower shades, one wall pink, one wall lavender and the last two peace-rose cream. At present he's working on a huge walk-in cage for Quick in the old coal-house by the back door. He's already plastered the walls and laid quarry tiles on the floor. Bron insists he makes the home big enough for future ferret friends.

Gabe has to give money each week for Bron. I told Henry I was uneasy taking it because he so rarely saw Bron, but Henry said he has to pay, it's the law and anyway she might change her mind one day and want to see her dad. She's in school full time now and talks to everyone bar Gabe.

Sometimes, like today, Bitch Singer of the Whip Tails views this cosy domesticity with alarm. Who am I? What am I becoming? Sometimes I have to search for the memories of that other life; dig out the likenesses of Striker and Kai and One-Eye. Were they real, is Bitch Singer real, or were she and those others fantasies grown by an injured brain? Did Dorrie invent a new world because she couldn't face the old? If I wake in the night or have trouble getting to sleep I wonder if Spartax's ludus or the red-techs labs ever did exist.

But sometimes in the night I hear Verrier's voice, echoing down the time stream, and I know he's real and out there somewhere, somewhen.

I was in the market this morning buying food for Quick and I heard Striker's voice in the queue behind me, I turned to look and course it wasn't him. All day he's been on my mind. I've heard his laugh, smelled the glue he used on his spikes, felt his arms about me. It's time to pick up Bron and I'm so down I could lock myself inside a cupboard and hide away for ever. But I can't. I've got to drive my cheap little dented car to the school.

It was Henry who got me driving. Gave me lessons and asked his friend the driving examiner to test me. 'My daughter's been ill, lost her confidence. Give her the once over, will you Charlie?' And after me driving him here there and everywhere he gave me the thumbs up and departed with a load of fruit and veg from Henry's patch.

I arrive at Henry's and Bronwen goes to tell Quick how his new home is getting on, while I drink coffee with Henry.

'You're looking peaky, Bit. What's up? It's not Gabe is it?'

'No. Nothing like that. I'm not sleeping well, that's all. Been getting these wild upsetting dreams. Hearing things, smelling stuff that isn't there.'

'That's only natural, your brain took a real knock. I suppose it's like a bruise, takes a while to fade. You've got too much time to dwell on bad times, why don't you do something.'

'What do you mean, do something? I'm on the go all the time, I'm fine.'

'Fine? You've just told me you're far from being fine. I think you need an interest, something totally new. After your mother died and before your accident I did Meals on Wheels three times a week and I felt all the better for doing something to help others. Here, look at this.'

He hands me a free newspaper and rings a section with his pencil. *Volunteers Wanted* it says. *Have you time to spare? Want to help a good cause?* I read on, learning about all kinds of organisations needing unpaid helpers. The one that catches my eye is from the local hospital where I woke up, asking for volunteers to push the newspaper and snack trolleys, distribute library books or spend time talking to the patients. I look up and Henry's watching me expectantly.

'Well, what do you think?'

'There's one from the hospital. They were good to me, perhaps I can do something for them.'

Henry beams, like he's really pleased, and we go out to give Bron a push on Dorrie's old swing.

I'm going to the hospital. I rang about volunteering and a hearty woman asked me to 'pop along' for a 'nice chat'. It's odd going back. I'm directed to a room on the ground floor with FOSTA on the door.

'Come in, come in,' breezes the voice from the telephone and I enter a crowded space mostly filled with a well-built woman with a floppy grey bun, lilac twin-set and pearls.

'I'm Margery Bullington, take a pew and welcome to FOSTA—Friends of St Andrew's.'

I smile and say my name.

'Well, ah … Bit, I understand you want to help out. What are you interested in? Hankering to be a trolley gal? Feel like reading to our visually challenged patients? Or do you fancy being a talker?'

'A talker?'

'Chatting to patients without visitors, or to recovering coma patients, bringing the outside world to them.'

I sit up, and she chuckles. 'That certainly spiked your interest.'

'Well, I was a patient here not long ago. I was in a coma for several months. I know from experience how hard it is to adjust. I think I'd like to be a talker.'

'Right you are. When can you start?'

'Now?'

'That's the spirit! I'll take you to Ward 6 and introduce you to Sister.'

And before I know it I've signed up for two hours every Tuesday and Thursday, half twelve to half two, leaving me time to pick up Bronwen from school. Starting tomorrow.

Sister Hastings gives me a badge that says Bit Hart, and hands me a list of names. First one is Maud Stevens, a stroke victim who has difficulty with words. After ten minutes I realise that her words come freely enough, she's just hard to understand. But I do my best, do a lot of smiling and hold her hand till she falls asleep. My face is aching when I go to my second visit. This lady, Florence Germain, is deaf so I try a sign or two and she smiles broadly flashing a trill of signs that leave me reeling. She understands, slows right down and we start a halting conversation. Our signs don't quite jibe, but I pick up her new signs and we get along just fine and I promise another visit soon. Hand to mouth she gestures thanks and I give her a thumbs-up.

Time's flown and there's barely time for the last visit. The third name on the list is Stuart Judge, a young man badly injured in a motor bike accident. His bed's empty, but as I'm leaving the ward a porter wheels him in. The nurse with him is Nurse Nell.

'Hello. It's Mrs Hart, isn't it?'

'Yes. I'm back to help. Signed on as a talker.'

She laughs, 'That's great. Is Stuart on your list?'

'Yes.'

'Right Stuart, let's get you on that bed.'

After nurse and porter manoeuver the silent Stuart onto the bed, she takes me aside, 'Stuart needs all the help you can give him. He has no family and his three best friends were killed in the pile-up. He won't be getting many visitors and you know how much your father did to speed your recovery.'

Once he's tucked in and his pillows well plumped, she leaves. I sit on an arm chair covered in the exact same shiny fabric as the one by the bed I woke in, and I study Mr Number Three.

He's pale and made paler by the dense blackness of his thick hair and under the new growth I spot scarring. He's staring straight ahead, focused on the middle distance. I shift, and the slick upholstery makes a sucky-creaking noise. His head turns and I get a first look at his searing blue eyes and long sweeping black lashes. His glance is magnetic and it's hard to pull away. I move again and the rude noise enables me to break the stare. He smiles.

'Name's Bit and I'm a volunteer visitor,' I say hurriedly and he screws up his eyes like he's trying to remember something. Hell's flames I've upset him all ready, gotta reassure him.

'You don't have to say anything and you don't have to stick with me, there are other volunteers. The idea is for you to hear words, listen to speech, get the old brain stimulated. They'll get you listening to familiar music, hear family stories, anything to jog the memories back.'

God, should I have mentioned family? I babble on, 'Don't worry if you haven't got the words. It takes a time to get them back. It's like you're a baby again; an awful lot has to go in before anything sensible comes out. Look I'm not just saying that, I've been where you are, been in another world—unconscious I mean. And I came out of it. I recovered and I'm talking well enough, now, aren't I?

He smiles at my words, a smile that breaks your heart.

'Okay, I'm babbling, but I'm nervous. This is my first day. Perhaps you'd prefer someone more experienced.'

His lips move like he's trying to speak, but no words come out, just a mumbled moan and that distresses him.

'Don't try speaking yet. If you're anything like I was, your lips'll feel like wood and trying to speak will be hard as pushing a rusted gate. But I promise it will come, it will happen. Listen and get limber, as a teacher of mine used to say.'

His hand moves, surprisingly quick and he grabs my wrist and I hold my breath as he stares into my eyes. Then his tears start welling and as they trickle down his face he lets me go and turns away. I stand and walk down the squelchy tiles to the nurse station and tell Nurse Nell I might have upset the patient.

'Did he cry?'

'Yes.'

'It happens. Cried like a baby when I gave him a mirror. Didn't you? It's a shock waking up not knowing anything.'

'Shall I come back Thursday?'

'Why not. Give it another go.'

'Right, see you Thursday for one more shot.'

43

It's Thursday and I'm in two minds whether to go back or not. Don't want to make the guy worse by saying the wrong thing. Henry rings to tell me he's ready to install Quick's palace and I tell him my worry.

'What shall I do, Henry?'

'Do as the nurse says, give it a go. Start with your ladies and if it doesn't work with the young man, then move on to someone else.'

'Sounds a plan. I'll go with that. Thanks.'

Henry's got a key so I don't need to be here when he comes. I get to the hospital early and find that Maud's gone back to her care home. However Florence is eager for more signing so I spend double time with her and I feel I'm really doing a good job. Now for Stuart Judge.

There's a different nurse on duty, but she's expecting me and says to go straight along. He's sitting in the chair today so I get one of the stacking chairs and sit beside him. He looks up, his blue eyes so fierce I feel nervous.

'It's me again, Bit. Remember?'

He stares. Does he want me to go? Better ask. He shakes his head. Right. Got to say something, but what?

'Want to know something about me? Well I was in a coma like you, for about six months, made a good recovery then ditched my gotch-eyed mate.' I stop dead, he's grabbed my hand in a tight grip. He's fighting to get a word out, 'Who?' he says, 'Who?'

'I'm Bit,' I say, but he's shaking his head, no. And then he croaks, 'No.' Lets go of my hand and shuts his eyes. The nurse comes up, 'Anything wrong?'

'He said something. I think he thought I was someone else.'

'That's progress, means he's remembering.'

'Shall I go?'

'He's quiet enough, so no, I'd keep talking if I were you, it might be painful for him but the sooner it all comes back the better.'

'Right I'll just chunter on till he goes to sleep. If he gets upset, I'll yell.'

'Fine.'

'Right then I'll talk about my daughter Bronwen and her pet ferret.'

Soon as I mention the word ferret he opens his eyes and looks at me again. He doesn't attempt to say anything so I keep going, telling him how we found Quick and how we're making him a new home fit for a king. I talk on and on about Quick and Bronnie, and he's taking it all in I can tell. I don't stop till my voice starts getting croaky and he's asleep.

Tuesday, and Florence's bed is empty. She's gone home to her daughter's and Stuart's top of the list. He looks up as I near the chair carrying my stackable seat.

'Want to hear Quick's latest escapade?' He nods. 'Bronwen was playing in the garden and he got through a gap in next-door's fence. They've got this soft old Alsatian dog and it brought Quick back to the fence in its mouth!'

He smiles a sad smile and I find myself telling him of another ferret. 'I named her Brown because of her warm chocolate colour. She came to me at a bad time, without her I'd have given up.' I draw a deep breath. 'I lost her a world ago, but she's with me all the time … like all the others I lost.' By now I'm deep in memories. 'She had a passion for small spaces and once she got into this really secure room. How she did it I'll never know. She bypassed locks, reinforced doors, alarms, the whole shebang. It was my old boss Spartax's place—supposedly everything-proof. But Brown got in and chewed a bar of hand-made perfumed soap. Seems ferrets go wild for the smell, anyway she chewed enough of the stuff to set her puking, and being a clean creature she puked neatly in one of Spartax's boots. Eily found her later, curled up on the rug nice as you like. Luckily Spartax found it funny so there wasn't any comeback.' I stop talking, haven't talked of Brown for so very long and can't stop the tears.

A hand gives me a tissue, Stuart's hand, and he's staring at me hard, every scrap of colour leeching from his face. He's biting his lips, his eyes like laser drills. He whispers something I don't catch and I lean forward.

'Bit, it's me, Striker.'

I sit back on my hard visitor's chair with fire and ice chasing through my body and the world, like my heart, on utter standstill. Then the hurdy-gurdy plays and the roundabout whirls again.

'Welcome home,' I say hugging him so tight I think he'll break. A picture of Kai and One Eye bursts into my mind. 'Two found and now just two more to go,' I tell my love, my Rat, my Striker.

Acknowledgements:- I owe thanks to You Write on for giving me the confidence to finish Rats, to The Writing Asylum for offering such constructive criticism, but most of all to the Triskele clan for settling me safely on the rocky road to publication.

Thank you for reading a Triskele Book.

Enjoyed *Rats*? Here's what you can do next.

If you loved the book and you'd like to help other readers find Triskele Books, please write a short review on the website where you bought the book. Your help in spreading the word is much appreciated and reviews make a huge difference to helping new readers find good books.

More novels from Triskele Books coming soon. You can sign up to be notified of the next release and other news here: www.triskelebooks.co.uk

If you are a writer and would like more information on writing and publishing, visit www.triskelebooks.blogspot.com and www.wordswithjam.co.uk, which are packed with author and industry professional interviews, links to

articles on writing, reading, libraries, the publishing industry and indie-publishing.

Connect with us:
Email admin@triskelebooks.co.uk
Twitter @triskelebooks
Facebook www.facebook.com/triskelebooks

Also from Triskele Books

The Charter by Gillian Hamer
Closure by Gillian E Hamer
Complicit by Gillian E Hamer
Crimson Shore by Gillian E Hamer

Behind Closed Doors by JJ Marsh
Raw Material by JJ Marsh
Tread Softly by JJ Marsh
Cold Pressed by JJ Marsh

Spirit of Lost Angels by Liza Perrat
Wolfsangel by Liza Perrat

Delirium: The Rimbaud Delusion
by Barbara Scott Emmett

Tristan and Iseult by JD Smith
The Rise of Zenobia (Overlord Book I) by JD Smith
The Fate of an Emperor (Overlord Book II) by JD Smith

Gift of the Raven by Catriona Troth
Ghost Town by Catriona Troth

Lightning Source UK Ltd.
Milton Keynes UK
UKOW03f1355071014

239734UK00002B/14/P